C0-DXE-201

COVER SIX SECURITY

Lisa B. Kamps

THE GUARDIAN: DARYL

Cover Six Security, Book 2

LISA B. KAMPS

Lisa B. Kamps

Dedication

For my husband, Jack, who kept me sane during this one and knew
when I needed that extra push to keep me going...
And who promised me a really long vacation, just because!
I love you, Honey Bear!
When do we pack our bags?

Lisa B. Kamps

THE GUARDIAN: DARYL
Copyright © 2019 by Elizabeth Belbot Kamps

All rights reserved. Except for use in any review, the reproduction or utilization of this work in whole or in part in any form by any electronic, mechanical or other means, now known or hereafter invented, including xerography, photocopying and recording, or in any information storage or retrieval system, is forbidden without the express written permission of the author.

Cover Six Security™ is a fictional security company, its name and logo created for the sole use of the author and covered under protection of trademark.

All characters in this book have no existence outside the imagination of the author and have no relation to anyone bearing the same name or names, living or dead. This book is a work of fiction and any resemblance to any individual, place, business, or event is purely coincidental.

Cover Design by Jay Aheer of Simply Defined Art
https://www.simplydefinedart.com/

Cover Six Security Logo Designed by Benjamin Mangnus of Benjamagnus Design Ltd.
http://www.benjamagnus.com/

All rights reserved.
ISBN-13: 978-1091048942

CONTENTS

Dedication v
Copyright vi
Other titles by this author ix
Special Acknowledgement xi
Prologue.. 13
Chapter One 16
Chapter Two... 31
Chapter Three 47
Chapter Four... 60
Chapter Five.. 65
Chapter Six.. 74
Chapter Seven 87
Chapter Eight.. 93
Chapter Nine..106
Chapter Ten 121
Chapter Eleven 127
Chapter Twelve..135
Chapter Thirteen..147
Chapter Fourteen 155
Chapter Fifteen 165
Chapter Sixteen 168
Chapter Seventeen 185
Chapter Eighteen 196
Chapter Nineteen 203
Chapter Twenty 207
Chapter Twenty-One 220
Chapter Twenty-Two..228

Chapter Twenty-Three	235
Chapter Twenty-Four	240
Chapter Twenty-Five	254
Chapter Twenty-Six	264
Chapter Twenty-Seven	269
Chapter Twenty-Eight	275
Epilogue	286
About the Author	293
The Protector: MAC	295
The Defender: RYDER	296

The Guardian: DARYL

Other titles by this author

COVER SIX SECURITY

Covered By A Kiss, A CSS Novella, Book 0
The Protector: MAC, Book 1
The Guardian: DARYL, Book 2
The Defender: RYDER, Book 3

THE BALTIMORE BANNERS

Crossing The Line, Book 1
Game Over, Book 2
Blue Ribbon Summer, Book 3
Body Check, Book 4
Break Away, Book 5
Playmaker (A Baltimore Banners Intermission novella)
Delay of Game, Book 6
Shoot Out, Book 7
The Baltimore Banners 1st Period Trilogy (Books 1-3)
The Baltimore Banners 2nd Period Trilogy (Books 4-6)
On Thin Ice, Book 8
Coach's Challenge (A Baltimore Banners Intermission Novella)
One-Timer, Book 9
Face Off, Book 10
First Shot At Love (A Baltimore Banners Warm-up Story)
Game Misconduct, Book 11
Fighting To Score, Book 12
Matching Penalties, Book 13

THE YORK BOMBERS

Playing The Game, Book 1
Playing To Win, Book 2
Playing For Keeps, Book 3
Playing It Up, Book 4
Playing It Safe, Book 5
Playing For Love, Book 6
Playing His Part, Book 7

THE CHESAPEAKE BLADES

Winning Hard, Book 1
Loving Hard, Book 2
Playing Hard, Book 3

FIREHOUSE FOURTEEN

Once Burned, Book 1
Playing With Fire, Book 2
Breaking Protocol, Book 3
Into The Flames, Book 4
Second Alarm, Book 5

STAND-ALONE TITLES

Emeralds and Gold: A Treasury of Irish Short Stories
(anthology)
Finding Dr. Right, Silhouette Special Edition
Time To Heal
Dangerous Passion

Special Acknowledgement

The idea for the Cover Six Security series came about when I started the Chesapeake Blades series—particularly book 2, *Loving Hard*. And the more I played around with it, the more it drew me in.

I had the story ideas. Names for the guys on the team. Their backgrounds. I was ready to go, my fingers itching to get the words on paper.

What I didn't have was a name for the security company. Ideas came to me, only to be deleted because...well, frankly, because they stunk. Then I got stuck.

Like many authors, I have a fabulous reader's group on Facebook: Kamps Korner. And that's where I turned to for help. I threw the question (okay, I begged) to the greatest bunch of readers I know—and they totally came through for me!

There were dozens of suggestions, all of them fantastic—which led to another dilemma: how do I pick one? There were a few that really stood out so I did what any smart author would do: I created a poll and let the readers pick...

And Cover Six Security was born.

Thank you to everyone who offered suggestions—there were so many great ones! And special thanks—and my undying gratitude—to Elizabeth Roney and her Marine husband for the wonderful suggestion! It totally fits. And in Elizabeth's words: "He [her Marine husband] said it would be a good pick up line explaining to the ladies what cover your six means!"

And it totally is—as you'll see in several of the upcoming books!

Elizabeth and your Marine husband—this one is for you! Thank you <3!

Lisa B. Kamps

PROLOGUE

She stood in line with the other passengers, patiently waiting to board. The urge to look over her shoulder was strong but she ruthlessly pushed it away. Nobody had followed her—she had checked and double-checked. Checked again before she made her way through security four hours before the flight was scheduled to take off.

Had wandered around the airport, searching for anyone who appeared out of place. For anyone who seemed to be searching for someone else.

Much like she was.

But nobody was following her. She'd lost them a few months ago, had managed to get away before they noticed her. She had time now, time where she didn't have to constantly look over her shoulder.

But how much time? Weeks? Months? Maybe. Enough time to allow her to take this quick trip.

Enough time to find the man her father trusted.

The line started moving, the passengers around her laughing and talking, their voices filled with excitement. She reached the gate agent, showed her the ticket and her passport. Held her breath, waiting.

But the gate agent only glanced at the passport, gave her a quick smile and nodded. Relief went through her and she hurried down the jetway, the floor bouncing beneath her feet. Of course the agent wouldn't question the passport. Why would she? She had already cleared security, had made it this far with no issues.

But she'd still been nervous, afraid the document would be studied too closely. Worried that they'd pull her out of line and question her—or worse.

She glanced at her ticket, looked up to study the seat numbers as she made her way along the plane's narrow aisle. Her seat was near the back, against the window. She would have preferred an aisle seat—she didn't like the feeling of being blocked in with no way to escape—but this would have to do. She slid into the seat, tucked her backpack under the chair in front of her, and quickly fastened her seatbelt. Around her other people were doing the same—but they were with their friends. Families. Loved ones.

She was alone. More alone than she'd ever been.

She turned her head to the side, looked out the window as the baggage handlers loaded luggage into the plane. Suitcases of all colors and sizes, one after another. She didn't bother searching for hers—she didn't have one. Everything she needed, practically everything she owned, was safely stored in the backpack by her feet.

A sudden wave of uncertainty washed over her and she nearly jumped to her feet, feeling the need to flee. She took a deep breath, fought the urge to run from the plane. She didn't have a choice, not anymore. She had to see this through. It was too important not to. She needed to do this. Needed to find the man her father trusted.

And then...she wasn't sure what she would do then. She had no intention of talking to him. Not yet. She just wanted to see him. Study him. Make up her own mind before she approached him.

Yes, her father trusted him. But she didn't. How could she, when she didn't know him? When she had never met him?

But time was running out. She would have to make a decision, and soon. She couldn't keep running the way she'd been for the last three years. Couldn't keep looking over her shoulder and jumping at every shadow, real and imagined. The time was coming when she wouldn't be able to manage on her own. When she would need help, more than even her father could give her. In fact, this trip had been her father's idea. If not for his insistence, she wouldn't be going.

But she was. She didn't have a choice. She needed to find the man her father trusted so much.

And then she needed to decide for herself if he had the power to slay dragons—

Or if he was nothing more than a myth. Nothing more than a fantasy she had carefully—desperately—built up in her mind.

CHAPTER ONE

The blonde was watching him.

Daryl "Zeus" Anderson raised the tall glass to his mouth and studied her over the rim as he took a long swallow. Sure enough, she looked away as soon as their eyes met. And shit, was that actually a blush creeping across her face?

It was either that, or she'd gotten sunburned sometime in the last hour she'd been sitting under that shaded canopy reading a book. It was one of those e-readers that didn't require you to turn any real damn pages so he couldn't tell if she was actually reading—or just pretending to read.

Because yeah, she'd pretty much been watching him for the past hour, ever since he'd strolled out to the bar for a serving of the hair of the dog that bit him in the ass last night.

And this morning.

Daryl glanced at his watch and frowned. No, make that this afternoon.

Fuck.

What the hell had been in those damn drinks they'd been tossing back last night? Nothing he could taste, he knew that much. No rum. No vodka. No whiskey. Or maybe it had been a combination of all three, the taste cleverly disguised by the other ingredients.

Whatever it was had been lethal—and dangerous,

because they'd gone down smoother than water before sneaking up on him and kicking his ass three ways from tomorrow. He hadn't lost control—he *never* lost control, it was too damn risky in his line of work. He remembered everything that happened—maybe a little too well because the sight of Chaos doing the limbo under those two beach bunnies wasn't something he *wanted* to remember but he couldn't seem to get out of his mind. He hadn't tossed cookies, hadn't passed out, hadn't staggered back to his bungalow—at least, not much.

But damn if his head hadn't come close to exploding when he finally rolled out of bed two hours ago with an extreme case of cottonmouth and clothes that looked like they'd been slept in for a week. Water had taken care of the cottonmouth and a shower and change of clothes had taken care of his appearance. But the head? Yeah, there was only one thing that could take care of that and he held the remedy in his hand.

Another swallow then he placed the glass down and shifted on the barstool, his gaze casually drifting over to the blonde. She had the e-reader held up close to her face, giving him a chance to study her without being too damn obvious.

He didn't remember seeing her before. She hadn't been in the crowd of onlookers at Mac's sunset wedding yesterday evening and he'd pretty much scanned the faces of every resort guest who had tried to get closer to see what the hell was going on. It was a damn wedding, what the hell else did they need to know?

Sure, maybe the bridal party was a little unorthodox. Not the bride or the groom, or even the bride's mother or groom's father, who stood as matron of honor and best man. It was the rest of the bridal party that no doubt helped draw attention to them. Who *wouldn't* look at the ten men, all obviously former military, all dressed in khaki shorts and relaxed island shorts, flanking the wedding couple? It wasn't like they *didn't* stand out. Especially here, at this secluded Caribbean resort.

But it wasn't like any of them had any say in the matter. Tabitha "TR" Meyers—no, not *Meyers*, her name was *MacGregor* now—had wanted all of them to join her and Mac when they tied the knot. Saying no wasn't an option. Then yesterday morning, before the wedding, her mother had suggested they all dress in those damn matching outfits and actually be a part of the ceremony.

Daryl had opened his mouth to say *oh hell no* but Boomer had beat him to it. Mac didn't have to say a word—the expression on that scarred face of his said it all.

They'd dress in those damn outfits and be part of the wedding or else. Coming from Mac, the *or else* was a threat to be ignored at their own peril.

They had definitely drawn attention, although the curious resort guests had tried to remain discreet about it. Daryl had still checked everyone out, and he hadn't been the only one. Crowds, even small ones, were always an unknown.

The blonde hadn't been part of the crowd and he was pretty damn sure he would have noticed if she was—even if she wasn't really his type. Not that there was anything wrong with her, because there wasn't. Straight blonde hair ending in a blunt cut just below her shoulders. Long legs. Lean build with just enough tone to advertise the fact that she did *something* physical.

Maybe the gym, maybe not. Average height—from what he could tell from where he was sitting. Average build. Not thin but not quite as curvy on the top as he preferred. Yeah, he was a tits guy. Sue him.

He reached for the beer and took another swallow, still studying the woman. What the hell was it about her that kept drawing his eye? Was it just because she kept watching *him*? Would he have noticed her if she didn't keep looking this way?

Like right now. Their gazes caught again and damn if she didn't look away and pull that e-reader up to hide her face.

And *that's* why he was drawn to her. She was...he was going to say *coy* but that was the wrong word. *Coy* implied making a pretense of being shy. *Coy* was playing a game—like his wife used to do every damn time she wanted something. If that didn't work, she'd turn on the fucking faucet and cry until she got her way. Until—

Fuck. Why the fuck was he even thinking of Melissa right now? That was nine years ago. A lifetime ago.

He bit back the scowl thoughts of his wife brought—thoughts and a shit-ton of bad memories he didn't want to face right now—and glanced over at the blonde. Sure enough, she was watching him again. And apparently he didn't hide that scowl well enough because her eyes widened and she quickly looked away, started gathering her things in a pile and shoving them in a tote bag.

Enough of these damn games. The blonde was cute, a perfect distraction to derail the sudden dark turn of his thoughts. He was on this island paradise for another twenty-four hours and there was no rule saying he had to spend it alone. If he had a chance for company other than the guys he'd come down here with, he was going to take it.

He slid off the stool and made his way over to the shaded canopy just as the blonde pushed to her feet. She tossed the bright-colored tote bag over her shoulder, turned around, then froze when they came face-to-face.

"Hey." Daryl nodded and offered her a smile. And fuck, he must look worse than he thought because those eyes of hers—a gorgeous hazel ringed in green—widened and for one fleeting second, he caught a glimpse of fear in their depths.

He automatically stepped back, not wanting to scare her any more than he already had. Or maybe it was just his imagination because the fear he'd seen was gone, replaced by nothing more dramatic than caution. Fair enough. Caution showed she had enough common sense to be leery when a strange guy approached her, even if she *had* been checking him out for the past hour.

"I'm Daryl." He started to offer his hand, reconsidered at the last second because she still didn't look all that comfortable. And hell, had he completely misinterpreted those glances she'd been shooting his way for the last hour? Yeah, probably, because she looked like she was ready to bolt. Or maybe even swing that damn tote upside his head, with the way she kept squeezing the braided handles in one fist.

Maybe if she could see his eyes, she wouldn't look so damn worried. He pushed the sunglasses up, forced himself not to wince when the sun sliced across his abused retinas. "Would you like to grab a drink? Maybe a bite to eat? My treat."

No smile. No nod. No shake of the head. Nothing. Just that wary gaze fixed on his as she kept clenching her fist around those braided handles of that damn tote. Yeah, he had definitely read the signs all wrong. Damn shame because now that he was closer, he could see she was definitely more than just cute.

And he needed his fucking head examined for just standing there waiting for an answer that obviously wasn't coming. He took another step back and raised his hand in a lame ass farewell gesture. "Sorry. Didn't mean to bother you."

He turned to leave, quickly scanning the small crowd by the pool and bar. At least none of his teammates were around to see him crash-and-burn. Christ, they'd never let him hear the end of it—

"Kelsey."

There was something about her voice that shot straight to his gut and unleashed a need he hadn't even acknowledged. Low, sultry, a little breathless even, like she'd just rolled out of bed after a night of hot, sweaty sex. Daryl schooled his expression, did his damnedest to hide his reaction when he turned back and caught her gaze for a brief second before she looked away. She pulled her full lower lip between her teeth, sucked on it long enough for his mind to go places it had no business going. She shifted her weight from one foot to the other and readjusted the tote bag on her shoulder. Her body language screamed her caution. Not just caution, but hesitation as well, like she couldn't decide if talking to him was a good idea or not.

She finally released that lower lip and with it, the band around his chest that had squeezed the damn air from his lungs. Her shoulders straightened and her chin came up just a notch and then, holy hell, she smiled. A small one, just enough to curl the edges of her soft mouth, but shit, it was enough to catapult her from cute to damn near mesmerizing.

"Kelsey." He repeated the name, watched a blush stain her cheeks when he said it. But she didn't look away, not until he moved forward and held his hand out. Her glance drifted to his hand and he felt her hesitation, like taking it would mean crossing some kind of line in her mind. Then her hand was in his, her grip stronger than he had anticipated despite the slight trembling in those slender fingers.

"About that drink—"

"I think I can manage one." Kelsey smiled again, just a brief curl of her mouth. "Especially since you're treating."

"Just doing my civic duty, ma'am. Dehydration can be an issue in this climate."

Her delicate brows shot up. "Your civic duty, hm?"

Daryl grinned then stepped to the side, allowing her to move beside him before leading her to the bar. He started to place his hand in the middle of her back, changed his mind at the last second and let it drop. "Of course. Is there anything wrong with that?"

"No. I just wasn't expecting anyone to be concerned about their duty—civic or otherwise—while on vacation."

"Old habits, I guess." He led them over to a shaded table near the bar and pulled the chair out for her. She shot him another of those odd glances then sat down, carefully tucking the tote bag between her feet. Daryl motioned toward the bartender then took the seat across from her. "So. Kelsey. Are you enjoying your vacation so far?"

Her eyes slid away, darted back to his. "I'll let you know tomorrow."

And whoa, okay. Was that a pick-up line or was he just reading into it? He started to ask—*how* he was going to ask escaped him at the moment—but the bartender had piss-poor timing because he came over for their drink order. By the time he walked away, Kelsey was already changing the subject.

"You're military."

It was a statement, not a question. Daryl shifted, ran one hand through his longer-than-regulation hair, offered her a quick grin. "Former military. What made you ask?"

"You called me *ma'am*. I thought maybe you might be from the south but you don't have an accent." She lifted one shoulder in a small shrug. "My next guess was military."

Observant woman. And why the hell did that thought send up a caution flag in his mind?

"Right on both counts. I'm originally from New York and I was in the Army until two years ago. How about you?"

"No military for me."

He had guessed as much, but that wasn't what he'd meant—and he had a feeling she knew it. "And you're from?"

"Oh, here and there. I, um, I've moved around a lot." Her eyes drifted down and to the side when she answered. Definitely evasive. Fine by him. She was entitled to her privacy.

"But you're American." A statement, one that drew a small smile from her.

"Red, white, and blue, through and through."

The bartender returned with their drinks—a beer

for him, a frozen piña colada for her, along with two glasses of ice water. Kelsey reached for her drink, her slender fingers gently gripping the plastic straw as she guided it to her mouth. The sleeve of her gauzy cover-up fell back, revealing a tattoo on the inside of her left wrist.

"Nice ink." And it was. Crisply drawn, the lines clear and bold. The Eye of Horus, a symbol of protection.

And probably a hundred other different things, too.

Kelsey placed her drink on the table then yanked the sleeve of the cover-up over her wrist, almost like she was trying to hide it. "Thanks."

Daryl nodded, his mind spinning as he tried to figure out what the hell else to say. Conversation was never an issue on those sporadic occasions when he was in the mood for company back home. Hit the bar, meet someone, have a few drinks, see if there was any chemistry. If there was, they'd get together. No strings, no expectations, no hassles.

Why the hell was this any different? Why was he searching his brain for conversation when all he had to do was invite her back to his bungalow?

Because this *was* different somehow and he had no fucking clue why. Maybe it was the location, a small private resort on this tiny Caribbean island. Maybe it was the leftover atmosphere of the wedding. Not necessarily romantic—at least, not like those chick-flick movies or popular novels—but not exactly...

He frowned, trying to figure out the right way to describe it—for maybe two seconds. Did he really care? No, he didn't. Especially not when Kelsey was watching him again with those hazel eyes.

Unreadable hazel eyes. That struck him as odd. Most people did a piss-poor job of hiding their thoughts and feelings. Excitement, wariness, anxiety, happiness, fear—you name it, it generally showed in a person's eyes. But not Kelsey's, not since that brief shadow of fear and caution he'd seen when he first walked over to her. Her body language gave away more than her eyes did but even that was subtle, reserved.

He realized he'd been staring when she sat back in her chair and raised one eyebrow in his direction. He shifted, cleared his throat, tried to come up with an excuse for being so blatant. He finally nodded toward the necklace around her throat. It was a polished black stone, hanging from a black leather cord. Nothing fancy, nothing special.

"Did you get that here?"

She reached up, curled her hand around the stone. And damn if another faint blush didn't just stain her cheeks. "No. No, I've had this for a few years."

He leaned forward, caught himself when she moved back the slightest bit. "What is it? Volcanic rock or something?"

She dropped her hand, nodded her head before reaching for her drink. "Volcanic glass, yes. Black obsidian. It's, um, for protection." She took a sip then waved her hand in a dismissing motion. "I mean, that's what someone told me. I have no idea if it really means that, I just like it."

Her gaze darted away from his, just for a fraction of a second. And yeah, the blush flaring across her cheeks grew a little deeper. Was she embarrassed? Why? It wasn't like he cared. If she wanted to believe some rock had mystical powers of protection, more power to her.

"Protection? Sounds like something I should look into carrying." Not likely. Not when he carried something a lot more lethal—and a hell of a lot more reliable—than some stupid chunk of rock.

But the words had the effect he had hoped for because they alleviated some of her embarrassment. The blush faded as she propped both elbows on the table and leaned forward, studying him with an earnest curiosity that surprised him. "And why would someone like you need protection?"

Daryl paused with the beer halfway to his lips, his brows shooting up in surprise. "Someone like me?"

Kelsey straightened, waved one hand at him. "You know—former military. You don't exactly look like you can't take care of yourself."

"Thanks. I think."

"You don't take compliments well, do you?"

Daryl laughed, more to cover the fact that he was actually fucking blushing than out of any amusement. "Oh. Is that what that was? I wasn't sure."

"It was." She leaned back, her steady eyes watching him for a few long seconds. "So, Daryl. What is it that you do?"

"Do?"

"Yeah, *do*. You know, to pay the bills. Private security? Hitman? Bodyguard?" A smile teased her mouth. "That was the winning guess last night at the wedding—that all of you were bodyguards."

What the fuck? Had that been nothing more than a casual question? Something to fill the gap in conversation? Maybe—but it struck too damn close to home, which automatically made him suspicious.

He took a long swallow of the beer to cover his pause then placed the glass on the table in front of him, cradling it between his hands. She was still watching him, that amused smile curling her full mouth. Curiosity danced in her eyes but there was something more there as well, something that said his answer held more importance to her than it should.

What. The. Fuck.

"I didn't realize you were here last night. On the beach, I mean." And yeah, that fucking bothered him, too, because he hadn't noticed her—and he should have.

"I wasn't, not really. I mean, I wasn't watching like everyone else." She tucked the hair behind her ear and leaned forward to take a sip of her own drink. And damn if watching her wrap those full lips around that damn plastic straw didn't make all his blood rush south.

He yanked his gaze from that perfect mouth—because yeah, his mind was working overtime on some serious fantasies right now and that was the last thing he needed—and met her gaze. "But you were here long enough to listen to what everyone was saying."

Kelsey lifted one shoulder in a careless shrug. "It was kind of hard not to. The wedding seemed to be the highlight of the excitement last night."

Yeah, he could see that. But he still couldn't figure out if she was merely curious, or if there was something else behind her seemingly innocent question.

"So." She leaned forward, a teasing smile on her face that didn't quite match the anticipation in her eyes. "Bodyguards? Or something else?"

"Not bodyguards."

She laughed, the sound husky, throaty. Too damn sensual for his own good. "I didn't think so. The groom looked like he was more than capable of taking care of himself."

She had that part right, at least.

Kelsey leaned back in the chair, rested her elbows on the armrest and carefully crossed her legs. The pose was open. Relaxed. Seductive? Possibly. He was picking up mixed signals and had no idea how to read them. Maybe this was the first time she had allowed herself to be picked up in a bar by a stranger. That would certainly explain some of the mixed signals.

But it sure as hell didn't ease that little niggling of suspicion in the back of his mind.

"If you're not bodyguards, then my next guess would be private security."

"Yeah? And why is that?" And why the hell was she so damn interested?

"You just have that certain look about you."

"Which look is that?"

She tilted her head to the side, studied him for a few seconds, then waved her hand in his direction. "Like you'd kick ass and worry about taking names later."

The chuckle escaped him before he could swallow it back. Did he really give a shit if she seemed more interested in what he did than he thought she should be? No, he didn't. Maybe it was odd but hell, for all he knew, she was just trying to convince herself she was safe with him.

He opened his mouth then snapped it shut when he saw a trio of men walking in their direction. Fuck. The last thing he needed was company, especially from those three. Boomer. Chaos. Wolf. And yeah, they had definitely spotted him and were heading his way, zooming in on him with the pinpoint accuracy of a surface-to-air missile.

He bit back a groan and barely refrained from

rolling his eyes. Kelsey shifted in the chair and looked behind her. Her entire body stiffened and she quickly turned back, some of the color draining from her face as she clutched the fancy glass between her hands. There was no misreading her now, not when her body language clearly screamed fear.

Daryl leaned forward, dropped on hand on her arm for what he hoped was a reassuring squeeze. "They're just my guys. They're perfectly safe."

At least, *she'd* be perfectly safe with them. But how would she know that? Kelsey had no reason to trust him, no reason to believe him. She grabbed his hand and for a split-second, he expected her to brush it off, to tell him not to touch her. Her fingers entwined with his instead, their grip almost desperate when the men finally stopped at their table.

Daryl looked up, met each of the men's curious stares, then shot a scowl in their direction that encompassed all of them. "Get lost."

All three men ignored him, their gazes now focused on Kelsey—who no longer looked like she was ready to bolt, despite the grip she had on his hand.

Wolf shoved his sunglasses to the top of his head and offered her one of his mega-watt smiles, the one that showed both fucking dimples to perfection. "Would your name happen to be Cinderella?"

Chaos slammed his shoulder into Wolf's with a muttered, "Jesus." But did he do the smart thing and drag Wolf and Boomer away? Fuck no. Of course not. Instead, he turned to Kelsey and offered his own damn smile.

Daryl bit back an oath and shifted in the chair. He was going to lean back—or maybe stand up and shove them all away—but Kelsey's hand still gripped his. And yeah, call him easy but no way was he going to let it go, not when he was enjoying her touch.

"Kelsey, meet the guys. Sebastian. Derrick. Ryder." He nodded to each in turn, his use of their actual first names sending a clear message to all three of them. Her gaze skittered to his—wary, uncertain—then moved back to the three men before offering them a fleeting smile.

She must not have been reassured because she pulled her hand from his and pushed her chair back. And dammit, she was leaving. There was going to be hell to pay later, involving some serious ass-kicking of three morons who didn't know when to fucking leave.

Daryl stood, shot another death glare at the three morons in question, then stepped toward Kelsey. No idea why. Maybe to offer to walk her back to wherever she had come from. Maybe to ask if she wanted to grab dinner later. Hell, maybe for no reason at all other than to be close to her. Damn if he knew.

And damn if it mattered because she turned to him, a hesitant smile curling her lips and a shadow of uncertainty in her eyes. But there was no uncertainty in that sexy voice of hers when she spoke.

"Do you mind if we go somewhere more private?"

Whoa. Yeah, okay. Private. He could totally deal with that. He nodded, moved close enough to place his hand in the middle of her back, and started guiding her away from his teammates.

But not before throwing one last glance in their direction, the command in his eyes unmistakable. "Take care of the bill for me."

CHAPTER TWO

The *somewhere private* ended up being Daryl's bungalow. And yeah, he'd hoped that was what she meant when she said it but now that they were here, he couldn't shake the slight hold of discomfort that had settled around him.

Probably because Kelsey was uncomfortable. She paced the small area, studying the colorful prints on the wall and the decorations artfully placed around the room to add a little more tropical atmosphere.

Thank God he'd made the bed before rolling out a few hours ago. He'd opted to forego daily housekeeping on general principle—the idea of anyone poking around his room made him twitch—but also because he didn't need it. Yeah, making the bed was a habit he'd never get out of. Not that she noticed because her nervous gaze never once darted to the king-size bed at the far end of the studio bungalow.

Talk about ignoring the elephant in the room.

He moved to the small kitchenette—nothing more than a counter along the far wall with a small refrigerator, sink, and a two-burner cookstove. A microwave was set into the cabinets above the counter and a four-cup coffeepot—these people couldn't possibly be human if they thought that was big enough—sat on the corner. He opened the refrigerator and pulled out two bottles of water, cracked the lid on one and stepped into Kelsey's path to hand it to her. She stopped, her body jerking in surprise before her eyes darted to his.

Yeah, definitely nervous. What the hell did she think he was going to do? Jump her? Not just no but hell no.

He moved to the small sofa perpendicular to the sliding glass door and leaned against the arm. "We can head out to the beach if you want. I'm pretty sure I can find us a few lounges away from everyone else."

"No." She shook her head, took a sip of the water and recapped the bottle then shook her head again. "No, this is fine. It's nice and cool in here."

Daryl nodded, wasted a few minutes studying the grain of the faux-wood tile floor. Wasted a few more minutes guzzling some of the water. Watched Kelsey as she glanced around the room, her right foot rolling back and forth as she stood there.

Yup, no doubt about it—she was nervous. Which made him wonder why the hell she had suggested coming back here in the first place. He pushed away from the sofa, ready to suggest again that they go outside, only this time it wouldn't be a question.

"Do you mind if I play some music?"

He hid his surprise, shrugged and nodded. "Sure. Help yourself." He expected her to pull out a cellphone, to call up a playlist and pop it into the notch in the alarm clock designed just for that. To his surprise, she moved toward the small entertainment system and turned on the stereo, scanning the channels before choosing one. Instrumental music infused with a touch of the islands drifted through the speaker. Mellow. Relaxing. Just loud enough to act as background noise to cover the awkward silence that had settled between them.

She glanced at him over her shoulder, a hesitant

smile tugging at her mouth. "Is this okay?"

"Yeah. Perfect." He eased back against the sofa arm, his chest tightening at the sight of her moving to the relaxing strains. Did she realize her body was gently swaying to the beat of the song? Slow, sensual, the ends of her hair swinging against her back, her hips swaying in a teasing rhythm.

Daryl's eyes drifted along her body, from the top of her head to the slope of her shoulders, to the way the cover-up fell over her firm ass. The hem pulled up just enough to tease him when her hips rocked to the left, then dropped when she moved to the right. Thank God her back was to him because he was certain she'd run screaming if she caught sight of the hunger and desire he knew was burning in his eyes. Then she turned around and Daryl dropped his gaze to the floor, forced himself to think of anything but that beautiful ass swaying in front of him.

"Are you married, Daryl?"

What. The. Fuck.

The question caught him so off-guard that he nearly squeezed the water bottle in half. Although maybe it was a fair question. Maybe she could sense the tension that rolled off his coiled body and thickened the air around them and wanted to be sure he wasn't already involved with someone. Fair enough.

He took another swallow of the water, recapped the bottle, and shook his head. "No."

Kelsey tilted her head to the side, those green-ringed hazel eyes studying him for a half-second too long. "Why did you hesitate before you answered?"

Had he? Yeah, probably. Stupid, because he had nothing to hide—he just didn't usually discuss his past, especially not this part. "I *was* married. A long time ago."

"Divorced?"

"No." The word was short. Clipped. It invited no additional conversation—but Kelsey didn't seem to realize that. She closed the distance between them, stopping a foot away, sympathy welling in her eyes. Her hand closed over his arm, her fingers cool against his hot flesh, and squeezed.

"I'm sorry. I didn't realize—you must have loved her. How long ago did she pass?"

A muscle twitched in his clenched jaw and for a second, maybe two, all he wanted to do was brush her hand away. To escape the suddenly suffocating confines of the room and head to the beach. To run, feel the soft grains of sand shift under his feet as he pushed himself, sweat dripping into his eyes and clouding his vision. To keep running, until he couldn't think, couldn't feel—

Until he could no longer see the sympathy and concern in the depths of those green-ringed hazel eyes staring up at him.

She actually felt *sorry* for him. Thought his abrupt answers were because of sorrow. Because he *missed* his wife.

Nothing could be further from the truth. Miss Melissa? No. Not in this lifetime. Not after what she'd done. And if that made him a cold-hearted son-of-a-bitch, then he'd gladly pay for the sin in whatever afterlife waited for him.

But he didn't brush Kelsey's hand from his arm. And he didn't turn and run. To his surprise, he heard himself answering her, the words coming from a distance he didn't quite understand. "Nine years ago. And no, I didn't love her."

Did the words shock her? Yes. Her fingers jerked against the hard flesh of his arm a second before she moved her hand. Her eyes widened, slid away from his as she pulled her lower lip between her teeth and sucked on it. "I'm sorry. I shouldn't have—it's not my business—"

"She was killed in a car accident." His voice was low. Flat. Emotionless. "About two hours after she told me she was filing for divorce and left." Memories and emotions sucker-punched him, coming out of nowhere, slamming his heart against his sternum and squeezing the air from his lungs. He bit down on the next words. They'd been buried for the last nine years, there was no reason to set them free now. Not here, not with the woman who was staring up at him with sympathy and understanding.

The words came anyway, fought their way up from that dark hole he'd shoved them into nine years ago. Harsh. Ragged. Painful. Shredding him even now, after all this time. "Our daughter was with her."

He heard Kelsey's gasp, saw her cover her mouth with one hand.

But it was another voice he heard, soft and crying, raspy with spent tears as tiny arms latched around his neck.

"Wanna stay, Daddy. Wanna stay with you."

"I know, Bean. But you need to go with Mommy for right now. Just for a little bit. Then Daddy will come get you."

Melissa in the background, her sharp voice bitter, threatening, telling him he'd never see Layla again unless she got what she wanted. Damn her, didn't she know what she was doing to Layla? Didn't she care? And God help him, at that second, he wanted to hurt her, wanted to throw her out the door and tell her to never come back. She must have seen something in his face, must have realized she had pushed too far this time because she backed off, gentled her voice and reassured Layla that she would see Daddy when he got home—in eighteen months.

And fuck, he had to do something. He couldn't let Melissa take off with Layla, not like this. Not when he was leaving in two days. He'd go to his CO, the Chaplain, somebody. Somebody somewhere would be able to do something. They had to because his next option would be going fucking AWOL and if that's what he had to do, then he'd fucking do it.

He dropped to his knees and set Layla on her feet, plopped a wet, noisy kiss on her forehead the way she liked then handed her the ragged stuffed bunny she carried everywhere. "You be a good girl for Mommy, okay? And Daddy will come get you as soon as I can."

"Promise?"

"You're my Bean. Of course I promise. And Daddy never breaks his promise."

Only that time, he had. The promise had been nothing more than empty words. Nothing more than a lie. Two hours later, Melissa was gone, killed on impact when her speeding car slammed into a tractor-trailer.

Layla was gone.

His entire world had ended, snuffed out between one heartbeat and the next. Life as he knew it was over. Life? Fuck, he hadn't cared about life after that. Hadn't cared about *anything*.

But he didn't say any of that. Looking at the expression in Kelsey's eyes, he knew he didn't have to.

He ripped his gaze from hers, uncapped the bottle and raised it to his mouth. Drained it in two long swallows. Fuck. What the *fuck* had possessed him to tell her that? He hadn't told anyone, not Mac, not any of the other guys on his team. The only person who knew was Reigs—Jon Reigler—and that was only

The Guardian: DARYL

because Daryl had ripped him a new one more than a year ago, telling him he had no fucking clue what he was missing out on before he reunited with his ex-wife—and his daughter.

And the memory—fuck, he never allowed himself to remember that day, or the weeks and months following. If it hadn't been for his CO, he'd have gone off the deep-end. The crotchety son-of-a-bitch wouldn't let him, though. Had forced him to channel all that rage and anger and despair into something more constructive, more lethal.

Captain Allen Davis had saved his sorry ass in more ways than one.

Kelsey's hand wrapped around his, eased the empty bottle from his strangling grip. He expected her to walk away. To turn around and leave. What woman wanted to listen to a fucking sob story from the guy who had picked her up and invited her to join him for a drink? But to his surprise, she didn't leave. She tossed the bottle in the trashcan near the small refrigerator then turned back to him, stepped close enough that the gauzy material of her cover-up brushed against his chest, his arms. Close enough that he could feel the heat of her body, smell the faint coconut scent of her sunscreen.

She leaned up on her toes, cupped his face between her hands, and gently brushed her lips against his.

"I'm sorry. I can't imagine what you must have gone through." Her voice was even softer than before, husky with sympathy and sorrow. And fuck, this was a bad idea. He didn't want her, not like this, not out of whatever fucked-up sympathy she was feeling.

Yeah, this was a definite bad idea. His emotions

were too close to the surface, the hold on his control too fucking tenuous. It would be too easy to lose himself. To just fucking let go and *feel* for the first time in nine years instead of just going through the motions. To use her to forget.

No, he didn't want to do that. Didn't want to use her that way. But the words stuck in his throat and he couldn't get them out. And then it didn't matter because her lips brushed against his once more and those stunning green-ringed eyes met his, filled with soundless reassurance.

Forget everything except this. Just us. Just for tonight.

Yet he still hesitated, held himself back—until her mouth closed over his. Sweet, warm, filled with promise.

And the desperate grip he had on what remained of his control snapped.

Daryl wrapped one arm behind her waist and pulled her closer, fitting her body to his. He cupped the back of her head and took over the kiss. Deepened it until her mouth opened on a small gasp. His tongue delved between her lips, tasted the intoxicating mixture of rum and coconut and something even sweeter—Kelsey herself.

She stiffened and for one horrifying second, he worried that he'd gone too far, pushed too hard. Then her body relaxed against his, supple curves and firm flesh pressing against him. One of her hands tangled in his shirt; the other wrapped behind his neck, her fingers playing with the ends of his hair.

It wasn't enough. Now that he had just a little taste, he wanted *more*. More of her touch. More of her taste. More of *her*.

A weak voice of reason whispered in the back of

his mind, warning him to slow down. Demanding he move away until he regained control. He shoved the voice away. He didn't want to slow down. He didn't want control—not if it meant holding a piece of himself back.

For the first time in nine years—longer than nine years—he allowed himself to *feel*. To give up the control he had fine-tuned and mastered over the last decade. He didn't want control—

He wanted Kelsey.

This woman. Right here.

Right now.

He swallowed her breathless sigh when he lifted the hem of her gauzy cover-up and palmed her ass through the bottom of her bathing suit. Even that thin barrier was too much. He wanted it gone, *needed* it gone. Needed to caress bare flesh, to trace the cleft of her ass, to dip his finger lower to that sweet, warm treasure between her legs.

He broke the kiss, dragged his mouth along her neck. Her head fell back, her breath escaping from slightly parted lips. Fingers dug into his arms and her sigh turned to a small moan when he nipped the delicate flesh between her neck and shoulder.

He claimed her mouth again, slow and demanding, savoring her taste. Reached between them, worked the buttons of his shirt and shrugged out of it, let it fall behind him. He grabbed the hem of her cover-up and pulled it up. Up. Higher, breaking the kiss long enough to drag it over her head.

Hunger ravaged him as he stared at her. Smooth skin pulled tight over lean muscle. Firm breasts hidden behind two triangles of black material held together by a simple string tie. The points of her nipples hardened as he watched, pushing against her bikini top, begging to be touched.

Demanding to be touched.

He reached out with one hand, traced the line of her delicate collarbone. Turned his hand over and grazed the peak of one hardened nipple with his knuckles.

Her head fell back again, her eyes closing as he teased that nipple. Back and forth, his touch light. A little harder, then lighter. Over and over until her chest rose and fell with each short breath. Until those breaths turned into sharp sighs. Until she staggered toward him, her hands reaching, searching.

Daryl caught her, closed his mouth over hers. Swallowed his own groan when her hands—slender and delicate and hungry—roamed over his chest. His shoulders. His arms.

And fuck! He wanted her now. Needed to drive his cock into her wet heat. Deep. Hard. Fast. Faster, until there was nothing left but the two of them. Until the world—the past, the present, the future—faded away. Just them.

Here.

Now.

He broke the kiss, dragged his mouth to her ear and nipped the small lobe. His voice was rough. Hoarse and ragged. "Don't move."

Her lids fluttered open and those beautiful eyes slowly focused on him. His heart slammed into his chest and the air rushed from his lungs when he saw the need swimming in their hazel depths.

"Don't move." He repeated the command, his gaze never leaving hers as he skirted the sofa and moved toward the sliding glass door. He reached behind him and threw the lock with one hand. Grabbed the edge of the drapes and slid them across the door, plunging the room into shadows. Still watching. Always watching, his gaze locked with Kelsey's the entire time.

He closed the distance between them in two strides. Could she see the hunger in his eyes? See his urgency? This overwhelming need that consumed him? Yes, she could. Her eyes flared, her pupils dilating. But she didn't move away, didn't step out of his reach. He held himself still, afraid to move, to touch, giving her a chance to flee, to tell him no.

She moved toward him instead, her arms reaching for him, her hands sliding along his biceps. His shoulders. His chest. He caught her around the waist and pulled her to him, his mouth crashing over hers. Hard. Hot. Wet.

Hungry.

He slid his hand up her back, pulled the two sets of ties that held her bathing suit top in place then dragged it off her. A sigh escaped her mouth and he ruthlessly swallowed it before pulling away. Her arms came up to shield herself but he pushed them away, caught her hands in his and held her arms out to the side. Then he raked her with his gaze, felt his mouth go dry and his balls tighten with need.

He'd been a fool earlier, thinking her curves were lacking. Her firm breasts were perfect. Small and beautiful. Soft mounds of pale flesh, the nipples a dark rose. He released one of her hands, trailed a finger along her arm. Across her shoulder and throat. Down. Slow, teasing, watching her skin pebble and flush where he touched. Down further until he cupped the slight weight of one breast in his palm. He teased the tight peak of one nipple with his thumb, heard the swift intake of her breath as her head fell back. Her chest thrust forward with the motion, offering herself to him.

An offer he had no intention of refusing.

He dipped his head, closed his mouth over the tight peak and sucked. Nipped. Teased. Pulled it into his mouth and savored the taste of her sweet flesh, reveled in the feel of flesh both hard and soft against his tongue.

Her sigh turned into a moan, deep and throaty, the sound shooting straight to his cock. He braced her with one arm behind her back, trailed his hand along the flat of her stomach. Down lower, dipping into the flimsy material of the bikini bottom.

Smooth flesh, hot and wet and deliciously bare, greeted him. And fuck, he damn near came in his swim trunks right there. Hunger shot through him. Powerful. Potent. He wanted to see those bare lips, run his tongue over that bare flesh.

Now.

He bent down, scooped her into his arms and carried her to the edge of the bed. Her lids fluttered open and she watched him through eyes glazed with need as he gently lowered her to the mattress. He slid her to the edge then eased the bikini bottoms down her legs. Dropped to his knees and spread her legs, murmuring words of reassurance when she tensed under his touch. Then he placed a kiss against her inner thigh, heard her long sigh, felt the tremor that ran through her body.

Kiss after kiss. Featherlight. Teasing. Higher and higher until he reached the decadence of that bare flesh between her legs. He reached up and spread the delicate flesh with one hand, ran the tip of one finger along her clit. Just a light touch. Teasing. Her back arched, her hips rocking toward him. Seeking. Silently demanding.

He leaned forward, dropped his mouth against her bare flesh, and kissed her. Ran his tongue along the hard flesh of her clit as he slid one finger inside her. Fuck. She was so fucking wet. So fucking hot.

So fucking sweet.

He slid his finger out, traced a damp line along her inner thigh. Down, then up. Back to the fiery treasure. Two fingers this time, in and out. Slow. Slower. Feeling muscles quiver as she rocked against his hand, his tongue.

Faster. A little deeper, until her sighs turned to sharp moans and her body writhed under his touch. His kiss.

Faster still, his tongue swirling around the hard flesh of her clit as he fucked her with his fingers. Harder, muscles gripping, holding—

Her back arched and she reached down, nails digging into the flesh of his wrists. Cries of need fell from her mouth, breathless and nearly incoherent. Daryl lifted his mouth from her sweet, wet pussy. Watched as her head tossed from side-to-side, as her teeth bit into her lower lip.

As she held his hand in place, her hips rocking against him, her pussy riding his fingers. Faster, faster...until she exploded around him, muscles clenching and unclenching. Wet. Hot. So fucking hot.

And fuck. He needed inside her *now*. Needed to feel that pussy clenching his cock instead of his fingers. He reached down with his free hand, shoved the swimming trunks past his hips and curled his hand around his cock. Stroking, hard and fast, his hand mimicking the pulsing squeezes of Kelsey's pussy.

Her body slowly relaxed and he eased his fingers from inside her, watched her chest rise and fall with each sharp breath. Still stroking his cock but slower now, controlling the urgency that had swept through him moments earlier. Kelsey pushed up on her elbows, a sleepy smile curling her mouth as she motioned for him to stand up.

He released his cock, pushed to his feet and stepped out of the swimming trunks. Kelsey's eyes raked his body, hunger flaring in their depths. She met his gaze, lifted one hand and curled her finger in a beckoning motion.

Daryl stepped closer, stopped and moved back, reaching for the wallet sitting on the nightstand. He opened it up, reached in and grabbed the condoms inside then tossed it to the side.

Two condoms. Two fucking condoms. They wouldn't be enough. Not nearly enough.

Kelsey pushed to her knees and grabbed the condoms from his hand, a small smile teasing her mouth. "We can get some more later."

It was a promise he had every intention of holding her to.

She tossed one packet to the bed, tore open the second one and leaned forward. Her hair fell over her shoulder, revealing another tattoo high up on her right shoulder. The triquetra—the Celtic cross. Another symbol of protection. Daryl reached out, traced the three-cornered interwoven knot and overlaying circle with the tip of one finger. She tensed under his touch, quickly looked up.

And he knew, with a certainty he couldn't explain,

that she was in trouble of some kind. The Eye of Horus. The obsidian. The triquetra—all symbols of protection.

"What are you protecting yourself from, Kelsey?"

Surprise flashed in her eyes, quickly hidden as she shrugged. "Nothing. Everything."

"Me?"

She shook her head. "No. Not you. Not tonight."

He wanted to ask her more, wanted to tell her he could help—and how fucked up was that? He'd just met her, knew nothing about her. After tonight, he'd never see her again. But he still wanted to reassure her, to tell her he was there if she needed him.

Then it didn't matter because her small hand closed around his cock and stroked. Long. Hard. She rolled the condom down his hard length then reached up. Hands closed over his shoulders, their grip stronger than he anticipated as she pulled him down on the bed.

Her mouth claimed his, igniting the need simmering deep inside him. He settled himself between her spread legs, groaned when she raised her hips and rocked against him. Seeking. Demanding.

He thrust into her with one deep stroke, swallowed a low groan when she tightened around him. When she matched his rhythm. Slow. Fast. Deep. Hard.

And with each stroke, he felt himself losing more and more control, until there was nothing left.

Just Kelsey.

Just him.

The two of them.

Here. Now. Tonight.

And somewhere deep inside, in the darkest corner of his soul, something shattered.

***

Daryl sank deeper into the covers, fighting a decades-old habit of rising early. There was no need to wake up. Not yet. Not when he was too comfortable. Content. Sated.

He stirred, stretched one arm across the bed, searching for Kelsey. He jerked to a sitting position and stared at the rumpled sheets, his mind fighting to process what his eyes were telling him.

Fighting to process what his heart already knew.

Kelsey was gone.

He glanced around the room, knowing before he did that there would be no sign of her. No colorful tote bag. No gauzy coverup. No simple black bikini.

Nothing except a handful of condom wrappers and the faint scent of coconut and sex. Nothing except the indentation of her head in the pillow she had used when she finally fell asleep, curled in his arms.

He looked closer, frowned. Reached out and fingered the chunk of raw obsidian hanging from a black leather chord resting on Kelsey's pillow. He hesitated, closed his fingers around it and held it in front of him, wondering why she had left it behind.

It's for protection. That's what someone told me. I have no idea if it really means that, I just like it.

Daryl pulled it over his head, adjusted the length, then climbed out of bed.

And told himself the chill skipping along his spine was caused by nothing more than the temperature of the cold room.

CHAPTER THREE

Three Months Later.

Kelsey stopped at the edge of the narrow alley. Despite the shadows of the encroaching night, she was careful to keep hidden behind the gnarled trunk of the ancient oak tree that backed up to Miss Theresa's house. How many times had she wished for a tree like this growing up, moving from base to base as her father was assigned to a new duty station? She had always wanted a tree house when she was a little girl, someplace special to hang out with her ever-changing handful of friends.

Someplace where she could go to hide away from the world, to daydream about what she'd be when she got older. A fairy princess. An astronaut. A scientist. An actress. President. A marine biologist. An engineer. Her dreams would change from month to month and year to year but it didn't matter. Her dad had always encouraged her, told her she could be whatever she wanted to be as long as she worked hard for it.

Not once, in all those years, had she ever dreamed she would be where she was today. Running, always running. Hiding, always hiding. Because it wasn't *her* dreams that mattered anymore. And she could live with that, had gladly given up those dreams in exchange for someone much more important.

Kelsey rested her head against the gnarled trunk, took odd comfort from the feel of the rough bark against her cheek and under her palms. *Please God, let her grow up to have those dreams like I did.*

It was the same prayer she uttered every morning and every night—and every hour in between.

Please God, keep her safe.

Please God, let her grow up.

But time was running out. Kelsey felt it deep down in her gut, knew it in the darkest corner of her mind where nightmares dwelled, waiting to lurch. To attack and devour.

How much time? Weeks? Months? Years? No, not years, not even close. Months, if she was lucky. Weeks if she wasn't. Not enough time. Never enough. Grady Byrne would never give up, not until he got what he wanted. Not until he won.

Kelsey couldn't let him win. She would die first.

She didn't want to acknowledge that that was a very real possibility—one that grew even more possible with each passing day. She'd been running for—she frowned, thinking, trying to separate the months from the years. Three years.

Three years, four months and she didn't know how many days. Ever since Blaine had died. Ever since Grady Byrne had discovered he had a granddaughter.

A granddaughter he would never see, not as long as Kelsey could keep running. Not as long as she drew breath.

But time was running out, may have already run out. Grady was getting close, she knew that with every ounce of mother's instinct running through her blood. Paige was safely hidden...for now. As long as Kelsey remained alive, as long as she didn't slip up and do anything stupid, Paige should stay safe.

Or was that nothing more than a wish she kept

repeating to herself in a vain attempt to make it true? She'd done her best, hidden Paige as well as she could with her father's help. Was it enough?

Please God, let it be enough.

That's why she was here now, answering her father's cryptic summons. She hadn't seen him in six months, had only spoken to him once in all that time: the week before she'd gone to that tiny Caribbean island, needing to see for herself if she could trust the man her father spoke so highly of.

Daryl Anderson.

Memory sliced through her and she closed her eyes, brushed off the pain that accompanied the memory. She had only meant to check him out, to watch from a distance. She had *never* planned on talking to him.

Had never planned on sleeping with him.

Kelsey still didn't understand why she'd done either of those things. Her father trusted him, that should have been enough. She should have never gone down there. Should have walked away the very first time their gazes met. Should have packed her small cache of belongings and disappeared long before he had come over to talk to her.

But she didn't. She *couldn't*. She'd been too mesmerized, too curious, too drawn to him. Or maybe she had merely been starved for human contact, for something deeper than the aloof and casual interaction with society that had become her new normal from the very first day she started running.

It didn't matter *why* she'd done those things. She'd done them and couldn't go back to change them, didn't think she would even if she was somehow given the chance. She had slept with him. And for that handful of hours, she'd felt...normal. Safe.

No, she wouldn't change any of it.

But did Kelsey trust him? With her body, yes. But with her most treasured possession?

She didn't know.

And she was very much afraid the time to make that decision was coming. Why else would her father have summoned her here to his place? The news couldn't be good, not when he knew how much was at stake. How risky her showing up here was.

The time was drawing near when she would be forced to decide: could she trust Daryl Anderson? She thought maybe she could—*maybe*. No, there was no logical reason for the trust. Nothing more than her father's own trust in him and the fact that she'd slept with him. She wouldn't sleep with anyone she didn't trust, even if it *had* been mere hours after meeting him. There was something about him, some inner strength she thought she saw. Something that had tugged at her, especially when she saw the pain he had tried so hard to hide when he talked about losing his wife. No, not his wife—his daughter.

Or had that been nothing more than sympathy? Had she thrown all caution and sensibility to the wind simply because she'd felt sorry for him?

No, she didn't think so. She would have never slept with someone she didn't trust on some basic, instinctual level before. Certainly, she hadn't changed that much in the last three years. But she couldn't be a hundred percent sure of that, was already second-guessing herself.

And second-guessing herself could get her killed and place her daughter in the hands of a madman.

Maybe she still had time. Maybe her dad's cryptic

message was for another reason entirely. She almost laughed. Was she really trying to convince herself of that fantasy? No, she knew better. Maybe she had a little more time before making a final decision regarding Daryl Anderson but that time would be measured in days, not weeks or months.

Kelsey adjusted the straps of the worn backpack then pushed back the sleeve of the oversized leather jacket and glanced at her watch. Not quite seven o'clock yet. She had another fifteen minutes to wait before she could move down the alley to the back door of her father's house.

Fifteen minutes.

Why did it feel like an eternity? Her stomach was twisted in knots and her palms were damp. Nerves? Excitement? Both. Nerves because she knew the probability of this meeting signaling the beginning of the end, knew that her time to make a decision was drawing near.

Excitement because, even with everything else going on, she was going to see her dad again. It had been too long and she missed him, almost as much as she missed her daughter. He was her only family, the one who had seen her through all the ups and downs of her teenage years after her mom had passed. The one who had taught her how to be strong and independent and fight for what she wanted, no matter what that happened to be.

She'd been so afraid to tell him when she learned she was pregnant, so afraid she'd see disappointment in his eyes. But there'd been no disappointment, only joy—and reassurance. And he'd been there for both of them, from the day Paige was born to the day Kelsey had started running. Supporting. Guiding. Helping.

Staying one step ahead of Grady Byrne for as long as they could.

Her father was sick. She knew that even though he hadn't said anything. She didn't know what was wrong with him but she'd been able to tell the last time she had seen him. His color had paled and he'd lost weight. But he was still larger than life, still the strongest man she knew.

Tonight, more than anything, she needed to feel his strong arms wrap around her in a big hug, the way he'd done when she was a little girl with a boo-boo. Needed to hear his gruff voice tell her everything was going to be okay. Just for tonight. Just for the first five minutes, even though they would both know it wasn't true.

Kelsey reached up, wiped a hand across her face to make sure there were no tell-tale tracks of tears. She yanked the baseball hat off her head and shoved it into a pocket of the jacket then ran both hands through her hair. It was shorter now than it had been a few months ago, cut into a no-nonsense shoulder-length style that released the natural wave she had always struggled to contain when she was a teen. The hair was back to her natural color now, too—at least, as close as the stylist could get to the deep brown-red locks she'd always had until Kelsey bleached and dyed it blonde before going to the Caribbean.

A small smile teased her mouth. Dad would have loved to see the blonde color. She'd have to be sure to tell him about it, during those first five minutes she saw him when they could act like nothing was wrong. When she could fall into the role of Daddy's girl that she so often missed now.

Kelsey rechecked her watch. It was time. She

looked around, noting her surroundings the way she had when she first got here. Nothing was out of place, nothing sent shivers of apprehension skittering along her spine. It would have made her feel more comfortable to have her car parked nearby but leaving it a few blocks away was a precaution she felt better taking.

She adjusted the backpack straps a final time then pushed away from the tree and headed toward her father's house. *Walk like you belong there and nobody will question you.*

That had been just one small piece of advice her father had given her over the years and she followed it now. Each step was confident and measured, not furtive or secretive. She walked like she belonged—because she did. This was her father's house. She'd been here before, more than once after he retired and settled down in this small neighborhood outside St. Louis. She'd even met a few of his neighbors, had teased him about Miss Theresa flirting with him.

She reached the back fence of her father's neat little yard, raised the latch on the gate and pushed. It opened soundlessly, swinging inward on well-oiled hinges. She closed it behind her then paused, looking around. Unlike many of the other houses in the neighborhood, there was no parking pad back here. Her father had taken it out not long after buying the house, replacing the concrete with a small brick patio and seeding everything else.

Neat flowerbeds lined the edges of the small patio, now dormant except for a few mums that hadn't quite reached full bloom yet. The vegetable garden was the same, the short rows neatly tilled under, waiting for the next spring when her dad would plant tomatoes and cucumbers and maybe some squash.

The only thing that didn't fit in with his garden was the well-maintained storage shed in the corner, which housed his gardening tools and a small workshop where he fiddled with woodworking.

It also housed one of his most prized possessions, a 1972 Kawasaki Z1 that he kept in excellent shape and still took out on the weekends. At least, he had as recently as six months ago. She remembered when he taught her to drive it, not long after she had turned fifteen. They were living in Louisiana at the time and she'd been pouting because she'd had to change schools and make new friends—again. Learning how to ride the old bike had acted like a balm of sorts, giving her a small taste of joy and freedom that continued to fill her over the next few years. The fact that her dad still rode it filled her with a combination of concern—and envy.

She pushed the twinges of nostalgia away and crossed the patio to the backdoor. The back of the house was dark but she could see the faint glow of lights coming from the front. Her dad was probably in the living room, either watching television or playing around on his laptop, catching up with news of the many guys he had served with.

Kelsey dug the key from her front pocket and slid it into the lock, turned the knob and eased the door open. She had only taken one step inside when she realized something was wrong.

Very wrong.

The smell hit her first, a faint sickly-sweet smell that turned her stomach and caused bile to burn her throat. She shook her head, denying what her heart already knew, and moved toward the living room.

Tears filled her eyes, clogged her throat and threatened to strangle her. Her father—the strongest man she had ever known, the person who had taken care of her for so long—was gone. He sat in his favorite recliner, his body sagging in death. His eyes were closed, almost as if he was sleeping, and for one desperately heartfelt second, Kelsey convinced herself that's all he was doing.

He was sleeping. Had dozed off waiting for her. She would call out to him and he'd open his eyes, make a gruff noise and pretend he hadn't fallen asleep.

Yes, that's all it was. He was sleeping, that's it.

Except he wasn't. The small hole in the center of his forehead told her that much.

"Daddy." She stepped toward him, stopped and covered her mouth to stop the wail building in her throat, knowing if she started, she'd never stop. "Oh, Daddy. No. No, no, no."

She hurried to the recliner and dropped to her knees beside him, ignoring the sights and smells of death as she wrapped her hand around his. Cold, so cold. Smaller than she remembered, frailer somehow. She closed her eyes, dropped her head against his still hand, and cried. Cried until she couldn't breathe, until her lungs ached and her body numbed.

Kelsey Ann, stop it. You've had your cry. It's time to get over it. You have things to do.

Her head jerked up and she looked around, expecting to see her father behind her. But he wasn't—he couldn't be, not when she still held his cold hand in her terrified grip. But it *was* his voice she had heard and he was right, she didn't have time to grieve. Not now, not when other things needed to be done.

"I love you, Daddy." She swallowed her tears and

pressed a kiss against the back of the lifeless hand then pushed to her knees. Panic washed over her, and fear, replacing the overwhelming grief from moments earlier. She needed to brush them all off, *now*. If she didn't, she'd be paralyzed into inaction and the only person who would suffer would be Paige.

Kelsey refused to let that happen.

That's my girl. Now go.

Yes. Yes, she had to go. How much time did she have? Was Grady Byrne still around? Because there was no doubt in her mind that this was his work.

No, he wasn't here. Not right now. Close, maybe, but she had time. Minutes, perhaps a few hours.

That realization, more than anything else, prompted her to move. For Paige, she needed to get out. Leave. Flee to safety.

Flee east.

But first she needed to get something—if *they* hadn't already taken it. No, they hadn't, she was sure of it. The tidy house hadn't been ransacked. Or rather, if it had been, they had put everything back exactly where they found it. She didn't know much about how Grady worked but she didn't think his men would be that meticulous.

She moved through the living room, bounded up the stairs to her father's room. There was enough light from downstairs that she could still see but even if there wasn't, she wouldn't have had any trouble. Her father had made sure she knew exactly where everything was, had made her practice looking for it with her eyes closed so she would never have any problems.

There, on the corner of his dresser, sat a small humidor. She went to it, raised the lid and fought back tears as the smell of her father's favorite cigars wafted out of the Spanish Cedar box. She slid her nail around the edge, lifted the corner of the thin wood tray her father had added until she could get her fingers under it to remove it. An envelope, maybe a quarter of an inch thick, rested at the bottom. She grabbed it, shoved it into the inside pocket of her jacket, then replaced the cigars. On an impulse she didn't stop to consider, she grabbed two of the cigars and placed them in the jacket pocket as well.

Kelsey moved to her father's closet, reached for the top shelf. Her fingers brushed against cold metal, wrapped around the edges of the heavy box and pulled it down. Her father's small gun vault. And oh God, why had he kept it locked up here, where it couldn't help? If he'd had his gun, maybe—

No, she couldn't think like that. Not now. Later, when she was far away from here, maybe. But not now.

She snagged the key from the top drawer of the dresser and opened the box, pulled out the pistol and released the clip, checked the chamber. Clear. She slammed the clip back in, double-checked to make sure the safety was on, then shrugged out of her backpack. She started to place the gun inside then hesitated. It wouldn't help her if she needed to use it and couldn't get to it.

But *would* she be able to use it? Would she be able to pull it on someone and shoot if necessary?

She thought of her father downstairs. Thought of the daughter she hadn't seen in six months. Yes. Yes, she'd be able to use it if she needed to.

She tucked the gun into the waistband of her jeans and tossed the other two clips—both full—into the backpack. A box of ammo followed. Then she shrugged back into the pack and headed out of the room. Impulse made her turn into the spare room that served as her father's office. There, along the far wall, was the shelf where he kept the mementos from a lifetime of military service. She made her way over to it, snagged the dog tags from the small hook next to the shelf and draped them over her head before tucking them into her loose sweatshirt. His jump wings went into her front pocket.

Then she raced down the steps, averting her gaze from her father's lifeless body. He was gone. She had said her goodbyes. There was nothing more she could do. Not here. Not now.

Biting back tears and grief, she made her way to the kitchen and grabbed the keys to the shed before letting herself out of the house. It was completely dark now, with very few lights shining from the neighbors' yards. She made her way across the small backyard and unlocked the shed, opened the door and let herself inside. Returning to her car was out of the question now. She had no way of knowing where Grady's men were, couldn't take the chance that they were already here, waiting for her to return to her car before fleeing. It was nothing more than instinct but she had nothing else to go on—and it was too risky to ignore the urgency propelling her forward, dictating each move she made.

She grabbed the helmet from the sleek handlebars of the motorcycle and dropped it over her head before raising the kickstand with her foot. She pushed the bike from the shed, paused long enough to close the door and lock it, then wheeled the bike through the gate of her father's backyard.

For two blocks she pushed it, sweat beading her

forehead, exertion and fear and urgency pounding in her chest, urging her forward.

You know what to do, Katydid.

Yes, she knew.

Head east. To safety.

To help.

But where? To West Virginia and the tiny off-grid cabin nobody else knew about?

Or to Maryland? To Daryl Anderson—the man her father swore would protect and guard her if things ever reached this point?

She didn't know, couldn't decide. Not yet, not when her mind was still reeling.

Kelsey swung her leg over the seat and started the motorcycle, felt the smooth power of the engine roar to life between her legs.

No, she didn't know, not yet. But she still had a little bit of time to figure it out—about fourteen or fifteen hours of travel along the back roads, following the route her father made her memorize more than six months ago.

West Virginia?

Or the man with the sun-streaked hair and eyes the color of liquid amber, with the reassuring smile and, she prayed, the strength to slay dragons?

CHAPTER FOUR

Grady Byrne curled his hand around the receiver, took a deep calming breath through his nose, just like his therapist had taught him. It worked only inasmuch as controlling his well-modulated voice when he spoke. It didn't do a damn thing to control the rage boiling inside him.

"What do you mean, you don't know where she is?"

There was a pause on the other end of the line, as he knew there would be. Despite the control in his voice—a voice that held the faintest of an oft-practiced lilt—the man on the other line could hear his anger. He'd be a fool if he didn't, a fool if he didn't realize how dangerously close he was to signing his own death warrant.

"She never came out of the house, sir. I had one man watching the front while I waited at her car."

"But she's not in there now, is she?"

"No, sir."

"Which means she obviously left the house. Did nobody watch the back?"

There was another pause, this one filled with muted stuttering. The blundering idiot! They were close, closer than they'd been in six months, when the woman and the girl had vanished entirely as if they had never existed. To be this close and fail—

No. Grady Byrne did *not* fail. The word wasn't part of his vocabulary. He would have never climbed his way out of the slums if he accepted failure. Would have never created an empire worth millions if he allowed failure.

Failure had no place in his carefully constructed world.

"N-no, sir. We thought, once she saw her father, that she'd run out the front. Call for help."

"She obviously didn't, now did she?" No, of course not. A woman who could evade him for three years, a woman who could disappear without the slightest trace for six months, wouldn't do anything quite so expected. His men had underestimated her—again.

Grady moved around the antique desk and lowered himself to the expensive chair. He didn't bother looking out the window—the bustling landscape of the old city beyond provided no solace. He hated this place. Hated that he'd been forced to move here to escape the reaches of the US government. They were nothing more fools that thought they could control him and his business ventures.

But there were other fools that needed to be dealt with first.

"Find the woman. I expect to hear news within twenty-four hours."

"Yes, sir. She couldn't have gone far, not on foot. We'll—"

"You imbecile! She won't be on foot."

"But her car—"

"She's not that careless. She'll find some other means of transportation. Just find her. And Michael?"

"Yes, sir?"

"Do not fail again." Grady slammed the phone

into the receiver, enjoying the brief flare of satisfaction the action gave him. The satisfaction was short-lived, quickly replaced by anger and impatience.

It was impossible to believe that a woman with such limited means and no connections could evade him for so long. Three years ago, he hadn't even cared about the woman—all he had cared about was the girl. His granddaughter. The child didn't even carry his name—or her father's name. That mistake would be rectified immediately—as soon as they found the woman. As soon as he had the girl.

If a man in Grady's position had any regrets, it would be that his own son, his own flesh-and-blood, had never known him. Blaine had been a bastard, raised by the woman who had caught Grady's eye for a very brief time. If he had known, if he'd had any inkling whatsoever, that she had been pregnant with a boy— his *son*—he would have taken the child away from her and raised him under his own tutelage.

But Grady hadn't known, hadn't learned about Blaine until it was too late. Until his son's life had been cut short by a drunk driver. The driver had paid for the mistake with his own life and Grady had attended his only offspring's funeral filled with regret over a missed opportunity.

Until he had seen the woman. The *girl*.

His son's daughter.

The girl would take his son's place. She would be raised with only the best, tutored and groomed to take over the empire Grady had fought so hard to build. Her presence would soothe the ruffled feathers of some of the men under him. He wasn't a fool, he'd heard the grumblings. The insinuations that he was getting old. The concern that there was no blood to take over his empire when he was gone. The arguments over who might possibly take his place.

The girl would solve all of that. She would be his legacy.

She *was* his legacy.

He reached into the center drawer and removed the worn photo, the edges curled and creased. It showed a two-year-old girl with auburn curls and wide green eyes—her father's eyes. *His* eyes. Perfect bow-shaped lips were parted in a smile, revealing straight white teeth. A stuffed bear was clutched in one chubby hand raised toward the camera.

The picture had been taken the day before his son's funeral—a day before Grady himself had approached the woman and made his offer.

To his surprise, she hadn't immediately accepted. He didn't miss the fury clear in her voice, in her eyes—fury that had been quickly masked. She had watched him for a long time before finally telling him she would think about it. Then she turned her back on him and walked away.

If he had known how stubborn she would be, Grady would have snatched the young child then. But he hadn't known, had erred on the side of caution, had convinced himself that her hesitation had been caused by grief. The woman would gladly accept his offer once she had a chance to think about it. How could she not? He had never considered that she would refuse. After all, everyone had a price.

And yes, he could admit—at least to himself—that part of him had been impressed by the woman's stubbornness. By her refusal to give up her child so easily. His granddaughter would have inherited some of that stubbornness and loyalty, which would serve the child well when she was being groomed.

But his admiration quickly evaporated when he learned the next day that the woman had taken off. Disappeared with no trace.

And all this time, she had somehow managed to stay two steps ahead of his men. Two steps ahead of *him*.

The woman would pay.

Soon.

Very soon.

CHAPTER FIVE

Exhaustion washed over him. *Washed?* Hell, it was a fucking tsunami, battering his entire body. The only thing keeping him moving forward was more than a decade of training and pure, stubborn habit. That—and the promise of a shower. A cold beer. Eighteen hours of uninterrupted sleep.

Not necessarily in that order.

Daryl ignored the bantering of the two men behind him. Chaos and Boomer were bitching about something but he had no idea what—and he didn't give a shit, either. The past week had been a total fucking blur as they moved around the country, chasing down the tiniest clues and leads before crossing into Mexico and intercepting an arms shipment before it landed in the hands of a drug lord. The job had been a last-minute favor for a friend high up in the chain of command of a no-name agency that didn't exist...on paper. It was easier—not to mention less sticky—for Daryl to take a couple of men and handle it. No muss, no fuss—and no chance of shit going publicly sideways if they screwed up. Not that they would but if something happened, nobody would be pointing fingers at any government official.

Bureaucracy at its finest. But what the hell—the pay more than made up for the bullshit.

He keyed his code into the rear door of the renovated warehouse that served as headquarters for Cover Six Security. There was a small beep, followed by the faintest click as the lock released. He opened the door, adjusted the heavy pack on his shoulder, then grabbed the even heavier duffel and walked inside. Fifteen more minutes and he'd be heading home to that shower and beer.

And his empty bed.

His booted steps echoed off the concrete floor of the cavernous back room they used for storage and training. He passed the duffel to Chaos. The other man raised one brow but didn't say anything as he took it. That was one of the advantages of being in charge: delegating.

Not that he did it often. He was too much of a fucking control freak—in everything. Tough shit. It worked for him, had worked for the last nine years, before then even. He never lost control...

Except for that one night, three months ago—

Fuck it. He pushed the thought to the back of his mind and locked it down. That night had been nothing more than a one-night stand, he'd known that going in. Hell, he hadn't *wanted* anything other than a one-night stand. Yeah, sure. That's why that hunk of obsidian still hung around his neck, tucked into his shirt where nobody could see it. Where nobody could question it.

"I'm going up front, get an update from TR." He tossed the words over his shoulder, received a nod of acknowledgment from both men. They had stopped their bickering, thank Christ, and were focused on cleaning up the gear.

Thirteen more minutes and he could head home.

That thought followed him as he made his way through the large room, pausing to enter his code into another reinforced door. The front of the warehouse was completely different than the rear, remodeled to hold small offices, a conference room, and the front reception area—all accessed through a crazy maze of hallways. He moved through that maze now, his mind on autopilot as he pushed through the last door and stepped into the reception area.

TR Meyers—no, not *Meyers*, she was *MacGregor* now and why the fuck was he still having trouble remembering that?—looked over at him then frowned. He didn't miss the way her nose wrinkled in distaste or the way she actually slid her chair back the tiniest bit when he approached. And shit. He didn't smell that bad, did he?

Yeah, maybe he did because she reached up with one hand and pinched her nose closed. Held her other hand out to stop him. "Don't come any closer. Seriously. You reek."

Daryl frowned, tilted his head and sniffed. "It's not that bad."

"That's because you've fried your nasal passages."

He started to argue, snapped his mouth shut when he realized she might have a point. They'd been out in the field for more than a week then spent the last thirty-six hours on the road pretty much non-stop. He hadn't showered. Hadn't even managed to sleep more than an hour or two here and there. But hell, she should be used to it by now. She'd been filling in as a temporary receptionist for damn near the last eight months, running the front office with a skill that bordered on scary-as-fuck.

She picked up a small stack of messages. "These are for you, most important on top. Not important enough that you need to call anyone back before you take a shower, though."

Daryl took the message slips, quickly scanned

them before tucking them into his front pocket. "Did Mac make it back yet?"

He didn't miss the hint of a smile playing around TR's lips when she nodded. "He got back yesterday. He's in his office working on reports."

"And everyone else?"

"All present and accounted for."

Meaning the handful of jobs that had been divided among the team had been successfully completed. The guys would either be home resting or doing personal shit, getting in time at the range, or working at the training field.

"And this came for you last week." TR held out a small package, one of those generic bubble mailers that was slightly larger than an envelope. Daryl took it, glanced at the front then frowned.

No return address but the postmark was from Springfield. Who the fuck did he know in Springfield, Illinois? Nobody came to mind but there was something vaguely familiar about the bold handwriting. He studied it for a few seconds, trying to place it, then gave up. "Anything else?"

"Nope, that's it."

He nodded, thought about shoving everything into his bag and simply heading home, changed his mind at the last minute. There was no sense going home then coming back later, not when he could take care of the messages now. It would only add ten minutes—fifteen, tops. He could deal with that.

He headed toward his office, frowning again at the small package, that hint of familiarity niggling at him. Curiosity washed away some of his exhaustion—a sure sign that he was more tired than he thought because any other time, he'd just toss the small package on his desk. Come back to it later, then approach it with an overabundance of caution instead of eyeing it with curiosity.

He dropped his gear bag to the floor then slid the chair out with the toe of one booted foot before dropping into it. He pulled the message slips from his pocket, went through them one-by-one before placing them near his keyboard. Not a single one of them needed an immediate response.

The package, however, was a different story.

Daryl eyed it for a few minutes, still studying that handwriting, still wondering why it looked vaguely familiar. He pulled the small pocketknife from his side pocket and eased it under the sealed flap, carefully slicing it open. He upended the envelope then stared at the contents for a long minute.

A small sheet of paper, folded precisely in half.

A thumb drive.

A house key.

What the hell.

He grabbed the note and unfolded it, stared down at the bold writing and the signature scrawled at the bottom. Confusion was slowly replaced by...not excitement, not in the traditional meaning, anyway. His pulse sped up for a brief second, adrenaline and awareness replacing the weariness that had been clinging to him for the last few hours.

Not just awareness, but wariness as well.

He absently turned on the computer, his eyes rereading the few short lines over and over as he waited for the machine to boot.

> I'm calling in the favor you owe me.
> ~Allen Davis

Below that was an address in St. Louis, Missouri.

Allen Davis. His old CO. The man who had saved his ass in more ways than one. He hadn't spoken to the man in years. Hadn't thought of him in almost as long—

No, that wasn't right. Hadn't he just recently thought of him, three months ago when they were in the islands for Mac's wedding? Yeah, he had. The day he'd met—

He pushed the memory away and grabbed the thumb drive, held it in his hand for a few seconds. Waiting. Ignoring the frisson of unease skittering along his spine. The reaction was only because he was tired. There was no reason—real or imagined—for him to be uneasy. Davis was calling in a favor. So what? The favor was long overdue as far as Daryl was concerned. Hell, for all he knew, the cranky s.o.b was going to order him out to wherever the hell he was living now—must be that address in St. Louis—to paint his house or some shit like that.

His mouth twitched in a quick grin. Yeah, that would be something his old CO would do. And Daryl would go, take a few of the other guys with him. They'd paint the fucking house, inside and out. Do whatever else the cranky s.o.b. ordered them to do while they were there. Because yeah, the man had saved Daryl's ass in more ways than one.

Daryl owed him.

He slid the thumb drive into the port then sat back, waiting for the computer to automatically launch whatever the hell was on the drive. A picture of a worn chair filled the screen. Shelves covered the wall behind the chair, filled with mementos of military life. Pictures and awards. A shadow box filled with ribbons. A small hook holding his dog tags. Another hook holding a pair of jump wings.

Daryl leaned closer, wondering why the hell Davis had sent him a picture of an empty chair. Then he heard a muffled cough. The slide of a shoe against a hardwood floor.

Not a picture—a video.

A few seconds later, the thin figure of an older man filled the screen. Just his back at first as he moved toward the chair, muttering under his breath. The man turned toward the camera and Daryl sat back, struggled to catch the breath that had been knocked from his lungs when recognition hit.

This wasn't just some unknown older man—it was Allen Davis. Thinner. Paler. Gaunt. His full head of hair had thinned, become more gray than dark brown. The man facing the camera looked to be in his seventies, not—Daryl frowned, did the math in his head. Davis was twenty years older than he was, which would make him fifty-three.

What the hell had happened to him?

What the hell was going on?

The man looking out at him from the computer monitor raised one long finger and pointed it at the camera. "This damn thing better work this time. I'm running out of fucking patience with this shit."

A ghost of a smile played around Daryl's mouth. The voice was as strong and gruff as he remembered. Blunt. Unforgiving.

Daryl blinked and the years melted away, morphing the image of the older man in front of the camera into the man Daryl remembered. Strong. Dedicated. Loyal. Hard-as-nails and tough-as-shit. Unstoppable.

The man cleared his throat, leaned back in the chair and stared into the camera. He narrowed his eyes and pressed his lips together, his mouth forming a thin line of impatience. Christ, Daryl remembered that look, had seen it plenty of times before—usually seconds before Davis exploded.

But there was no explosion. Not this time. Instead, the older man blew out a heavy sigh, the sound weary. Defeated. His gaze never wavered from the camera, held Daryl's own attention as if he was there in person, sitting on the other side of his desk.

"I hadn't planned on doing this, son. Believe me, if I had any other alternative, I wouldn't. But time is running out and I need your help."

Daryl leaned forward, nudged the volume up. That frisson of unease grew, pebbled the flesh on his arms and the back of his neck.

"I need your help." The man repeated the words, slowly shook his head and uttered a harsh laugh. "Those words don't come easy for me. Or for you. Hell, for any of us. But there it is: I need your help."

Another pause as Davis glanced down at his hands. He turned back to the camera, anger flashing in his eyes. "I'm dying. I'm not telling you that for your pity so just knock that shit off now. I'm telling you that so you understand why I need your help. So you understand how important this is. I've been keeping tabs on you, Anderson. And I'm damn proud of you. Of everything you've accomplished. Call me arrogant but I like to think I had a hand in getting you where you are today."

Davis leaned to the side, coughed, swore beneath his breath. "Damn cancer. Yeah, you heard me. Cancer. Stupid fucking disease. Eats away at you, chipping away at everything you've got. Day-by-day until you look in the fucking mirror and see a stranger staring back at you. And now my time is running out. Doctors say I might have six months. Maybe a little more, maybe a little less. And that's why I need your help: my time is running out."

Davis leaned forward, fiery stubbornness lighting his eyes. The force of his gaze held Daryl's. Commanding. Ordering. Demanding. Just like he had nearly a decade ago. "I'm calling in that favor you owe me. Never thought in a million years that I'd ever do such a damn thing but here I am, doing it anyway. I need your help, son. I can't go into details here—too damn risky. I'll explain when I see you in person. Yeah, I'm asking you to drop everything and get your sorry ass out here. Now."

He coughed again, the sound wet and thick, the force of it bending him over. He straightened, wiped his mouth with the back of his hand, pursed his mouth in distaste. Then he stared into the camera once more, not bothering to hide the fear and worry shadowing his eyes. "My daughter's in trouble, son. And you're the only one I trust to keep her safe."

CHAPTER SIX

A chilled breeze rustled the branches, pulling the last remaining leaves from the trees. They skittered along the sidewalk, collected on the small front porch and tangled in the edges of what remained of the yellow crime scene tape.

Daryl stared at the house, dread filling the hollow pit of his stomach.

Too late.

He was too late.

Anger ripped through him, mingled with the sorrow taking root in his heart. There was something else there, too. Something more than anger, more than sorrow—

Regret.

Failure.

His CO, his mentor—his *friend*—had called on him for help and Daryl had failed.

He'd left as soon as he could, within an hour of watching the video. Chaos had arranged the private charter flight while Boomer broke every posted speed limit getting him to the small airport forty-five minutes from the office. The small jet had been waiting for him, had taken off as soon as Daryl had climbed aboard and shoved his pack under the seat. He'd ignored the sense of urgency pushing him, told himself he was overreacting. That Davis himself had been overreacting. That the situation wasn't as dire as the older man had made it out to be.

He'd actually fucking convinced himself during the nearly-three-hour flight that everything was fine. Whatever trouble Davis's daughter was in couldn't be as serious as he was making it out to be. He'd get to his CO's house and they'd have a beer, sit down and figure out what the hell was going on. Solve it by putting their heads together then kick back and talk about old times.

Only Daryl had been wrong. There'd be no sitting down. No figuring things out. No reminiscing over a beer.

He was too late.

He had failed.

What the *fuck* had happened?

Daryl glanced around the tidy neighborhood, wondering what the fuck to do next. He needed answers. *Now.* Standing out here on the fucking sidewalk as darkness descended around him would get him nowhere. But where the fuck did he go? He needed to find out what happened and *when*.

He had the key Davis had sent him. Did it go to this house? Probably. Even if it didn't, Daryl would have no trouble getting inside. But did he really want to draw attention to himself by going in through the front door? The sidewalk and street were empty but he knew people had seen him, had noticed the curtains of the house two doors down flipping back as whoever was inside looked out.

No, he wouldn't go in the front door. Too obvious. He'd go back to the rental car, pretend to drive off and circle the block, find someplace to park then come back on foot. The small alley would provide plenty of cover as he made his way around the back.

He turned, started back toward his car when he heard the sound of a door opening. It came from the house two doors down, the same house where he'd noticed the curtains moving. Daryl kept walking, watching the woman standing on the small porch from the corner of his eye. She was in her late forties, maybe early fifties. Short dark hair, generous build. Skin-hugging denim clung to her curves. Her hands twisted in the edges of a bulky zippered sweatshirt, holding it tight against the evening chill.

He had just reached the rental car when she moved forward, the first few steps hesitant. Daryl didn't say anything, pretended he hadn't even noticed her. Her steps quickened when his hand closed over the door handle and she called out to him, her voice cautious, maybe a little hopeful.

"Excuse me." She reached the end of her walkway, keeping a safe distance between them. "Are you looking for Allen Davis?"

Should he tell her yes? Or would it be better to deny it? To throw off suspicion for when he returned later and entered the house on his own? He almost settled on the latter then changed his mind at the last second. There was something about the way the woman was watching him, with an air of expectancy and even hope.

"Yes, ma'am. I was." He glanced up the street, looked back at the woman. "Do you know what happened?"

A visible chill shook her and she tightened her grip around the edges of the thick jacket. "Someone broke into the house and...and he was murdered."

Murdered.

Anger washed over him once more, replaced by sorrow and regret. He turned his gaze back to the vacant house, to the loose section of frayed yellow tape that fluttered in the cold breeze.

Too late.

He'd been too fucking late.

He swallowed against the emotion in his throat and made a mental note to have Chaos pull up everything he could find. Then he turned back to the woman. "I'm sorry. I didn't know."

The woman nodded and Daryl thought she may have blinked back tears but he couldn't be sure. "He was a friend of yours?"

A friend? Yes. No. Allen Davis had been much more than a friend, in ways he couldn't begin to define. "Yes, he was. It's been a few years since I've seen him. I was coming out to visit but—"

But he'd been too late. Too damn late.

Light from the corner street lamp reflected from the line of earrings in the woman's right ear when she tilted her head to the side. She watched him for a long minute, studying him.

No, not studying—*measuring*. Sizing him up. She finally nodded, almost to herself, then tossed a quick glance around them. She stepped closer and lowered her voice, emotion flaring in her dark eyes. "He was expecting someone. What's your name?"

He hesitated, weighing the pros and cons of telling her. None of the cons mattered if this woman would be able to help. If she had information about Davis. Hell, maybe she had information *from* Davis.

"Daryl."

"And your last name?"

Again, just a split-second hesitation before he answered. "Anderson."

Recognition flared in her eyes, quickly concealed by a careful blink. So Davis *had* mentioned him to her.

But why? What did she know? He started to ask but she interrupted, asking another question that completely surprised him.

"Would there happen to be another name you go by?"

What the fuck? The woman was being cautious—not necessarily a bad thing. But what the fuck did she know? What had Davis told her? Maybe nothing. Maybe this was just an overabundance of caution.

No, it was more than that. The simple fact that she had asked for another name told him that much. A first and last name would be more than enough for most people—unless they'd been told to ask for more. Davis knew his code name. Hell, the man had been the one to give it to him—and it had nothing to do with a god-complex the way TR had joked all those months ago.

The woman kept watching him. Waiting. There was no doubt in Daryl's mind that she knew the answer, no doubt in his mind that Davis had been the one to tell her. But why?

He met the woman's direct gaze with one of his own. "There is but before I answer, I have a question for you."

She hesitated, her thin brows pulling low over her eyes for a fraction of a second. "Fair enough. What?"

"Who are you?"

"My name is Theresa. Theresa Martin."

"And how did you know Davis?"

Sadness shadowed her eyes but only for a brief second. She blinked, looked away, looked back. "We are—were...friends."

He didn't miss the sorrow in her voice, or the sheen of moisture quickly blinked away. More than friends, then. And Davis had obviously trusted the woman. That was good enough for him—for now.

He extended his hand. "Some people call me Zeus."

She sagged in relief, caught herself and reached out to accept his hand. Her grip was stronger than he expected, her fingers trembling just the slightest bit against his. "He said you'd come. I didn't think—I thought it was too late."

"Ma'am?"

She released his hand, glanced around then stepped back and motioned toward her house. "We should go inside and talk. It would be less obvious. And I have something to give you."

Curiosity overrode caution as he followed Theresa into the house. The inside was neat, tidy despite the overstuffed furniture and collection of knick-knacks that lined several shelves on the near wall. A stack of books rested on the floor in front of an end table. A basket of colorful yarn and several long needles sat on the coffee table. The beginnings of what might be a hat or hell, maybe even a sweater for all he knew, rested next to the basket, obviously forgotten. Had she placed the knitting work aside to watch him? Possibly. Or maybe someone else lived here with her and the knitting belonged to them because Theresa didn't look like the knitting type.

He took a few minutes to study her more closely as she closed the door and shrugged out of the thick sweat jacket. In addition to the piercings lining her ear, she had a small one by the corner of her nose. A discreet jewel, maybe a diamond or a crystal of some kind. Small enough not to be noticeable at first.

Her long-sleeve t-shirt was emblazoned with the logo of a popular motorcycle company. She pushed the sleeves up, revealing an intricate tattoo of fairies and ivy on the inside of her right arm.

A hundred different questions rolled through his mind—and the first dozen centered around his surprise that Davis and this woman had been friends. More than friends. How had his tough-as-nails, spit-and-polish former CO become involved with the woman in front of him? A woman who, by all appearances, was the man's complete opposite?

Then again, maybe that was reason enough. And who the hell was he to judge in any case?

Theresa turned toward him. Shifted her weight from one foot to the other. Ran her hands along the legs of her dark jeans. "Would you like something to drink? Ice tea? Coffee? Water?"

"No, thank you, ma'am."

A hint of a smile curled her lips, quickly faded. She ran her hands along her jeans once more then pointed to the sofa. "Have a seat. I'll go get the letter."

She moved the room, leaving him alone. Instead of sitting, Daryl took the time to study the framed photographs resting on the shelves and hanging on the walls. They were all candid shots, featuring the woman and several different friends—including Davis. One in particular caught his attention. Davis had his arm around Theresa's shoulders, bright smiles on both their faces. Two motorcycles—a Kawasaki and a Harley Davidson—sat off to their right, nearly lost in the dramatic background of the Grand Canyon.

Footsteps paused behind him, then resumed a little more slowly. Theresa stopped next to him, a nostalgic smile on her face. She reached out, traced the couple in the framed photograph with the tip of one brightly-painted nail.

"That was taken last Spring. Before..." Her voice trailed off and the smile faded from her mouth. She sighed, straightened her shoulders, then held out a thin envelope. Daryl's name was scrawled across the front in his former CO's bold writing. "He left this for you. In case..." She stopped, cleared her throat. "I guess he was worried something might happen. I didn't believe him. Thought he was just worrying too much. I...I was wrong."

Daryl accepted the envelope, stared down at it for a few seconds then looked back at Theresa. "What *did* happen?"

She shrugged, moved toward the sofa and sat down with a sigh filled with weariness. Sorrow. Disbelief. "He was shot."

Daryl kept his face carefully blank but inside, he was reeling. Davis had been shot? When? By who? And why? Was this connected to his daughter somehow? What the fuck was the girl involved in and how the fuck had her father been dragged into it? He curled his hand into a fist, slowly released it. "When?"

Theresa pulled her lower lip between her teeth then sighed again before sagging against the back of the sofa. "Eleven days ago. I—we were supposed to have breakfast but he didn't show up so I went over, thought maybe he was sick. He—he hasn't been well."

"He said he had cancer."

"Yes. I thought—" She shook her head, took a deep breath. "I went over to check on him and...he was in his recliner and I thought he was sleeping but...he wasn't."

She squeezed her eyes closed then a ran one shaking hand over her face before dropping it in her lap. Daryl reached over, closed his hand over hers and gently squeezed.

"I'm sorry."

Theresa nodded then took another deep breath before opening her eyes. A sad smile teased one corner of her mouth. "The police haven't been able to learn anything yet, at least as far as I know."

"They don't have any leads?"

Theresa shook her head. "I don't think so. They don't think it was robbery related because the house looks like it always does and no valuables are missing."

He heard something in her voice, something she *wasn't* saying. He leaned forward, studied her face. "Except?"

She laughed, the sound hollow. "Allen said you were perceptive. No, nothing valuable was missing—at least as far as the police know."

"But?"

"His dog tags are gone, along with his jump wings. And...his motorcycle is missing. He kept it in the shed behind the house. As far as the neighbors know, he sold the bike last year. It's not even registered in his name anymore."

"I don't understand."

"He was being careful. Changed the registration to my name so nobody could trace it back to him."

Daryl frowned, wondering what the hell he was missing. Why would Davis do something like that? And why did he need to be careful?

Theresa must have sensed his confusion because she offered him a sympathetic smile then kept talking. "He kept the bike for his daughter. In case she needed it. I—I think she was here that night."

What the fuck? "You think she had something to do with—"

"No. God, no. Not even close. I—I think she found him."

Anger washed over him. What kind of woman was Davis's daughter that she'd take off instead of getting help for her father? Once again, Daryl wondered what the hell the girl was mixed up in. "You think she found him but instead of calling for help, she just took off?"

"She wouldn't have had any choice."

"I don't—"

"I think maybe you should read whatever Allen left for you." There was a hint of steel in the woman's voice, an edge of command that dared him to do otherwise. She pushed to her feet and turned toward a doorway leading to the rear of the house. "I'll be in the kitchen. Let me know when you're finished and I'll take you over to Allen's."

Daryl waited until she left the room then stared at the envelope in his hand. He swore softly then pulled the small knife from his pocket and slid it under the seal. The envelope contained a single sheet of paper. Daryl pulled it out, unfolded it—and choked on a startled laugh.

The damn thing was written in code.

He stared at it, his mind arranging and rearranging the letters, trying to make sense of it. Dammit, he wasn't a fucking cryptologist, how the hell—

His last thought echoed in his mind. *He wasn't a cryptologist.* Davis was well aware of that fact, wouldn't have written something in a code Daryl wouldn't be able to understand.

He studied the letters and numbers, his mind sifting through memories, finally latching on the one he needed. He closed his eyes, pictured his hard-ass CO giving them shit about hurried communications.

Heard the man's gruff voice belt out instructions, telling them any fucking idiot could figure it out if they knew where to start. Daryl had been the fucking idiot in question, barely eighteen and full of piss and vinegar, convinced surviving BCT had given him the skills to conquer the world.

He'd been wrong. So fucking wrong.

Davis had set him right.

He opened his eyes, looked at the numbers and letters one final time, seeing the message he'd been meant to see.

A single name that meant nothing to him: Grady Byrne.

Below that, two sets of coordinates, clearly marked *first* and *second*, with a twisted arrow directly behind the second.

The final few lines were a personal message to him, one that did nothing to explain what was going on.

> If you're reading this, it means I'm not around and my girl is on the run. I told her to go to you but I don't think she will—she's not one to trust easily, not even on my say-so. Find her. She needs you, whether she admits or not. Yeah, she knows who you are and she'll have to learn to trust you. She has no choice. She can explain everything to you then, including that second set of coordinates.

Daryl reread the note, trying to make sense of it. What the hell kind of game was Davis playing? A deadly one, yes. But what the hell else was going on?

Steps sounded to his right and he glanced up, noticed Theresa leaning against the doorframe, watching him. She pointed to the note. "Does that answer any of your questions?"

No, it didn't. The only thing that might help was the name. *Grady Byrne*. It meant nothing to him, didn't spark even the faintest recognition. He'd have Chaos run it, see what he could find. But he didn't share any of that with Theresa. He simply shrugged then carefully folded the note and placed it back in the envelope before tucking it in his inside jacket pocket.

"Do you know his daughter?"

"I've met her a few times but I haven't seen her recently."

"Is there anything you can tell me about her that might help?"

"Like what?"

Daryl rose to his feet, curled one hand into a fist and jammed it into his pocket before he did something stupid, like punch a hole in the wall. How the fuck was he supposed to help when he had absolutely nothing to go on?

"A name would be a good start." Yeah, a damn good start because Davis hadn't once called his daughter by name. "A picture. Why she's running."

"Allen didn't tell you her name?"

"No, he didn't."

"Then I don't think I should, either." She raised her hands, stopping his argument before he could make it. "I'm not being difficult. It's just—I don't know what name she's going by."

"How about her given name? That might be a good start."

"I'm sorry but I made him a promise. If he didn't tell you, then I certainly can't."

Daryl wanted to shout at her, tell her he was one of the good guys. That he was the one Davis had asked for help. But yelling would do no good, he knew that from the stubborn set of her shoulders as she stared at him. And part of him admired her loyalty and her integrity. He swallowed back his frustration, ran one hand through his hair.

"Is there anything you *can* tell me?"

Theresa tilted her head to the side and watched him for a long minute before answering. "I know she's a good kid. She loves her father. I know that the trouble she's in isn't her fault. I know she's been running for at least three years and Allen did his best to help out. And I know...despite what the police think, I know he died protecting her."

Her voice broke and she quickly blinked away tears, took in a shaky breath as her gaze dropped to the floor. She ran a hand across her eyes then looked up, her gaze fastened on his with steely determination and a glimmer of hope. "Are you the man he always told me you were? Are you going to do as he asked and help?"

The silence stretched around them as Daryl watched her. *Fuck*. He knew the answer, had known it as soon as his old CO's face had come up on that video he'd sent. He didn't have a choice.

"Yeah. I'll help."

He just wished to hell he knew what he was getting into—and wondered if it was already a foregone conclusion that he'd fail.

CHAPTER
SEVEN

Grady Byrne leaned against the edge of the desk, a smile on his face. He was well aware of the image he presented, had practiced it long enough in the decades of fighting to get where he was today.

Mature and trustworthy. Not quite grandfatherly but close, with his full head of striking silvery-red hair and sparkling green eyes.

Self-assured. Confident, with straight posture that gave the illusion of height. Of strength.

He took great care with his appearance, choosing only the most-expensive suits, carefully tailored to make his average frame more impressive. Everything about him screamed success. Encouraged trust from those around him.

The woman huddled in the chair in front of him didn't appear to trust him. Such a pity.

She was a small woman, in her late-twenties. Short blonde hair and blue eyes shadowed with fear. A narrow face with an unfortunate overbite. Thin lips, pale and trembling.

She was afraid of him, despite his attempts at making her feel comfortable. The apparent lack of trust on her part rankled him. Who was she to sit there and stare at him in fear, instead of the respect he deserved?

No matter. If her husband failed again, he would make sure she had a genuine reason for her fear.

"Amy, lass. You mustn't fret. No harm shall come to ye."

The woman cast a nervous glance over her shoulder, staring at the men stationed behind her, their hands on her shoulders, holding her in place. She turned back to Grady, offered him a smile that was nothing more than a slight stretching of trembling lips.

He hid his distaste, casually glanced at the expensive gold watch on his left wrist. Swallowed back his irritation as the minute hand jumped.

Michael was late. Damn the fool. Had he bungled his job again? Grady was running out of patience. Why was it so difficult for his men to do the job they were supposed to do? A simple task. Find the woman. Discover the location of the child. Dispose of the woman and bring the girl to him.

His granddaughter.

His legacy.

She should be with him now. For each day that she wasn't, he lost the loyalty of several more men—men who were convinced he was no longer capable of running the organization.

His organization.

Anger swept through him, anger he was quick to hide. How dare they! How dare they question his abilities. His plans. How dare they question *him*!

They would learn. All of them.

As soon as he had the girl.

As soon as Michael completed the job he'd been given—

The phone rang, breaking the tense silence that had fallen over the room. Amy jumped, a whimper of fear falling from her lips. Grady stepped toward her, backhanded her across the mouth then knelt beside her.

"Now lass, there will be none of that. Is that

clear?"

Tears fell from the woman's eyes, trailed down her cheeks and mingled with the blood from her split lip. She nodded and Grady smiled, gently patted her on the shoulder then reached for the phone.

"Michael. I take it you have news for me, then?"

"Yes, sir. We think we found her."

Grady clenched his jaw, exhaled through his nose. "You *think*?"

"Yes, sir. We think—that is to say, we're sure she's in West Virginia."

"West Virginia?" Grady swallowed an oath, forced his voice to remain calm. "And where, pray tell, are you at this moment, Michael?"

A long pause, followed by a quick breath. "In Louisiana. Sir."

"And is there a reason you're in Louisiana when you believe the woman is in West Virginia?"

"We thought—" Another quick breath, the sound hinting at the slightest edge of panic. "It was a mistake, sir."

"A mistake." Some of the anger boiling inside him drifted into his voice. Grady didn't care, not anymore. "Tell me, Michael: why do you now think she's in West Virginia?"

"We did some checking. The father's friend has a cabin. In the mountains. We think she may have gone there."

"And you didn't think to check this *before* heading to Louisiana?"

"No, sir. We thought—no. No, we didn't. It was a mistake."

"Yes, Michael, it was. I trust there will be no more mistakes?"

"No, sir."

"Good. This friend of the father's—what is his name?"

"It's a woman, sir. Theresa Martin. She—she lives two doors down from the father."

Damn the fools! Why hadn't they thought to check for this information eleven days ago? Eleven days!

Fury ripped through Grady, momentarily stripping away the cultivated veneer he carefully presented to the outside world. The woman—Michael's wife, Amy—must have caught a glimpse of it, must surely know what fate he had planned for her because she whimpered, struggled against the two men holding her in place.

Grady pushed away from the desk, held the phone to his side and backhanded the woman again. A small scream filled the air, followed by pitiful crying.

He returned the phone to his ear, wondered if Michael had heard. Yes, he had—the ragged breathing, short and panicked, coming through the line assured him of it. "Your wife is a lovely woman, Michael. So very...petite. Fragile."

"S-sir?"

"We were just having a nice little chat, Amy and I. Such a lovely lass. It would be such a shame if anything happened to her."

Another pause, this one much longer. "Yes, sir."

"Get the woman for me, Michael. Find out where the girl is. Bring her to me. No more mistakes. No more excuses." He slammed the phone down, cutting off the man's terrified stammering. He walked around the desk, removed a square of linen from the top drawer and stared out at the darkness as he carefully wiped a smear of blood from his knuckles.

He released a sigh, spun the chair around and faced the two men standing stoically behind the woman. Neither man looked at him.

"Daniel, find out what you can about Theresa Martin. We may need to pay the woman a visit." Yes, a visit might be in order. But not yet. Not until he heard from Michael. If the man succeeded, there would be no reason to risk a return to the States. Not that entering would be risky, not when he had ways to avoid being caught.

"Yes, sir."

Grady leaned back in the chair, studied the blood flowing from the woman's mouth and cheek. Her head was bowed, her shoulders shaking with sobs.

Disgusting. Did the woman have no backbone? No strength? No, of course she didn't. She was worthless, even as a pawn to ensure Michael did what he was supposed to do.

He nodded to the woman. "Remove her from my sight. Get someone in here to clean up the mess her sniveling has left on the carpet."

Both men nodded, grabbed her by the arms and pulled her to her feet. Daniel's gaze met his then quickly slid away—but not before he saw the briefest glimpse of fear in their depths.

"What do you want us to do with her, sir?"

Grady waved his hand in a dismissive gesture. "Get rid of her. I have no use for worthless, sniveling women."

"Yes, sir."

"And Daniel?" The other man turned, waiting. "I think I'd like pictures. Lots of colorful, vivid pictures. Michael will want something to remember his wife by, yes?"

Daniel nodded then helped the second man drag the screaming woman from the room. The door closed behind them, plunging the office into blessed silence.

Grady spun the chair around, stared out at the twinkling lights of the landscape spread out below the window.

Tonight had been the first time he'd seen fear in Daniel's eyes. Daniel, of all people. More than fear, he'd seen impatience. Disgust.

No, it must have only been Grady's imagination, fueled by his own impatience and disgust over this entire business. Three years. There was no excuse for it. None at all. His granddaughter—his *legacy*—should already be here by his side. Should have been here three years ago.

Yes, what he'd seen in the man's eyes was merely his imagination. Grady refused to believe otherwise. Daniel was one of his most loyal supporters, would be by his side for years to come.

Helping him rebuild his crumbling empire.

Soon. Very soon.

His granddaughter would be by his side and those who had doubted him—who doubted him still—would pay.

Yes, they would definitely pay.

CHAPTER EIGHT

"I got that info you wanted."

Daryl closed his eyes, clenched his jaw so damn tight he heard his back teeth grinding. The edge in Chaos's voice told him the info wasn't going to be good. Had he expected anything different? Fuck no, not after the last five fucking hours. Hell, more than five, if he counted back to the minute he sat down and popped that fucking thumb drive into his computer.

He was running short on sleep. On food. On fucking patience. Why should Chaos have any information that even remotely resembled good news?

Daryl reached across the seat and grabbed his gear bag, dug around one-handed until his fingers closed over the stash of candy bars he kept tucked in there for emergencies. Chocolate and peanuts. Yeah, it totally worked for him.

He propped the phone between his ear and shoulder and tore open the wrapper. "I'm listening. What do you have?"

"Nothing good. Where the fuck are you?"

"I'm sitting in the damn rental truck TR arranged in a parking lot outside the shitty little airport *you* had them fly me into." Daryl bit into the candy bar and chewed. Swallowed then reached for the bottle of water on the seat next to his bag. "Now what information do you have?"

"Grady Byrne is a fucking crime boss."

The phone slipped from his shoulder. Daryl

lowered the candy bar and grabbed the phone with his free hand before it hit the floor. He stared at it for a few stunned seconds before raising it back to his ear. "Come again?"

"Grady Byrne is a fucking crime boss."

"Yeah, I heard what you said. I need you to elaborate."

"Crime boss. You know: organized crime. The Mafia."

"The Mafia? With a fucking name like *Byrne*? Are you sure about that?"

"Pretty damn sure. Although maybe I should have said *mob* instead of *Mafia*. Irish mob, to be exact."

"What the fuck? Is that even a thing?"

"Apparently." There was a faint rustling of papers in the background, followed by the sound of someone tapping on a keyboard. "From what I've been able to dig up so far, he has a penchant for comparing himself to all the big names who've gone before him."

"So he's what—a wannabe of some kind?"

"I didn't say that, no. The man has some violent history in his background. Fled the country about ten years ago to avoid serving time for drug trafficking and tax evasion. Last known address is Canada. Before that, he had business concerns in Boston."

Daryl took another bite of the candy bar, barely tasting it as his mind ran in a hundred different directions. How the hell was Davis—or rather, his *daughter*—connected to a criminal? Or maybe there was no connection, maybe Chaos had pulled the wrong name.

"Are you sure you have the right Grady Byrne?"

There was a long pause where Daryl could actually *feel* the other man's stunned ire. "There are dozens of men by that name. This is the only one worth discussing. You tell me, boss-man—would your buddy mention anyone who *wasn't* worth discussing?"

The answer to that was easy: no. His former CO would have known Daryl would run a check on the name. Hell, anyone would have. There was no reason to mention a name if there wasn't anything about it that would stand out, if there wasn't anything about it that might give Daryl some clue as to what the hell was going on.

"Point taken." Daryl finished the last bite of the bar then shoved the empty wrapper into the bag. "What else do you have on him?"

"Information from the last five years is slim. He's either been very careful, or he's lost what little prominence he had. My guess is the latter."

"Why's that?"

"He may have made millions doing business, but he was never what you would call a major player. Looks like he started off small enough, slowly built up from there. Mostly the drug trade and arms trafficking, from what I can tell."

"But you said he fled the country?"

"Yeah. He was facing charges on the trafficking and tax evasion—because hey, our friends need to stick with what works, right? But I get the impression he's not the kind of man you want to cross. There's a lot of dead bodies attached to his name, going back twenty years."

And ending as recently as eleven days ago—

If this guy Byrne had anything to do with Davis's death. Daryl still wasn't seeing the connection, couldn't stretch his imagination far enough to see his former CO mixed up with anything illegal.

Except it wasn't Allen Davis who was mixed up with anything. At least, not directly. It was his daughter. What had Theresa said?

He died protecting her.

Protecting her from *what*? What the hell was the girl mixed up in?

Daryl closed his eyes and pinched the bridge of his nose. Hard. There was a connection missing—a huge one. And no matter how hard he tried, he couldn't figure it out. Was that really so surprising? It was difficult as fuck to complete a puzzle when you only had ten pieces of it to work with. The way he figured it, he was missing at least nine-hundred-and-ninety of those damn pieces.

And he had no fucking clue where to start looking for them.

No, that wasn't right. He *did* know where to start: about an hour from here, in some God-forsaken patch of West Virginia wilderness. It would be a thirty-minute drive, followed by at least thirty minutes hiking. In the dark.

If the coordinates Davis had left him were correct. And *if* they actually led to his daughter. Daryl had a hundred percent confidence in that first part. The second? Not so much.

"Were you able to get anything on Davis?"

"Yeah. Right now, the police are calling it a home invasion. No leads. No evidence." Chaos paused, lowered his voice. "It was a single tap to the forehead. Small caliber. No defensive wounds."

"What the fuck? Are you sure about that?" Chaos had to be wrong. No defensive wounds? It wasn't possible. The Allen Davis he knew wouldn't have gone down without a fight.

"Sorry, boss-man. I'm looking at the report and the crime scene photos. No defensive wounds. Not even a scratch. Do you want me to send them to you?"

Daryl almost said yes, changed his mind at the last second. "No, I don't need them."

And he didn't. If Chaos said there were no defensive wounds, Daryl believed him. Even if didn't, he wasn't sure he'd want to see the photos. It had nothing to do with death itself. Fuck, he'd seen enough death in his time, had even pushed more than his fair share of people straight through death's door. Death didn't faze him.

But he didn't want to see his former CO like that. Didn't want to see the strong man he remembered reduced to nothing more than a corpse, stripped of all human dignity once life escaped the shell of the body.

"Are you going to tell anyone what the hell is going on yet?" Chaos's voice pulled him from the dark turn his thoughts were taking. He shifted in the seat, ignored the creaking of springs under his ass, and pulled the map from the side pocket of his pack.

"I'm not sure."

"You're not sure? Is that code for mind my own fucking business?"

"No, it means I'm not sure."

"Yeah. Hang on a second."

There was a muted rustling sound, followed by some gruff swearing. A second later, Mac's gravelly voice exploded in his ear.

"What the fuck is going on out there?"

Daryl deflected the question with one of his own. "Why the hell are you at the office when you have a wife at home, waiting for your ugly ass?"

"TR happens to like my ass and unless you want

her to kick *yours* for calling it ugly, you need to start talking. What the fuck is going on?"

"I'm not sure yet."

"Bullshit. You race out of here like the world's coming to an end then call back and have Chaos pull all sorts of fucking intel." Mac paused, lowered his voice. "Allen Davis was your old CO, wasn't he?"

"Yeah, he was. A long time ago."

"I'm sorry. I saw the reports. It doesn't look good."

"Yeah. Thanks."

"Was he mixed up with this Grady Byrne?"

"I don't think so. Not directly."

"Then what does one have to do with the other?"

"I'm still working on connecting those dots."

Another pause. "You heading to those coordinates you sent Chaos?"

"Yeah, as soon as I get off the phone with you."

"I looked at the topo. It's not exactly a Sunday hike."

"Not exactly like I haven't done worse."

"But you're going in alone."

"Yeah."

"Do you have any idea what the fuck you're walking into?"

Daryl thought about blowing him off and just as quickly dismissed the idea. "None at all."

"Then wait. We can be out there in two hours, tops. Go in as a team—"

"No." Daryl shook his head, repeated the word. "No. Not happening."

Mac exploded again. "You're out of your fucking mind. If any one of us tried a bullshit stunt like this, you'd go fucking nuts and ride our asses. Just wait. Two hours, not even—"

"Not happening, Sergeant."

"Fuck that *sergeant* shit. You had one stripe on me. Don't let it go to your fucking head."

Daryl laughed. The sound was tired. Weary. Maybe a little edgy—but it was still a laugh, something he needed without even realizing it. "Still not happening, Mac. I need to see what's going on first."

"There's a damn good chance you're going to be off-grid and unable to make contact once you start on foot."

"Probably."

"Do you have your sat phone?"

Daryl looked at the gear bag on the seat next to him and bit back a low growl. No, he didn't have his sat phone—or the other equipment he usually carried out in the field. His bag contained nothing more than the basics—because he hadn't planned on being in the field. Because when he tore out of the office yesterday afternoon, it had been with the intention of doing nothing more than visiting an old friend.

Fuck it. He had the basics. That was one of the advantages of flying charter because it allowed him to carry those basics—which happened to include his PK380, extra clips, and extra ammo. That was plenty enough. For now.

"No. It's back in my office with the rest of my gear."

"Son-of-a—" The curse disappeared in a rough sigh, followed by a few seconds of heavy silence. "Why are you doing this? At least tell me that much."

"I owe him, Mac." And it was as simple as that. Would Mac be able to hear what he *didn't* say? Yes, he would. He'd been around long enough, knew all about the bonds of brotherhood forged by something much stronger than blood.

"You've got twenty-four hours."

"Forty-eight."

"Twenty-four and you're damn lucky I'm giving you that much. Whatever you're doing, you better get your fucking ass in gear because the clock is ticking." There was a soft click, followed by dead silence.

Daryl tossed the phone into the cup holder then spread open the map and studied it in the dim overhead light of the truck's cab. There wasn't a direct route to his destination, no matter which way he looked at it. He'd be on the highway for ten minutes, then a series of backroads until the roads simply disappeared. At least to where he was going. Hell, there wasn't even any old fire trails that he could see.

Mac was giving him twenty-four hours. Fine. With luck, he'd reach the spot he had mapped out within an hour of starting out, maybe a little more. Daryl had no idea what was there. A cabin, if he was lucky. Not a damn thing, if he wasn't. He was erring on the side of optimism and betting on a cabin. Something small. Off-the-grid. Self-contained.

Isolated as fuck.

It was a good place for someone who didn't want to be found to disappear—if that same someone knew what the hell they were doing. This was Davis's daughter, though, so he gave her fifty-fifty odds. Maybe a little higher. No way in hell could she have Davis as a father and *not* learn at least a little something about survival.

Unless she was a total fuck-up. If that was the case, all bets were off. The problem was, Daryl had no way of knowing if she was a fuck-up or not. He didn't

The Guardian: DARYL

want to think she was, just because she was Davis's daughter. Then again, she was somehow involved with some fucking Irish gangster.

The fact was, he wouldn't know until he got to where the hell he needed to go—and that wouldn't happen until he put the truck in gear and started driving.

Twenty-four hours.

With luck, this would be over in three. He hoped like hell that was the case because a lot could go wrong in twenty-four hours—and that itchy feeling on the back of his neck told him to expect the worst.

Ninety minutes later, he was questioning not only that itchy feeling but also every last bit of sanity he thought he possessed. More than once, he wished he was back in the desert, navigating dry sand and barren mountains. Anything would be preferable to this fucking dense forest growing sideways on a fucking mountain in the middle of the fucking night. He had no NVGs—night vision goggles—and was essentially making his way blind. The half moon offered some illumination—when it wasn't hidden by the dense branches overhead. He used his small flashlight sparingly—just enough to check his coordinates against the map. Anything more and he risked giving away his position, not to mention ruining his night vision.

And just where the *fuck* was this damn place? It should be close but there was nothing around him except trees and more fucking trees.

Daryl paused, grabbed the water bottle from the side pocket of his pants and raised it to his mouth for a long drink. Sunrise would be in another twenty minutes and while light might make his trek easier, he'd prefer finding the damn cabin—or hut or tent or whatever the fuck it was Davis had sent him to—before that. He had planned to approach in the dark, do a little reconnaissance around the perimeter then find a spot where he could lay low and watch for a little bit.

That plan was pretty much shot in the ass. At best, he might have a chance to do a quick survey. At worst, he'd be walking up blind, his opportunity for surprise destroyed by the dawn.

That's if there was even anything here. Daryl was beginning to have his doubts. And if there *was* something here, the chances that anyone had managed to find this damn place were slim.

Isolated? Talk about fucking understatements.

He walked for another ten minutes, stopped short when he caught the first whiff of woodsmoke. Just the faintest odor drifting on the breeze, barely noticeable. Daryl closed his eyes, tilted his face up and sniffed. Yes, definitely woodsmoke.

He opened his eyes, swore to himself when he noticed the change in light. Just a subtle difference, where the darkness wasn't quite as complete as it had been minutes earlier. He'd either lost track of time or had miscalculated the sunrise. *Why* didn't matter, only that he had.

He swore again, moved silently in the direction of the smoke, pausing between each careful step. The growth was thinner here, growing thinner with each step that took him closer to his destination.

And yeah, there was a definite destination at the end of this journey. He wasn't sure if that was a good thing or not. There was a fleeting sense of reassurance that he hadn't been sent on a wild goose chase—

And a good deal of trepidation because he had no idea what waited for him. Davis's daughter? Maybe.

Maybe not.

But who the fuck else could it be?

He paused again, frowned when he noticed another smell in the air. Blinked, resisted the urge to rub his eyes. Was he fucking imagining things?

No, he wasn't—that was fresh coffee he smelled.

What. The. Fuck.

He moved even closer, dropped into a crouch behind some thick cover when the silhouette of a small cabin came into view. There was a thirty-foot clearance around the cabin, at least from what he could see. That would make sneaking up on it tricky, especially if the person—or people—inside were keeping an eye out for unexpected company.

Dawn was creeping across the sky, slowly pulling back the cover of night. If he wanted to get closer to the cabin without being noticed, now was the time.

Fuck. There were a million things wrong with this scenario. A million fucking things that could go sideways—and none of them ended in his favor. He was putting a lot of faith in Davis, in the belief that his old CO wouldn't send him here if it was a trap. *That* was the one thought propelling him forward: Davis's daughter was here, hiding out. The older man wouldn't have sent her somewhere dangerous.

Unless she was dangerous herself and Davis just didn't know it.

Daryl pushed the thought from his mind and carefully circled the cabin, staying out of view until he'd completed a full three-sixty. His first impression had been right: the cabin was small, maybe twenty feet by twenty feet. A shed backed up to the rear and next to that, a huge stack of firewood that could last an entire winter. There was no rear door, which sent a dozen alarm bells ringing through Daryl's head. There should be at least one more exit and yeah, one of those windows would work in a pinch but a door would have been a little nicer.

And it would have made things easier for him.

Time was running out. Unless he wanted to do this in the full morning light, he needed to move now. He mapped the route in his mind, circled to the spot he'd already picked out. Waited until the count of three—

Then took off at a low run toward the west corner, approaching from a diagonal, heading toward the shed and woodpile. They'd give him enough cover while also getting him close to a window where he could look in.

And hope like hell nobody was looking out when he did.

He reached the corner of the building. Paused, his breath held, listening. There was no cry of surprise, no shout of warning. He waited a full minute. One more. Still nothing. He pressed his back to the wall, eased closer to the shed. All he had to do was get between the shed and the woodpile. Once he was there, he could hunker down and wait, keep an ear out and take a look inside.

He was against the shed now, moving sideways, using his hand to guide him to the end. Another foot, no more. Daryl turned his head to the right, his gaze searching the empty clearing he'd just darted through. Still no sign—

"Don't. Move."

Two thoughts slammed into his consciousness

simultaneously.

The first was that he had fucked up. Big time. The fact that something cold and hard pressed against the back of his head told him that much. He didn't move. Didn't turn his head. Didn't fucking breathe.

The not breathing had nothing to do with the first thought and everything to do with the second—

Because he recognized that voice. He'd heard it in his dreams every fucking night for the last three months. Low, sultry. A little breathless, like she'd just rolled out of bed after a night of hot, sweaty, sex.

Daryl said a quick prayer that the woman on the other end of that fucking weapon didn't have a twitchy finger. He slowly eased his hands out to the side and spoke. Just one word, but that was all he needed to say.

"Kelsey."

CHAPTER NINE

Kelsey.

She recognized the voice. It was *him*. Daryl. She almost sagged in relief, caught herself at the last second. It would be too easy to let her guard down, too easy to fall into his arms and ask him to take care of everything, the way her father promised he would if she went to him.

But she couldn't. Letting her guard down could prove fatal—and not just to her. How could she trust anyone? She couldn't, not when there was so much at stake.

Those thoughts took fewer than two seconds to play in her mind—and those two seconds proved to be her undoing. Before she could move, before she could even react, she was flat on her back against the cold ground, a large hand clamped over her mouth, a familiar heavy weight stretched out on top of her. The gun she'd been holding so carefully was ripped from her hand as a pair of lethal amber eyes stared down at her in anger.

Kelsey tried to scream, struggled to move, to get out from underneath Daryl's heavy weight. Panic made her flail and her fists pummeled his back. His shoulder. His head.

She heard him grunt, the sound low and dangerous, but she didn't care. She hit him again. Desperation made her swing blindly, made each glancing blow weak and ineffective.

"Dammit, lady. Stop." The tone was one she recognized immediately, carrying the same authority and command that she sometimes heard in her father's voice.

But she didn't listen. She couldn't. She needed to get free. To run away. To find some other place to hide because oh, God, he'd found her. What if he wasn't the only one? What if there were others who had found her? They could be making their way through the woods even now, sneaking up on her, ready to kill her.

A fresh surge of panic raced over her, giving her a burst of strength. She arched her back, bucked beneath the man stretched out on top of her. Kicked her heels against the dirt and swung out with one fist. She felt her knuckles scrape against bare skin, heard a muttered oath, felt the heavy weight pinning her to the ground shift and for one fleeting second, she thought he was moving, that she could push to her feet and take off—

But she wasn't free. Instead of rolling off her like she had hoped—prayed—he just grabbed both of her hands and pinned them over her head. His powerful legs straddled her thighs, squeezing, keeping her from kicking out.

The fight left her as quickly as it had come, leaving her limp and tired. Exhaustion stole over her as adrenaline fled. As failure washed over her and with it, harsh reality.

She was going to die. Maybe not here. Maybe not by the hands of the man staring down at her with anger flashing in his eyes. But soon. She was going to die and there would be nobody left to protect Paige. Nobody to keep her safe from the madman who wanted her for his own.

She stared up at the man straddling her. Oh God,

how could she have *ever* felt sorry for him? How could she have ever pitied him? This wasn't the man she remembered. *That* man was gentle. Kind. *This* man was deadly. A warrior created for death. She saw it in his eyes, in the steel set of his jaw. Felt it in the restrained strength and power thrumming through his body.

He shifted, adjusted his hold on her pinned wrists, using only one hand now to keep her in place. Kelsey struggled, fought back a cry of desperation at her ineffectiveness. One hand. He was only using one hand! She should be able to break his hold, should be able to free herself—

"Stop it before you hurt yourself." He didn't even look at her when he issued the harsh command, like he knew she was no threat. She struggled again, winced when his hand pushed harder against her wrists.

"You're hurting me."

His amber gaze shot to hers and for one brief second, she thought she saw humor in their depths. He was laughing at her! At her struggles, at how easily he'd been able to overtake her. Then he blinked and the humor was gone.

"Hurting *you*? Lady, I'm not the one holding a gun to your damn head." The gun in question rested less than a foot away. He reached for it, ejected the clip. Hard amber eyes met hers in silent warning for a brief second before he freed her hands and sat back, slid the rack back and ejected the chambered round. He caught it in his free hand, stared at it for a brief second, then met her gaze one more time.

"Shit." The muttered oath fell from his mouth a split-second before his strong jaw clenched. He shook his head then pushed to his feet, refused to help her as she scrambled to her elbows and tried to stand. She struggled to her knees, was trying to get her unsteady legs under her when he held the gun out to her, grip first.

"Next time, just pull the fucking trigger. Don't hesitate. Don't give a warning."

She stared at the gun, looked up at him as a wave of nausea washed over her. "You'd be dead if I did that."

"Yeah—and I would have deserved it."

Kelsey pulled her gaze away from his, stared at the gun he was still holding out to her. She hesitated, finally took it, looked up at him once more. "Can I have the clip back?"

He laughed. He actually laughed at her! The sound set her nerves on edge, caused anger to settle in her stomach. She pushed to her feet, glared at him until he finally stopped laughing and shook his head.

"Lady, do I look that stupid to you?"

"Stop calling me *lady*! I have a name."

"Do you?" He advanced on her, anger flashing in his eyes—anger she didn't understand. She took a hasty step back, collided against the edge of the woodpile. "Care to tell me what it is?"

She frowned. His question made no sense. He knew her name—had said it a second before he tossed her to the ground. Had murmured it in her ear through the long hours they had spent together that night in the Caribbean. "You know my name."

"Do I? Is that really your name, or just something you made up when you were playing your little game a few months ago?"

"Game?" She shook her head, confusion warring with uncertainty, anger, weariness, and sorrow. It was too much, all of it. Being on the run. Hiding. Worrying about Paige. Finding her father.

She blinked back the tears burning her eyes and shook her head again. "I wasn't playing a game."

He stepped closer, the anger in his gaze scorching her. "Weren't you? I guess I'm just supposed to believe that meeting this summer was nothing more than a fucking coincidence. Is that it?"

"I—" She stopped, fought desperately to calm her mind, to *think*. Why was the man holding her prisoner with nothing more than his presence so angry at her?

Kelsey gave herself a mental shake, forced herself to focus on something much more important. Not on the man's anger—but on his *presence*.

Here.

Now.

At this hiding place that nobody else was supposed to know about.

She adjusted her grip on the pistol, felt the reassuring weight in her hand even though she knew it was useless for self-defense now. The most she could hope to do with it was swing it hard enough to catch him in the jaw. Maybe in the temple, if she was lucky. Hit him and then run. Keep running as she followed the escape route she had planned more than a week ago when she first got here. Keep running and hope that she could stay ahead of him.

But not yet. He was expecting her to do something like that, she could see it in the way he watched her. In the way his entire body seemed so attuned to hers. She needed to distract him. To get him to let his guard down, if only for a few seconds.

"What are you doing here? How did you find me?"

"Your father sent me."

His answer knocked the breath from her lungs. Brought tears to her eyes. She'd only meant the question as a distraction—but it had backfired. *She* was the one reeling now, trying to catch her breath. Her balance.

He was lying. Her father couldn't have sent him. Her father was dead.

Which meant he was one of *them*. One of Grady's men.

She swung her arm up sideways, aiming the broad side of the gun at his head. He jerked back before she could make contact. She took advantage of that small reaction and shoved both hands into his chest, pushing him away before darting to the side and tearing off at a run. Legs pumping, feet sliding as they sought for purchase against dirt and dead leaves.

Run. Move. Escape.

Those three words echoed in her mind, screaming, urging her forward. But it was useless, she'd been doomed to fail before she even started. Strong arms wrapped around her waist from behind, lifted her as she kicked back with her feet. As she thrashed and swung and tried to break the iron grip squeezing her.

The grip didn't budge and she felt herself being carried around the side of the cabin. She kept kicking with her heels, aiming for his knee, his thigh, *anything*. Her heel connected with something hard and she heard him grunt, felt warm breath brush against her ear as he swore.

But his hold never loosened, his steps never faltered. And oh God, where was he taking her? Was he going to kill her now? Or would he torture her first, make her tell him where Paige was before he killed her?

Would he believe her when she told him she didn't

know?

An image of Paige's face from the last time she saw her flashed in front of her. Thick auburn curls and wide green eyes—eyes that had once been filled with laughter and happiness but were now too serious. The perfect bow of her pink mouth, a mouth that hadn't smiled in far too long. Tears filled Kelsey's eyes, trailed down her cheeks at the thought of never seeing her daughter again.

At the realization she had failed the most important person in her life.

"Please don't hurt her. Please. I'm begging you, please don't hurt her." The words ripped from her throat, over and over, filled with the same desperation that made her keep fighting him. She had to keep fighting, she couldn't give up, not if there were even a small chance she could escape.

The arms around her didn't budge as he carried her, not toward the woods as she had first feared but toward the front of the cabin. Toward the door. Renewed panic seared her and she struggled even harder to break free.

"Dammit, Kelsey, stop fighting me! I'm not here to hurt you. I'm not here to hurt anyone so just stop!"

She heard the words but didn't believe them. He was lying, the same way he had lied about her father sending him. He was going to hurt her and then he was going to go after Paige—

And there was nothing she could do stop him.

She kicked out with her legs when he reached the door of the cabin, tried to catch the doorframe with her foot. Anything to slow him down. Anything to keep him from dragging her inside. But it was useless. He simply turned to the side and stepped through, carrying her like she was nothing more than a sack of rice.

He kicked the door closed with his foot then moved to the center of the room, pausing as he looked around. A different kind of fear erupted in her chest when he walked toward the bed and she kept fighting, raking her nails over the heavy jacket covering his arms, over the bare flesh of his hands and wrists.

He swore again and tossed her to the bed, fell on top of her and caught her hands and pinned them above her head. She shook her head from side-to-side, arched her back and kicked out with her feet but it was no use. She couldn't move, not with the way he was pressed against her, using the weight of his body to pin her to the bed.

"Please. Please don't. Please—"

"Dammit, Kelsey. Stop! Listen to me." He caught her face in one hand, the gentleness of his grip surprising her into stillness. "Look at me. I'm not. Going. To. Hurt. You. Do you understand that? I'm not going to hurt you. But you're going to hurt yourself if you don't stop fighting me."

She struggled to catch her breath. Struggled to understand his words. Told herself she couldn't believe him. He was lying, she'd be a fool to believe him. But there was something in his eyes, something besides the anger that had flashed in their depths when she tried to hit him earlier.

Concern. Worry.

No! No, it was an act. She couldn't believe him. Couldn't fall for whatever game he was playing now.

She shook her head. Tried to free her wrists from his one-handed grip. "Let me up. Please."

He hesitated, the doubt clear in that deep amber

gaze. To her surprise, he released her hands—but he didn't move from the bed. She was still pinned in place by his body, stuck between one strong arm and his hip. Could she move fast enough to escape? No. The only thing she could do was wait. Hope he let his guard down. Hope he moved away from the bed long enough that she could make a desperate dash for the door.

She held her breath, scrambled toward the headboard. He still didn't move, just kept watching her as she pushed herself to a sitting position and eased away from him. Surprise filled her again, that he would allow her to move that far away from him.

Far.

She was only kidding herself. That hard body was mere inches from hers and that amber gaze never wavered. Yes, she was sitting up now, resting against the headboard, but she wasn't far away from him.

And she was nowhere near being free.

She slowly bent her legs, still waiting for him to stop her. He didn't so she drew them against her chest and wrapped her arms around them. "Why are you here?"

"I told you: your father sent me."

"You're lying. My father's dead."

Sympathy flashed in his eyes. "I know. I'm sorry."

She swallowed against the tightness in her throat that threatened to strangle her. Repeated the question, more forcefully this time. "Why are you here? Don't say Dad sent you. We both know that's a lie."

Instead of answering, he shrugged out of his pack and placed it to the side. Then he reached into a side pocket of his tactical pants and pulled out a crumpled envelope. He held it out to her, waited patiently for her to take it.

She reached for it with trembling fingers; tears burned her eyes when she saw the bold handwriting on the front. There was no mistaking it as her father's handwriting. The name on the front was Daryl's.

She opened the envelope, pulled out the single sheet of paper and carefully opened it. The note was in her father's handwriting but she couldn't read it, any more than she could read the letter that was in the small packet she had taken from his house that night almost two weeks ago.

The night her father had died.

Kelsey blinked back tears then looked over at Daryl. He still watched her, his gaze guarded despite the sympathy she saw in his eyes. "Where did you get this?"

"From a woman named Theresa."

Was he lying? She couldn't tell. She didn't think so but how could she be sure? She didn't know Daryl, not really. She didn't know him at all. "When?"

"Last night. When I went to see your father."

"Why did you go to see him?" Kelsey expected him to lose patience at her questions but he didn't. He just sat there, his gaze never leaving hers, as if they were doing nothing more than catching up on gossip after months of not seeing each other. And God, how she wished that was true. How she wished life could be that simple again. But it wasn't.

And it never would be. Not anymore. Not for her. Not for Paige.

"Your father sent me a message, asking for my help. I didn't get it until yesterday afternoon."

"You were too late."

"I know. I'm sorry." He hesitated, moved away from her the tiniest bit. "I got to your father's place last night. Spoke with Theresa. She told me what happened and gave me that."

Kelsey looked at the note again, at the bold letters that were jumbled together and made no sense to her. Did she believe him? *Could* she believe him?

She was surprised that part of her wanted to—and that was dangerous. Very dangerous.

"You can read this?"

"Yeah."

"How do I know you didn't write this? How do I know this isn't a trick of some kind?"

"You don't."

He wasn't foolish enough to say she'd have to trust him, which was a point in his favor. She *didn't* trust him. She didn't trust anyone.

But she didn't think he was lying, either. Her father had been the one who had told her to find Daryl. Had been the one to reassure her that he'd help her when she needed it. It was because of her father that she had taken that impulsive trip in July. She had needed to see the man her father spoke so highly of, needed to form her own impression of him before she made any decisions.

And then she'd slept with him and any impressions she may have formed were forever clouded in those long hours she'd spent in his arms.

"You were there that night. The night he was killed."

Kelsey's head snapped up before she could stop herself, before she could hide the surprise at his words. It was a statement, not a question. "How do you know that?"

He leaned forward, reached out and snagged the chain draped around her neck. He tugged, pulled her father's dog tags from beneath her shirt. "Theresa said his dog tags were missing, along with his jump wings and motorcycle. She told me she thought you had been there. That you had found him."

She freed the dog tags from his hand and tucked them back into her shirt. Ignored his unasked question—she didn't have to answer, not when it was obvious he already knew—and asked one of her own.

"If Dad sent you, if you knew it was me, why were you sneaking around the cabin? Why not just knock on the door?"

"The only thing your father gave me were the coordinates to this place. I had no idea what—or who—was here." A muscle jumped in Daryl's jaw and for a brief second, those amber eyes hardened as he watched her. "And because I didn't know it was you. Your father never mentioned your name. Even if he had, there would have been no reason for me to think it was you. To connect it back to some random woman I'd met three months ago."

Some random woman.

Both the words—and the tone of his voice—made her flinch. Kelsey swore to herself, told herself there was no reason to let the words to bother her. After everything that had happened, everything that could still happen, she had no business being upset at what he said. His opinion of her paled in comparison to everything else, held no importance whatsoever. Let him have his dig—it meant nothing to her.

She ignored his jab and held the letter out to him. "Will you read it to me? Tell me what he said?"

Daryl's gaze held hers for so long that she thought he was going to say no. He'd take the letter back, fold it up, and tell her it was none of her business.

But he surprised her again because he reached for the letter, carefully smoothed it out against one hard thigh. "It lists two sets of coordinates. The first one is this location. He was very clear that I needed to come here first."

Excitement filled her and she leaned forward, her eyes scanning the note. "The second set. Do you know what they are? Where they're for?"

"Yeah, I do."

Kelsey looked up, wondered if he could see the excitement she was trying so hard to hide. "Where?"

Daryl shook his head, the finality of the movement shocking her. "No. Not until I get some answers and you tell me what's going on."

Kelsey sat back, crossed her arms in front of her and said nothing. He watched her for a long minute then looked back at the note.

"The rest of the note is fairly brief. Straight forward." He cleared his throat, started reading. "*'If you're reading this, it means I'm not around and my girl is on the run. I told her to go to you but I don't think she will—she's not one to trust easily, not even on my say-so. Find her. She needs you, whether she admits or not. Yeah, she knows who you are and she'll have to learn to trust you. She has no choice. She can explain everything to you then, including that second set of coordinates.'*"

God, that sounded so much like her father. Kelsey could actually hear his voice, picture the frown that had probably been on his face when he wrote it. Could see him sitting at the beat-up old desk he refused to replace as he scribbled the note in that ridiculous code.

And she got the message meant for *her* as well, whether it had been deliberate or not.

She needs you, whether she admits it or not.

She'll have to learn to trust you. She has no choice.

Kelsey squeezed her eyes closed in a vain attempt to stop the tears, felt them trailing down her cheek anyway.

I'm scared, Daddy.

I know you are, Katydid. But you have to trust him. He can help you.

Her father's voice was close. So close. If she opened her eyes and looked to her left, would she see him? Would he be standing next to her, the reassuring smile on his face somehow easing the stern frown she knew she'd see? Kelsey was so sure she'd see him that she actually opened her eyes, turned her head—

But there was nobody there.

Nobody except Daryl Anderson, the man her father had sent to her.

He watched her, his face void of any emotion, his eyes carefully blank. Minutes passed by, marked by nothing more than the sound of their breathing. Daryl finally looked away, giving her time to wipe her face as he carefully folded the letter and placed it back in the envelope. He shifted away from her, finally giving her much-needed space.

Space she could use to flee. To try to escape.

Kelsey didn't move. The time for running was over, had been over for a long time.

"He also mentioned a name. Grady Byrne. Does that mean anything to you?"

She nodded, wondered if the fear and disgust showed on her face. Maybe. Maybe not. It didn't matter because Daryl leaned forward, the strength of his gaze holding her prisoner.

"Are you going to explain? Tell me what the hell's going on?"

Kelsey sucked in a deep breath, struggled to find the words. *Any* words. She'd kept this secret for so long, she didn't know where to start. *How* to start. It wasn't easy, fighting against the survival instinct she'd developed out of desperation over the past three years. Of being on the run. Of hiding. Of never telling anyone. Never trusting anyone.

Did she trust Daryl? Maybe. Did she trust him enough? No—but she trusted her father. And her father was right: she didn't have a choice. Not anymore.

"Grady Byrne is after my daughter. And he'll stop at nothing to get her."

CHAPTER TEN

Kelsey had a daughter.

Daryl studied her face. The tear-stained cheeks. The dark smudges of exhaustion under green-ringed hazel eyes. The pale complexion and thinned lips. She looked so different from the woman he had met a few months ago. The woman he'd spent the night with. Her hair was shorter, a deep brown-red with mussed waves instead of long, straight blonde. She'd lost weight. Not much, but enough to make her look fragile. Helpless.

She was anything but helpless. The memory of the gun held against the back of his head chilled him. If her finger had slipped, if she hadn't hesitated or given him a warning, he'd be dead right now.

Even after he'd disarmed her, she hadn't been helpless. She'd fought him, each swing and kick fueled by a panicked desperation he now understood. No, she hadn't been a match for him and he'd had to force himself to hold back. To be gentle with her even as she kicked and scratched. He'd have marks from her attempts to get away, no doubt about it.

But she hadn't screamed. Not once. Her struggles had been quiet. Even when she had begged for him not to hurt her, her pleas had been quiet. Hoarse, ragged. Desperate.

But still quiet.

Kelsey had a daughter.

His mind reeled with the information. With the implication. Davis's insistence that Daryl help made more sense now. Kelsey's own desperation made sense. A few more pieces of the puzzle fell into place—but not enough to give him even a small glimpse of the whole picture. Not nearly enough. The new information was just one more twist in the crazy game of cat-and-mouse he'd been sucked into over the last twenty-four hours.

He pushed off the bed, glanced around the cabin. Small. Self-contained. Nothing more than basic necessities: the bed; a small table and two chairs; a cast iron wood stove. A free-standing utility sink with an improvised counter sat next to the woodstove. The counter was no more than two feet long, constructed of raw wood. A two-burner camp stove sat on top of it and, taking up an entire burner all by itself, was a coffeepot.

Daryl's steps echoed against the rough plank floor as he made his way over to the camp stove. A shelf hung over the sink and counter, maybe three feet long. Canisters were neatly lined along the shelf, their contents clearly labeled. Coffee. Sugar. Flour. Tea.

What the fuck? *Tea?*

He ignored the canisters and reached for the two enamel-coated mugs that were stacked on top the matching plates. He sat the mugs side-by-side on the counter then hefted the coffee pot and filled each halfway with the steaming brew.

Daryl hesitated then grabbed the sugar canister. Located a spoon and dumped a generous amount into each mug. He didn't usually use sugar but what the hell—he'd need the boost it would give him. So would Kelsey.

He took one mug and moved back to the bed, held it out for Kelsey. She stared at it like she didn't know what the hell it was then looked up at him. "I don't use sugar—"

"Tough shit. Take it."

Damn if it didn't look like she wanted to argue with him. He narrowed his eyes, silently daring her to push. To his surprise, she accepted the mug, held it between both hands and took a careful sip.

He turned his back on her—not the brightest move since part of him fully expected her to knock him over the head with something or throw the coffee at him. Maybe both. It wouldn't matter if she tried, not when he was faster. He grabbed the second mug and one of the heavy chairs, dragged it over to the bed and turned it around so he could straddle it backward.

Then he just sat there, sipping strong, too-sweet coffee and watching the woman curled against the headboard. Minutes dragged by, each one filled with tense silence. Kelsey stared into the coffee mug, taking an occasional sip but otherwise not moving. She appeared as unfazed by the silence as he was. Should that surprise him? Even when he'd first met her, she had been quiet. Maybe a little reserved, like she wasn't accustomed to talking to people. He had chalked it up to a natural shyness but now...no, she wasn't shy. She just wasn't used to being around people. Wasn't used to trusting anyone.

Too damn bad. She'd have to learn to trust him. She didn't have any choice, not if she wanted his help.

"Tell me about your daughter."

Her head shot up and she watched him through narrowed eyes filled with suspicion and wariness. "Why?"

Daryl swallowed back a growl of frustration, schooled his face into a blank mask and met her gaze.

"The more information I have, the more I can help. Now tell me about your daughter."

She watched him for a long minute, finally looked away with a shaky sigh. "Her name is Paige. She just turned five."

He waited but she said nothing else. And yeah, that was real fucking helpful. If he wanted information, he'd have to pry every single word from her—something they didn't have time for. "Kelsey, I'm not the enemy here. I can help you but only if I know what's going on."

"Why?"

"Why do I need to know what's going on?"

She shook her head, looked over at him again. "No. Why do you want to help me?"

Daryl clenched his jaw. Inhaled deep through his nose then forced himself to relax. "Because your father asked me to."

"And that's it? He asked, so just like that, you're going to help?"

"Yeah. Just like that."

"Why? What's in it for you?"

He clenched his jaw again. Christ, this was going to be harder than he first thought. "Nothing is in it for me."

"Then why are you going to help?"

"Because I owe your father." She kept watching him, the unasked question in her eyes. *Why?* He heard it as clearly as if she had said it out loud. He hesitated, wondering how much to tell her. And fuck, it wasn't like she didn't already know—she did. At least, part of it. Because he had run his fucking mouth to her, spilled his own secrets during their time together down in the islands.

He raised the mug to his mouth, took a long swallow of the too-sweet coffee. Took another one, more to kill time as he gathered his thoughts. "Your father helped me get through some things a long time ago." He darted a glance at Kelsey, quickly averted his gaze. "Back when my daughter died. He was my CO at the time, knew I was close to losing my shit. He, uh, he helped me get my head on straight. Helped me channel all the shit I was going through."

Davis had been the one responsible for helping Daryl keep his sanity. And he'd been the one responsible for fast-tracking him into the Ranger program, for making sure his package went through.

"I'm sorry. I didn't know."

"There'd be no reason for you to know, would there?" Did his voice hold an edge of accusation? Yeah, it did. Tough shit. She'd met him under false pretenses, had never bothered to tell him who she was. Their meeting hadn't been an accident, he was certain of that.

But now wasn't the time to go into that. Later—if it even mattered. Right now, Daryl wasn't sure it did.

He took another sip of coffee, lowered the mug. "Where's your daughter now?"

Kelsey hesitated. Turned her teary gaze toward him and shook her head. "I don't know."

"What do you mean, you don't know?"

"I don't know. I—I haven't seen her in six months. I'm hoping Dad told you where she is because if he didn't, I might never see her again."

The bottom dropped out of his stomach, allowing a blast of icy air to freeze him. What the *fuck* was going on? Instead of getting answers, he was being handed riddles—

And not a single thing made sense.

He hated fucking games. Hated being strung along. Hated being played. And Daryl couldn't shake the feeling that all three were happening right now.

He leaned forward, not bothering to hide his impatience. His anger. His frustration.

"I think maybe you better start at the beginning and explain. All of it. *Now*."

CHAPTER ELEVEN

Start at the beginning.

Kelsey stared into the coffee mug, focused on the swirl of dark liquid that was too strong and too sweet to drink. Focusing on that was a hundred times better than watching that amber gaze stare at her.

Angry. Judging.

She didn't understand either one, couldn't figure out why he seemed so angry. Did it matter? No, it didn't. At least, it shouldn't. Daryl Anderson meant nothing to her other than a means to an end—and then only if he could help her. If he could do that—and her father seemed to think he could—then she didn't care what he thought of her. If he could find her daughter and somehow end this nightmare that had been going on for far too long, he could glare at her with all the contempt in the world and she'd dance for joy about it.

She shoved the lie from her mind and took a deep breath, ran a shaking hand over her face. Start at the beginning, he'd said. Kelsey wasn't even sure where the beginning was. Back when Blaine's mother had disappeared from the monster who was his father? When she'd hidden his existence because she knew what would happen?

No, not back that far.

She took a long swallow of the coffee, grimaced at the taste but didn't put the mug down. Holding that mug between her hands, *focusing* on it, helped to ground her somehow. Gave her the illusion she was in control.

She hadn't been in control for three years.

"I met Blaine my junior year of college—"

"Who's that?"

She glanced up, frowned at the man leaning toward her like he still expected her to bolt at any second. "Blaine Walsh. Paige's father."

He nodded, motioned for her to go on. His face might as well have been carved from stone for all the expression he showed but Kelsey could still feel his judgment. Too bad. She didn't care. She *couldn't* care.

"We met in my junior year of college. He was helping me in my Energy and Thermodynamics class—that was one of the requirements for mechanical engineering." She smiled at the memory. Her first impression of Blaine had been one of the quintessential nerd. Shaggy, dark-ginger hair. Clothes that never seemed to fit him right. A distracted air that clung to him except when he was focusing on his work. The only thing missing from the stereotypical image was a pocket protector and glasses. Kelsey hadn't cared about the pocket protector but she'd been happy about the glasses. Blaine had the most gorgeous green eyes she had ever seen, deep emerald green with flecks of gold. Those eyes had been her downfall.

She pushed the memory from her mind, tightened her hands around the enamel mug. "We started dating after a few months." Because Kelsey had asked *him* out—Blaine was too shy, too sweet, to ever make the first move. The man watching her didn't need to know that, though. "A few months later, we learned I was pregnant."

"You're married." It was a statement, not a question—and Kelsey didn't miss the accusation in his voice.

"No, I'm not married. By the time I realized I was pregnant, the relationship had already run its course. We were better suited as friends, not lovers. And Blaine *was* my best friend. He was also a great father."

And he had been. Paige had been his pride and joy. Blaine had joyfully admitted to anyone who would listen that his little girl had him wrapped around her finger. The bond the two had shared had been unbreakable; the connection between them had been almost magical. Special. Paige had been a bigger daddy's girl than Kelsey had ever been.

"You said *was*. Where is he now?"

"Blaine was killed by a drunk driver a little more than three years ago. He, uh, he was walking down the street to pick up dinner when the driver swerved and ran up on the sidewalk." She closed her eyes against the tears, tried to push the memories away. The frantic knocking on her door by several of the neighbors. The shrill ring of the telephone as she raced out of her apartment. The silent prayers she kept repeating to herself, telling herself over and over that it was a mistake. That her neighbors were wrong, that it wasn't Blaine that had been hit but someone else.

Except some prayers went unanswered, a lesson Kelsey had learned the hard way that night—and in the days following. Blaine was gone. Her sweet, gentle Blaine, who had never hurt a soul, was gone. She'd never see him again. Never watch as he swung Paige around and around in dizzying circles. She would never again hear his rich laughter or see his eyes light up in wonder at something Paige had done.

She opened her eyes, pulled in a shaky breath as she wiped her cheek on her shoulder. Had she expected sympathy from the man sitting so close, his hands loosely folded around his own coffee mug as he braced his arms over the back of the chair? If she had, she would have been disappointed. No emotion showed on his face, in his eyes. He just sat there, watching her with a detachment that sent a chill racing over her.

"You loved him." It was a statement, not a question. A statement laced with accusation. Kelsey met his blank gaze and nodded.

"Yes, I did. I still do." Let him think what he wanted, she didn't care. She'd be damned if she explained herself to him, if she defended the way she felt. Blaine had been her daughter's father, a part of both their worlds that could never be replaced. A piece of her heart had been ripped out the day Blaine died and that hole still existed. It might be smaller now but it would always be there because nothing could fix it. Nothing—and no one—could replace Blaine.

"What does any of this have to do with Grady Byrne? Why is he after you?"

"He's not after *me*. At least, he wasn't. Not at first. He wants Paige."

"Why?"

"Paige is his granddaughter."

"Blaine was his son?"

Kelsey nodded. "Yes. His *only* child, from what I understand. But he didn't know about Blaine, not until after the accident."

"How did he find out?"

"I'm not sure."

"Did Blaine know about him?"

"Yes. His mother finally told him when he was in high school. Blaine did some research and find out what kind of man Grady was. He told me about him—

right before Paige was born. He wanted me to know, to make sure I stayed away if I ever happened to see him. Neither one of us ever thought it would come to that. Blaine's mom had been positive that Grady didn't know about him. She'd only been two months pregnant with him when she ran away—"

"Ran away?"

"Yeah. That's how Blaine described it—that she ran away. I'm not sure exactly what happened, I never asked."

"But Byrne found out about him anyway."

Kelsey nodded, raised the mug to her mouth and sipped. The coffee was cold now, even more bitter. She didn't care—she needed the caffeine. The sugar. The distraction of doing something ordinary and mundane.

"Grady showed up at the funeral. I—I didn't even know he was there at first. Not until it was over. He, uh, he came up to me after the graveside service. Introduced himself. And then..." Her voice trailed off and she squeezed her eyes against the memory, pressed one hand against her stomach to control the nausea.

"And then?"

"He said he wanted Paige. That she was his granddaughter. His *legacy*. That was the word he used. He said he would make sure she was raised in luxury and given every opportunity in life." Kelsey shuddered, opened her eyes and nearly spit the next words. "He offered me two-hundred-and-fifty thousand dollars for Paige. Like I would *sell* my own daughter."

There was a long pause filled with nothing more than the sound of the chair creaking as Daryl shifted position. "What did you do?"

She raised her head, met his blank gaze with her own fiery one. "I told him I'd think about it and walked away. Then I took Paige and disappeared that night. We've been running ever since."

"Why did you disappear?"

His calm question—his entire *demeanor*, so relaxed and casual—angered her. Kelsey swung her legs over the side of the bed, stood up and started pacing. She was only slightly surprised he let her but she didn't care. She needed to *move*, to rid herself of the pent-up energy and frustration and fear bottled up inside her.

"I didn't have a choice. I knew he wouldn't stop. That he wouldn't take *no* for an answer."

"But you gave up your daughter anyway."

Kelsey spun on her heel, curled her hands into fists and stared at the man who had just accused her of the most heinous thing she could imagine. "She's my *daughter*. I would *never* give her up. Never. I would die first."

"But you haven't seen her in six months. You don't know where she is."

"I didn't have a choice!"

"Why?"

"Grady's men found us again. Six months ago. I don't know how. I—I guess I let my guard down. Thought that we were safe, that they weren't looking for us anymore. But I was wrong."

"What happened?"

"We were shopping. There was this new toy Paige wanted and she wouldn't stop asking for it—and she never asks for anything. So I took her to the mall and bought it for her. We were walking around, getting ready to go for ice cream, when a man tried to grab her. She screamed and I hit him. Grabbed Paige and ran to the car and took off. And I kept going, didn't stop until I knew it was safe."

Kelsey wrapped her arms around her waist, warding off the chill of the memory. Paige's sharp scream. The determination flashing in the man's eyes as he held her daughter's arm hard enough to bruise her tender flesh. The flare of recognition that exploded in her when she met the man's eyes. He'd been with Grady that day, at the funeral.

Anger and panic had washed over her, paralyzing her for one frightening second before instinct took over. Before survival kicked in. Not just survival but a wave of protectiveness that nearly blinded her. She swung out. Hitting. Kicking. Screaming until people started rushing their way. Screaming until the man finally let go. She scooped up her crying daughter and ran, leaving the shopping bag behind.

She ran both hands through her hair, sucked in a deep breath and let it out in a rush. Exhaling fear. Emotion. Worry. "I called Dad from a truck stop and waited there for him. He showed up a few hours later and—he took Paige. Took her somewhere safe."

"And you don't know where."

Was that accusation she heard in his voice once again? No, it was nothing more than her imagination. Her own guilty conscience rising up, accusing her again of abandoning her daughter. Kelsey shook her head—in answer to his question, and in denial of the guilt that had been with her since that night.

"No, I don't. It was Dad's idea. If I didn't know where she was, I couldn't accidentally lead Grady's men to her."

Daryl was quiet for a long time. So long that she actually wondered what he was thinking. Did he believe her? Did she care if he didn't?

She shouldn't care. It shouldn't matter at all what

he thought. What he believed. But to her dismay, it did—because she needed his help. Without him, she might never see Paige again.

Kelsey tried to convince herself that was the only reason she cared but she failed—for reasons she didn't understand. Reasons she didn't even want to think about right now.

Daryl drained his coffee and stood. Dragged the chair across the floor and placed it in the exact spot where it had been earlier then calmly rinsed his mug out and placed it back on the shelf. Only then did he turn around and look at her, his eyes expressionless.

"Is Kelsey your real name?"

She blinked in surprise, almost asked why he cared. But she was too tired to play games. Too tired to verbally spar with the man carefully watching her. "Yeah, it's my real name."

"Why tell me? Why not give me a phony name?"

She almost asked him what he meant, stopped before she made a fool of herself. He didn't mean *now*—he meant *before*. The first time they'd met. "I—I don't know."

He nodded, glanced around the cabin, finally met her gaze. "Grab your gear. We're leaving."

Hope blossomed deep inside and she quickly squelched it. She couldn't afford to hope, not yet. Not until she knew for sure what he meant by *leaving*.

"Where are we going?"

His amber gaze held hers for a long minute. What she saw in their depths made the hope deep inside her spring to life once more.

"We're going to get your daughter."

CHAPTER TWELVE

The trip heading back to the dirt road where he had parked the rental truck was marginally easier than the hike in—but only because he wasn't making his way through the dark this time. Weak light filtered in through the empty branches overhead, adding an almost ghostly glow to everything. Daryl checked his watch to gauge their time. It had taken him just under two hours to reach the cabin once he started out. Going back shouldn't take as long—theoretically, anyway. But he wasn't traveling by himself and he had to account for extra time for Kelsey.

He stopped next to the thick trunk of a dead tree blackened with rot and turned to study her progress. She wasn't far behind him, her shorter stride steady and competent. A knit hat covered her head and the bulky coat she wore practically swallowed her small frame. A sturdy walking stick was clenched in one gloved hand; the other hand was loosely wrapped around one of the shoulder straps of her oversize backpack. She had her head down, watching each step as she carefully maneuvered the small downward slope.

For some odd reason, the image of a wizened old hermit came to mind. He didn't know why—Kelsey was neither wizened nor old. And she didn't look like a hermit; at least, not how he imagined a hermit would look. But the image was there, whether it made sense or not, and he almost grinned.

Fuck.

Yeah, he needed more caffeine. The second cup he'd had as he waited for Kelsey to gather her things had helped but the effects were already beginning to fade. He thought he'd have time for a third while she packed but she was faster than he gave her credit for.

Not that she had much to pack. The woman traveled light, he had to give her credit for that, at least. That didn't mean her pack wasn't heavy. It was nothing more than a regular backpack—a larger one, but still just a backpack. It wasn't a hiking pack, didn't have a waist strap. And it wasn't designed to carry any kind of weight over any distance. Whatever weight was in it, no matter how light, would be resting entirely on her shoulders instead of her hips.

He watched her approach, studying her face. Her expression. Her gait. Looking for any sign of weariness. Of weakness. They hadn't been walking for long, not even twenty minutes yet. But he had no idea what kind of shape she was in or what kind of conditions she was used to. He didn't want her tripping or falling, didn't want to push her if she needed a break.

Judging from the impatient glance she threw his way, she didn't want a break. Tough shit. There was no need to rush. No need to hurry. Nobody was chasing them and hurrying back wouldn't get them to where they were going any faster.

Then again, maybe he *should* push her. Move so fast that she was completely exhausted by the time they reached the truck. If he did that, he wouldn't have to listen to her scream and argue when she learned where they were going.

Because he wasn't taking her to get her daughter. No way in hell. He planned on taking her back home, holing her up somewhere safe and having one of the guys keep an eye on her. Then *he'd* go get her daughter and bring her back.

And figure out where the hell to go from there. If Grady Byrne was still looking for them—and there was no reason to think he wasn't, not unless Kelsey was lying—then finding her daughter wouldn't solve anything. It would reunite the two of them, yeah. But it wouldn't put an end to whatever danger they were in.

Fuck. He was still wrapping his head around everything she'd told him. Part of him didn't want to believe it—it was too much like one of those awful mobster movies that played on television late at night. But her pain and desperation as she told him the story had been real. Her panic and fear when she had first tried to run from him at the cabin had been real.

And Davis being murdered was real, too. What had Chaos said about Grady Byrne? *There's a lot of dead bodies attached to his name.* If even half of what Kelsey had told him was true, there was a good possibility that she could end up on that list of bodies.

Bullshit. Not on his watch.

And not just because Davis had asked for his help.

She came to a stop next to him, reached up and adjusted the straps of her pack then tossed him another impatient look. "You didn't need to stop. I'm fine."

Was she? Maybe. Maybe not. He couldn't tell. She seemed fine—except for the smudges under her eyes and the worry shadowing her gaze. Part of him couldn't quite believe she'd been running for three years. How had she managed to stay ahead of Byrne for so long?

He knew the answer even before the question completely formed in his mind: her father. Allen Davis would know how to help her disappear, would have been able to give her support along the way.

Disappearing wasn't as hard as people thought it was, even in this time of constant connection through technology, not if you knew what you were doing.

And Davis definitely knew what he was doing.

It was what she had told him about the last six months that surprised him the most. That she had willingly given up her daughter, had willingly allowed the separation in order to keep her daughter safe.

And fuck. She had a daughter. She was still in love with her daughter's father. He had to fucking remember that. Had to forget about that fucking night in the Caribbean, separate *then* from *now* and stay focused on what he needed to do.

Keep her safe—and stay the fuck away from her.

Daryl didn't fully trust her, wondered if there were things she wasn't telling him—hell, he *knew* there were things she wasn't telling him, like how the hell she had managed to be in the Caribbean the same time he was—but she had been honest about hiding her daughter. For the most part, she'd been detached when talking about everything else, like she was merely reciting a story. But her outburst when he accused her of giving up her daughter had been too real to be fake, too raw to be manufactured.

Yeah—or maybe he was just a fucking sucker for a sob story. Maybe he was letting that damn night they'd been together in the Caribbean cloud his fucking judgment.

Maybe—except for Davis. His old CO wasn't a bullshitter, wouldn't ask for help if he didn't need it. And if Davis thought the threat was real, then it was fucking real.

Daryl reached behind him and yanked a bottle of water from the side pouch of his pack. He twisted off the lid then held it out to Kelsey. "Drink."

"I'm not thirsty—"

"Too bad. Drink."

She narrowed her eyes then grudgingly accepted the bottle. Brought it to her mouth and took several long swallows before handing it back to him. "Your turn. Drink."

Daryl almost cracked a smile at the way her tone matched his. Unlike her, he didn't argue, just upended the bottle and drained it. He started to recap it then stopped, instincts going on high alert when something around them shifted and changed. The few early birds that had been singing stopped, plunging the woods around them into an eerie silence. That damn itchy sensation appeared on the back of his neck. He didn't wait, didn't look around—he just grabbed Kelsey's arm and pulled her to the ground, covering her body with his a split-second before the bark of the trunk he'd been leaning on exploded.

"Fuck!" The oath came out in a low growl, more of an I-don't-fucking-believe-this swear than a shit-we're-in-trouble swear. Who the fuck was out there shooting at them? Was it some other homesteader taking offense at them coming too close at whatever might pass for their home?

That was nothing more than wishful thinking. The shot had been a hell of a lot more than a warning shot—and too damn close for comfort.

Daryl shrugged out of his pack, reached inside his coat and pulled the PK380 from his shoulder holster. He had eight rounds in the clip and one in the chamber—more than enough.

He hoped. If not, he had two more clips ready to go.

How many people were out there? One? Two? More? He cocked his head to the side, listening through the slight ringing in his ears. There, off to the left, the tell-tale crack of a branch breaking. Just beyond that was the sound of a foot slipping in leaves, punctuated by a small grunt.

Another sound several yards to the right of those two. Wheezing, like someone was trying to catch their breath.

Yeah. It helped that they sucked at being quiet.

That made three. Were there more? Daryl listened for another few seconds, his ears attuned to any sound that didn't belong.

Whoever they were, they were doing their damnedest to be quiet—and failing. They must have been waiting. No way in hell would they have been able to sneak up on them without him noticing. Then again, he hadn't exactly been quiet. Hadn't thought he *needed* to be quiet, not out here, near the cabin in the middle of BFE that nobody else was supposed to know about.

Three men. The odds weren't bad, wouldn't make him think twice at any other time. But he wasn't alone, he had to think of the woman laying deathly still underneath him.

Was she hurt? He didn't think so. He knew she was breathing because he could feel the movement of her pack digging into his gut with each shallow rise and fall of her chest. But she was quiet, hadn't even screamed in surprise when he grabbed her and threw her to the ground. Hadn't flinched when the bullet hit the tree next to them.

As far as positions went, they weren't in a bad spot. Not the best spot, but it was better than the incline a few yards behind them. Why the hell hadn't the shooter—or *shooters*—fired then? They would have had a better chance of hitting their targets if they had.

He didn't know and for now, he was damn glad they hadn't. Damn amateurs. They'd pay for that mistake.

Later. Right now, he had to come up with a plan. Draw them out. He glanced around, studied the terrain, looking for a better spot. There, an old log, about ten yards away. He could make it with no problem—but could Kelsey?

He couldn't risk it—couldn't risk her safety. He didn't like the idea of leaving her where they were but for right now, it was the best option.

He slowly slid off her, easing his weight from her prone body. She turned her head, kept it lowered as her wide-eyed gaze met his. Her face had drained of color, making the small scratch on her chin stand out even more.

Rage tore through him, surprising him with its strength. It was a scratch, nothing more. A scratch that was probably *his* fault because of the way he threw her to the ground.

Something he'd had to do because of those assholes. Yeah, the bastards would definitely pay.

"Are you okay?" He mouthed the question, saw understanding flare in her eyes. She nodded but didn't say anything else, just rested her cheek against the dirt and leaves and twigs.

He wanted to lean down and press a kiss against her forehead, tell her how proud he was of her for staying so calm. Any other woman he knew would have screamed, would be hyperventilating in fear. And what the fuck was wrong with him? They had three fucking assholes waiting to open fire on them and he was fucking laying here thinking of kissing her because she was *quiet*? So she wasn't screaming. Big fucking deal. She was probably in shock.

And if he didn't get his fucking head out of his ass and come up with a plan, she could be dead in five minutes.

He pulled his gaze from hers and studied the terrain once more. Trees. Lots and lots of fucking trees—and even more dead fucking leaves on the ground. That would make moving around without being heard a little trickier. Not impossible, but definitely tricky.

That log was still his best bet. It would give him the best line of sight and still provide enough cover for him. He studied the ground between here and there, realized luck was with him. A plan quickly formed in his mind and he leaned down, caught Kelsey's gaze with his own.

"Stay here. Don't move." Her eyes widened and she shook her head, curled one hand around his shoulder as if that would keep him in place. He closed his hand over hers and gently eased it away, then leaned even closer and mouthed the words again.

"Stay here. Don't move." And damn if it didn't look like she was ready to argue with him. He clenched his jaw, shot her a warning look that would have had his men shitting in their boots. Then, because why the fuck not, he dropped a quick kiss against her forehead. Yeah, he needed his fucking head examined. But what the hell—it shut her up. She was still staring at him, her mouth opened in a small circle of shock as he pushed to his feet and ran in a crouch to the next closest tree.

Just as he expected, gunfire echoed behind him. Five shots. *Pop-pop-pop. Pop-pop.* Two guns—not three.

Why the fuck were only two of them firing? Where was the third guy?

He heard hushed voices, low and gruff, the words inaudible from this distance—but he heard enough to make out two distinct voices. Again, he wondered about the third guy. Had he heard wrong? Had there only been two to begin with?

No, there was nothing wrong with his hearing—there had definitely been three. The two clowns who had just fired, too close to each other to be effective, and Mr. Wheezy several yards to their right.

Daryl really, really wanted to know where Wheezy was right now.

The pair weren't even trying to be quiet. Hell, he could track their movements by the sound of their feet scuffling in the leaves. By the sound of their hushed voices as they spoke to one another.

And then, damn, one of them actually cleared his fucking throat like he was preparing to make a speech. Daryl had to fight the urge to roll his eyes as he eased around the trunk, searched for the tell-tale movement that would give away their exact position.

There, twenty yards away, at his eleven. Piece of cake. He sighted in, took aim—

"We just want the girl. Not you."

What. The. Fuck. Were they fucking serious?

Daryl squeezed the trigger, felt the small jump of the weapon in his hand, smelled the reassuring acrid scent of gunpowder. From twenty yards away came a surprised grunt and a wet gurgle, followed by the sound of a body crumpling to the ground.

Damn. He'd been hoping for the head shot but his aim had been off the slightest bit. Still not bad considering it had been a blind shot. Yeah, too damn bad—for the other guy. As far as Daryl was concerned, dead was dead.

There was a moment of stunned silence followed a high-pitched burst of outrage. Damn guy screamed like a fucking girl—or like someone had jammed his nuts in a vice and was squeezing the hell out of them.

Now there was a thought—

More shots, fired in rapid succession. It didn't matter because Daryl was already moving, heading toward his next position.

Pop. Pop-pop-pop. Pop. Pop-pop. Pop.

Click.

Well hell, now didn't that just suck. The guy must not have been paying attention. Asshole was totally not having a good day—and it was about to get even worse.

He sighted in, took aim and started to squeeze the trigger—

Stopped when he heard a low-pitched trilling that wasn't quite a whistle. Once. Twice. Three times.

Three shooters.

All three accounted for.

Daryl lowered his weapon and bit back a laugh. Pushed to his feet and brushed the leaves and dirt from his pants before moving toward that awful whistling sound. Mac emerged from the brush where the two shooters had been. A few minutes later, Chaos strolled out from behind a thick cropping of trees, a fucking grin on his face like he was doing nothing more than going for a leisurely stroll.

"I thought I told you twenty-four hours."

There was zero remorse on Mac's face when he shrugged. "Guess my watch is busted."

Daryl wanted to call bullshit but he didn't. Hell, he

would have done the same damn thing if their places had been reversed so he should have expected it. And it wasn't like the help wasn't appreciated.

Chaos motioned behind him with a brief nod of his head. "Any idea who they are?"

"No, but I'd bet they're connected to Grady Byrne somehow. Did you get anything off them?"

"IDs which are probably fake. All three of them had phones." Chaos patted the side pocket of his tactical pants. "I'll tear them apart when we get back, see what I can find."

Daryl nodded, his expression turning grim. "We need to find out how the hell they found this place. Nobody is supposed to know about it."

"You sure about that?"

"Pretty sure. Davis wasn't a fool. There's no way anyone could have connected this place back to him." He'd have to ask Kelsey, maybe she knew.

Daryl turned around, expecting to see Kelsey marching up behind him, demanding answers. She wasn't there. Was she still laying low? Possibly, although she hadn't impressed him as the type of person to cringe in fear once the danger passed. Hell, not even when the threat was right on top of her—

Unless she had taken off.

Fuck!

Why hadn't he considered that? She'd tried to run before, why wouldn't she run now? This would be the best time, when he was distracted. When he wasn't close enough to keep an eye on her—or stop her.

His feet were moving before his mind ordered them to. He'd gone two steps when the sound of weapon firing froze him in place. He dropped to the ground, weapon in hand, scanned the area around him.

Mac and Chaos had done the same thing behind him.

The shot had come from where Kelsey had been hiding. Fuck. Fuck damn shit. Had there been a fourth guy? Had he somehow fucked up? Fear and rage tore through him as he hurried forward—

Only to be stopped by another sound, this one an incredulous roar of disbelief in a voice he instantly recognized.

Boomer.

"Son-of-a-bitch! She tried to fucking shoot me."

CHAPTER THIRTEEN

Kelsey was going to be sick.

Nausea had been burning her stomach for the last hour, eating away at her as they marched through the woods. Was it odd that she used that word? *Marched*. She wouldn't have thought of it under normal circumstances but it seemed to fit now—probably because of the men surrounding her. Two men walked in front of her, two men behind. Maybe she was supposed to feel more protected that way but she felt like a prisoner instead.

Especially since the man she had almost shot was right behind her.

She glanced over her shoulder, met his dark gaze then quickly looked away. The chill in those eyes pebbled her skin and made her stomach twist and roll even more.

Oh, God, three men were dead—because of her. They'd been coming after *her*. What would have happened if Daryl hadn't found her first? Would *she* be dead already? A small part of her brain—the part that was always detached from her emotions, the part that could look at things logically and coldly analyze them—wondered about the timing of their arrival. Had Daryl somehow led them to her? Would they have found her if not for him?

She didn't know. All she knew was that three men were dead and she had nearly killed a fourth. Those three men should mean nothing to her—they were

Grady's men. They would have surely killed her just like they had killed her father.

The nausea exploded, tightening her gut, burning her throat. She didn't have time to speak, just pressed her lips together and took off at a run. Men yelled, called her name, but she ignored them. She couldn't stop—wouldn't stop. Wouldn't humiliate herself in front of them.

She stopped behind a scraggly bush, bent over as her body emptied the meager contents of her stomach. Her throat burned. Tears filled her eyes—not because of her body's traitorous act but because she couldn't get her father's image from her mind.

And God, she didn't want to remember him like that. Had succeeded in forgetting for the last twelve days. Why now? Why couldn't she replace the image of the last time she'd seen him with another image from a lifetime of memories? One of him laughing and smiling. Of pushing Paige on a swing or just sitting in his recliner, reading one of his favorite books?

The tears came faster, scalding her face as she bent over the bush. She pressed her hand against her stomach, willed her traitorous body to stop. Seconds went by, maybe minutes, before she reached behind her, searching blindly. Her hand brushed against rough bark and she fell backward, using the tree to brace herself as her knees finally gave out and she collapsed to the ground.

She curled her arms around her bent legs and dropped her head to her knees. But the tears wouldn't stop. Her shoulders shook with silent sobs, grief and regret tearing through her.

It was too much. All of it. The running. The hiding. The worrying and the fear. Never knowing what would happen next. Never knowing if she'd ever see her daughter again.

Never knowing if today would be the day she died.

But she was still here.

Her father was dead.

Three men she didn't know were dead.

She had nearly killed a fourth man. A man she didn't know. A man who had been trying to help *her*.

But she was still here. Still alive.

And she didn't know why. Didn't even know if she cared anymore. If not for Paige, she wouldn't. If not for her daughter, she would have given up long ago.

Part of her wanted to give up now.

Leaves rustled beside her, steps moving closer as a shadow fell over her. Kelsey didn't have to look up to know who it was. It was *him*. Daryl. Mortification swept over her though she didn't understand why. She didn't know him, not really. Why should she care if he witnessed her breakdown?

Because breaking down was a sign of weakness— and Kelsey didn't want to be perceived as weak.

That thought only made her cry harder. She pressed her face against her knees, tried to make herself stop. Willed the tears to end. Sucked in deep, cleansing breaths of air.

She needed to calm herself down. She was overreacting. Coming completely unglued. This wasn't like her. She didn't have breakdowns. She didn't lose control.

Kelsey Ann, this has nothing to do with losing control and everything to do with being human. Stop being so damn hard on yourself.

Her father's voice again, so loud and clear he could be standing right next to her. She didn't bother to tilt her head up, didn't bother to look around. If she did, she'd be giving into the insanity of wishful thinking. Of hoping the voice was *real* and not just a byproduct of finally losing her mind. Her father wasn't here—he would never be here again.

The man next to her—not her father but the flesh-and-blood man—crouched beside her. She turned her head away from him, angrily wiped the tears that kept streaming from her eyes. God, she was tired. So tired. Tired of running. Tired of hiding. Tired of being afraid.

Tired of doing everything on her own.

Tired of being alone.

"You okay?" Daryl's voice, low and even. *Real.*

"I'm not weak." And God, he must be laughing at her. How could she claim such a thing when she was nothing more than a sniveling mess? Even her voice was weak. Raspy. Hoarse. Pathetic.

"Never thought you were." He shifted, moved from a crouch so he was sitting next to her, his back against the trunk, his shoulder brushing hers. Something nudged her arm and she looked over, carefully keeping her face averted from his gaze. He was holding out a bottle of water—and a small square of material, neatly folded.

For a reason she didn't understand, the sight of that folded bandana made her start crying again. She swore to herself, tried to edge away from him as embarrassment swept over her. Arms closed around her—familiar arms, strong and capable—and she stiffened, started to pull away...

Then gave in and sagged against him. Buried her head against his chest and stopped fighting. Let herself cry until there were no more tears. Until she was limp and spent, drained. Physically. Mentally. Emotionally.

He didn't say anything, just sat there and held her, his hand rubbing gentle circles against her back. And it would be tempting, so tempting, to just stay where she was. To let the man holding her take care of everything.

There's nothing wrong with asking for help, Katydid. It takes a stronger person to ask for help and a fool to turn it down when you need it.

Her father's voice again. But was she really hearing it—or was it nothing more than a memory? How many times had he said those exact words to her when she was growing up? Whenever she tried to figure something out on her own. Riding a bike. Taking apart a lawnmower. Teaching herself how to braid her own hair because she wanted to show off to her dad. Always pushing herself, stubbornly convinced she didn't need help. Stubbornly convinced she could figure it out on her own.

I don't know how to ask for help, Daddy.

I know you don't, Katydid. You never did. Don't you think it's time you learned?

Was it time? Kelsey couldn't answer that question, wasn't even sure where to start or how to go about asking.

Maybe she didn't need to. Daryl was here now, wasn't he? He was already helping—because her father had asked him to. What kind of man would drop everything to help someone he hadn't seen in years? What kind of man would track down someone he didn't know, someone who didn't want to be found, just because an old friend had asked?

Only a man like her father would.

Kelsey eased away from Daryl, shivered at the loss of warmth from his body. She took the bandana from his outstretched hand, mopped her face with it in an attempt to erase all signs of her uncontrollable crying.

"You okay?" He asked the question again, like she hadn't completely fallen apart the first time he said those words.

She nodded, not sure she could get any words past her raw, swollen throat. Something nudged her in the side again and she looked down, saw the bottle of water Daryl was holding out for her.

"Drink. You don't want to get dehydrated."

She uncapped the bottle and raised it to her mouth. The cold liquid eased the burning in her throat, soothed the ache in her chest and somehow revived her flagging spirits. She drank half the bottle then recapped it and handed it back.

"You worry about dehydration a lot, don't you?" She noticed the confusion in his eyes so she nodded toward the bottle. "You said the same thing in the islands. Told me I needed to stay hydrated." Did he even remember that? Or had she placed more importance on his concern than it deserved?

"Yeah, I guess I did." His gaze shot to hers then quickly dropped. "Do you need a few more minutes?"

"No." But she didn't move and neither did he. Kelsey closed her eyes and rested her head against the trunk, tried to empty her mind of everything but the peace and quiet around her. Yes, it was peaceful now—but it hadn't been that way an hour ago. Not when the three men—Grady's men—had been shooting at them.

Not when she had nearly shot one of Daryl's own men.

"I—I didn't mean to shoot him." The confession fell from her lips before her mind even realized she was going to speak. And she wasn't sure why she was telling him, only that something inside her had decided he needed to know.

When she realized how close she had come—

If the man hadn't had the reflexes of a cat and moved in time—

She really hadn't meant to shoot him. She had reached into Daryl's pack, found her pistol tucked inside along with the clip. It had been nothing more than survival instinct, a need to protect herself against the men who were shooting at them. She'd been on edge, every sense on high alert even when she saw Daryl walk out to greet men he obviously knew. She'd heard them talking, had let out a sigh of relief—

And then she'd heard the noise behind her, the rustle of leaves crunching beneath heavy steps. She rolled over, saw the huge shadow coming toward her. She didn't think, just raised the gun and pulled the trigger and—

A shudder raced over her when she thought again of how close she'd come to taking an innocent life.

"He should have known better than to approach you from behind." There was something in Daryl's voice that made her look up. Humor? No, that couldn't be it—there was absolutely nothing funny about what had happened. Whatever she had heard—or thought she heard—was gone when he spoke again.

"Either way, I'm glad you didn't. Boomer's too valuable to the team." He pushed to his feet, reached down and offered her his hand. Kelsey hesitated but only for a second before accepting it. His grip was strong. Warm. Gentle. The way she remembered from their time together—

She pushed the thought away, quickly dropped her hand after he helped her stand. "Team? What team?"

"My team. Cover Six Security."

"I don't understand."

"You weren't too far off when you asked if I was in private security. Down in the Caribbean."

Had she? Yes, she had—but it had been nothing more than a wild guess, a way to fill in the gaps in their conversation. She'd known he was former military—her father had told her that much. But beyond that, she hadn't given it much thought.

She nodded toward the men standing a few yards away. "Those men work for you?"

"In a roundabout way, yeah. And now they work for you."

Kelsey wanted to ask him what he meant—not that they worked for him, she understood that part. What she didn't understand was the *why*. Why did they work for her now? Why were they even here to begin with?

She didn't get a chance because Daryl led her back to the three men who had been waiting for them. None of them said a word—they didn't even give her more than a passing glance when she finally joined them. Did that mean they hadn't noticed her breakdown?

No. Nothing got past the notice of these men. Which meant they were pretending it hadn't happened.

Fine, she could pretend to.

She took her place in the center of the line and started walking. Each step brought her closer to her daughter, closer to the end of this long nightmare.

Unless that was nothing more than pretend, too—and that was something she refused to believe.

CHAPTER FOURTEEN

Daryl studied the woman beside him. Even sleeping, she was tense, huddled into herself. Her arms were crossed in front of her, her hands tucked under her armpits. A frown creased her face and she shook her head, just once. Several strands of hair fell across her cheek and his fingers itched to brush them away. To pull her into his arms and coax her into relaxing against him, the way she had their one night together.

The way she had a few hours earlier, when she stumbled to the side of the makeshift trail they'd been forging and become sick.

He needed his fucking head examined. Relaxed? He didn't think the woman he couldn't seem to look away from knew what the word meant. Could he blame her? No, not after learning what she'd gone through the last few years.

As far as comforting—you needed to trust someone to let them comfort you. Like her father had warned, Kelsey Davis wasn't one to trust.

He eased his bulk from the seat and moved two rows back. The plane they were on was another small private charter, big enough for eight people. Theoretically, there should be plenty of room for the five of them.

There wasn't.

He wedged himself between Mac and Chaos, nodded at the phone in Mac's large hand. "Did you make the calls?"

"Yeah, everything's going to be handled. Bodies will be disposed of, no questions asked."

At any other time, the words would have reassured Daryl. Not this time. There *would* be questions. Maybe not from the authorities—their contact would make certain of that—but no way in hell would Grady Byrne *not* notice three of his men missing. No way in hell would he *not* question it.

Fuck it. He'd deal with that later.

He turned to Chaos, nodded to the secured laptop opened and braced against his legs. Daryl had already told all three of them what was going on. At least, the abbreviated version:

Kelsey was Davis's daughter.

She'd been running from Byrne for three years.

Her daughter was Byrne's granddaughter.

She'd given her daughter to Davis six months ago to hide and hadn't seen her since.

Abbreviated version? Shit, that was pretty much all he knew.

"Find anything?"

"Yeah, enough. And you're going to fucking love this. It's ingenious. I'll give it to your friend—he knew what the hell he was doing."

Daryl clenched his jaw, had to control the urge to punch the man in the mouth just to see that cocky fucking smile disappear from his face. "Care to elaborate?"

"To start with, you were right about the coordinates being flipped." Chaos turned the laptop to the side so Daryl could see it and pointed at the enlarged map on the screen. "If anyone got hold of them, they'd end up near Oelrichs, South Dakota."

Daryl leaned forward, frowned at the screen.

"Where the hell is that?"

"Yeah, exactly. *But*—if you flip the latitude, you end up here." Chaos typed something into the computer and brought up another map. "Portales, New Mexico. Just like you said. Want to know what's an hour outside Portales?"

"You mean besides dirt?"

"Actually, it's not as barren as you think—"

"Save it, Chaos. What's there?"

"A children's home."

"No shit."

"Yeah, no shit. Like I said, ingenious. He hid her in plain sight."

Which was the best place to hide something. Or, in this case, some*one*. He was still having trouble believing that Kelsey didn't know. No, scratch that. He had trouble believing that she went along with it willingly. He remembered the pain and anguish of losing Layla, remembered how he'd spiraled out of control, convinced life wasn't worth living. Anger had swallowed him whole, made him lash out at everything and everyone. No way in hell could he imagine willingly giving her up.

Except Kelsey hadn't given up her daughter—she'd placed her in hiding. Would he have done the same thing in her place? Fuck, no. He would have gone after the bastard chasing her down. Would have turned the tables on Grady Byrne and made the son-of-a-bitch pay.

But Kelsey didn't have his resources. Neither did Davis. Hell, Daryl hadn't had his own resources back then, either. It had taken him years to build the contacts, years of cultivating careful relationships in the shadows before being able to call in some favors and get to where he was now. To get CSS up and running. But he'd done it. *They'd* done it—him and Mac and Jon. And once they'd started, things had taken off faster than they expected.

But that was now. Back then, all those years ago when he'd lost Layla—no, he hadn't known what the fuck to do.

If he'd been in Kelsey's shoes, would he have done the same thing? If he had known what would happen, would he have taken Layla from her mother and put her in hiding?

He didn't even have to think of the answer—it was a resounding *hell, yes*. Because he remembered how fucking helpless he'd felt the day Melissa had walked out. Remembered how fucking *inept* he'd been, not knowing what to do or who to go to for help. All he'd been able to focus on was Layla's tear-streaked face as she clung to her bunny and made him promise he'd see her soon.

Yeah, you better fucking believe he'd have taken her that day if he'd known what was going to happen.

Fuck.

Daryl clenched his jaw, closed his eyes. Reached up and pinched the bridge of his nose. Anything to put that fucking day behind him.

He needed to get that image out of his head. Needed to leave it in the dark corner of his soul where he'd forced it to hide nine years ago. He'd spent a year after the accident fighting for his sanity, for something resembling normalcy. For direction.

Allen Davis had given it to him. And now he'd given him something else as well, placed something even more important in Daryl's hands: the safety of his daughter. His granddaughter.

Now he just needed to figure out how the fuck he was going to make that happen.

"Let me guess: we're heading to New Mexico."

Daryl opened his eyes, met Mac's steady gaze then slowly shook his head. "No."

"No?"

"No." Daryl repeated the word. From the way both men were staring at him, he knew they thought he'd just lost his mind. Hell, even Boomer popped his head over the back of the seat and gave him the hairy eyeball.

"Why the fuck not?" The question came from Mac, his gravelly voice making the words even harsher.

"Think about it. The girl has been there for six months. Nobody knows where she is. She's safe. We move her from there and we run the risk of this Byrne finding out somehow."

"How's he going to do that? If we squirrel them away somewhere, he'll never find them—"

"Like he wasn't supposed to find that damn cabin?" And yeah, that still fucking bothered Daryl. How the hell had those men found them? They sure as hell hadn't followed him—which meant they'd discovered it some other way.

"Then what the hell do you plan on doing? You can't keep them separated—"

"The hell I can't—"

Boomer snorted. "Yeah. Good luck with that."

Daryl ignored him and kept talking. "At least until I'm certain Byrne isn't going to be a problem."

"And how are you going to do that? Take him out?"

"If I have to, yeah."

"Jesus." Chaos leaned closer, lowered his voice.

"Have you lost your fucking mind? This isn't like taking down a lone wolf terrorist or some random crazy fuck. It's like a damn cell: you cut the head off and another grows right back. You take him down and his entire organization will come after you."

"Then I deal with that when it happens."

The three men stared at him, saying nothing. Yeah, he knew he sounded fucking ridiculous—not to mention blood-thirsty as hell. That wasn't how they operated. Going in and leveling anything—or anyone—in their path was so far out of procedure that even he wondered if maybe he was losing his mind. No, not his mind—his impartiality.

Even knowing that, he couldn't think of a better plan because no matter how he looked at it, Kelsey and her daughter wouldn't be safe until Byrne was stopped. Therefore, he had to stop Byrne. It was as simple as that.

Simple. Yeah, sure it was.

"You sure you're not letting emotion get in the way of your judgment on this one?"

Daryl's gaze shot to Boomer's. He narrowed his eyes, ground his teeth. But he didn't say anything—because Mac beat him to it.

"What the fuck are you talking about?"

Boomer motioned toward the front of the plane with a quick tilt of his head. "You don't recognize her? No, wait, you wouldn't. You never came out of that fucking bungalow." Boomer's gaze shifted to Chaos. "But you should."

Chaos shifted in the seat, leaned forward and craned his neck in an effort to see up front. And shit, could he be any more fucking obvious?

He sat back with a frown. "What are you talking

about?"

"You don't recognize her?" There was surprise in Boomer's voice. Daryl wanted to reach up and wrap both hands around the man's neck and fucking strangle him. But it was too late because he kept talking. "Long blonde hair. Legs that went all the way up to her—"

"That's enough—"

"Holy shit." Chaos leaned forward again, shook his head, then turned toward Daryl. "No fucking way. She's the one you hooked up with at Mac's wedding."

"What?" Now Mac was leaning forward, craning his neck to look up front. "How the hell did I miss that?"

"You missed it because you never came out of that fucking bungalow."

"The hell we didn't."

"No, you didn't. At least not for the two days we were there after the wedding."

Mac ignored Boomer's taunt, turned to Daryl with a frown. "So you know her?"

"Not really, no."

"But you knew who she was?"

"We weren't exactly exchanging names and phone numbers, no."

"Wait." Chaos leaned forward, lowered his voice even though there was nobody to overhear him. "Did she know who you were? When she met you down there, I mean."

Daryl placed both hands flat against his thighs. If he didn't, there was a damn good chance he'd throttle all three men, starting with Chaos and ending with Mac. "Yeah, she knew who I was."

"Jesus." Chaos sat back, shook his head. "She fucking played you."

Daryl wanted to deny it. Wanted to argue with Chaos and tell him he didn't know what the fuck he was talking about. Wanted to smash his fist into the faces of all three men so they'd stop looking at him like that. The problem was, he couldn't. Not when Chaos was right. Yeah, he'd been played. Maybe not in the way Chaos actually meant but the fact remained that Kelsey had known exactly who he was when he walked up to her that afternoon three months ago.

And she hadn't said a damn thing to let him know.

"She's the one you told me about?" Mac's voice was pitched low enough that only Daryl could hear it. "The one who left you that fucking rock around your neck that you won't take off?"

Daryl shook his head and stood up, cursing himself for ever saying anything to Mac. He didn't bother to answer, didn't bother saying anything as he moved toward the front of the plane and took his seat next to Kelsey. She was still huddled in on herself, still sleeping.

She didn't even stir an hour later when the plane touched down at the small airport in Middle River. Daryl leaned over, gently shook her shoulder—

And was rewarded by a fist clipping his jaw.

"Fuck!" Yeah, he should have fucking seen that coming. Dammit. He grabbed her wrist to keep her from swinging again, watched as panic ebbed from her shadowed eyes when she finally realized where she was, who she was with. Her arm relaxed and she tugged against his hold until he released her. She looked around the plane, twisted her head to the side and peered out the window.

"Where are we?"

"Martin's State Airport."

"Where is that?"

"In Maryland." Daryl stood, grabbed his bag and hers then moved to the side, waiting for her to stand.

"Is—is Paige here? Are we going to get her now?"

And fuck. That flare of hope in her eyes sliced something deep inside him. He pushed it away, ignored it, shook his head.

"No."

And just like that, the hope morphed into anger. She shot to her feet and stepped toward him, stumbled and caught herself. "You said we were going to get Paige—"

"And we will." At least, *he* would. No way in hell would he be taking Kelsey with him, not when he had no idea what kind of danger they might be facing. "But there are things we—"

"You said—"

"I know what I said." He kept talking as if she hadn't interrupted. "But there are things we need to take care of first. Plans we have to make."

Her green-ringed hazel eyes met his for a long minute. He almost expected her to start arguing, to lash out again and demand to be taken to her daughter *now*. Or worse, to start crying again. He didn't think he could handle that again—seeing her break down once was more than enough, especially since he got the feeling that she wasn't a woman prone to emotional outbursts.

Unless she was trying to shoot someone.

And fuck. Yeah, that wasn't even funny.

To his surprise, Kelsey simply nodded. "Then where are we going?"

"Someplace where you'll be safe."

She kept watching him, those eyes of hers

carefully blank. He expected another argument, or at least another dozen questions. Instead, she simply reached for her bag. Daryl hesitated, finally handed it to her. She hoisted it over one shoulder, stepped around him, and headed for the exit without another word.

CHAPTER FIFTEEN

There was a soft knock on the door, so soft that Grady would have missed it if he hadn't been listening for it.

Waiting for it.

He placed the pictures in a neat pile, his gaze lingering on the top one as he admired Daniel's handiwork. A face, battered beyond recognition except for an unfortunate overbite. Blonde hair, stringy and matted with blood. A petite body, the limbs broken and mangled, the skin blistered and sliced.

Poor lass. There had been no dignity in her death. No courage or fight—not that he had expected any.

Poor lass, indeed. She hadn't died well. Not at all.

A smile played around the edges of his mouth as he tucked the pictures into the middle drawer of the expensive desk. Satisfaction wound through him—the punishment meted out by Daniel's talented hands would serve as a lesson to all.

Yes, a lesson.

But he was still on edge. Restless. Impatient.

Grady smoothed the front of the silk tie, adjusted the platinum-and-gold cufflinks at his wrists. Ran one hand over his hair, smoothing it so it wouldn't look as if he'd been running his fingers through it for the past several hours as he waited for news. Then he cleared his throat, his voice calm and controlled when he spoke.

"Come in."

The door opened and Daniel appeared. Shadows darkened the skin below his eyes and stubble covered his chin. His dark hair was disheveled, as if he himself had been running his hands through his own hair before coming to see Grady.

Not a good sign. Not a good sign at all.

Grady straightened, pinned his most loyal man with a narrowed gaze. "What is it?"

"We received a call from someone who has contacts in West Virginia."

"Yes? Did your brother finally succeed? Does he have the woman? Do they know where my granddaughter is?"

Daniel's lips flattened in a tight line. His gaze—cold and carefully blank—shot to Grady's. For several seconds, the man said nothing. His gaze skittered away and he slowly shook his head. "No, sir. Michael and the others are gone."

Grady lurched to his feet, placed both fists against the polished surface of his desk. "Gone? What do you mean, *gone*?"

"They were killed, sir. Not far from the cabin where the woman was hiding."

Killed? No, that couldn't be. How? Not by the woman—she didn't have the means. The skill. Yes, she was stubborn. Creative. Determined. But to be able to kill his own men?

Grady yelled, a venting of pure anger and frustration that echoed off the paneled walls. In a rare burst of fury, he swept his hands across the desk, sending everything on it flying. A Waterford crystal paperweight. His Mont Blanc fountain pen. A stack of files and his prized first edition of James Joyce's *Ulysses*—a book that had never been opened, a story that had never been read.

He stared at the destruction around him, forced himself to calm. To inhale deeply through his nose, exhale slowly through his mouth. Again. One more time, until his fury gradually abated.

He turned to Daniel, noticed the man hadn't moved. He stood still, his gaze carefully averted from the mess littering the floor. "How?"

"Michael was shot." Daniel paused. Swallowed. "In the throat. The other two men had their necks snapped."

Grady swore. Curled his hands into fists and stared out the window. "Someone is helping her."

"Yes, sir."

"We need to find out who."

"Yes, sir."

Grady turned, caught Daniel's gaze and smiled. The man was careful enough not to flinch, smart enough to show no emotion. "I believe it's time we pay this Theresa Martin a visit. I believe she may have some information for us."

"Make the arrangements. I want to leave within the hour."

"Yes, sir." Daniel nodded then left, quietly closed the door behind him. Grady turned back to the window, the chilling smile still in place.

Yes, it was time to pay this woman—the father's friend—a visit. Any information she had would soon be Grady's.

And then he would do what he should have done long ago—

He would go after the woman himself. Find his granddaughter and bring her home.

CHAPTER SIXTEEN

The *someplace safe* Daryl had mentioned on the plane turned out to be his house. At least, Kelsey figured the driveway they pulled into belonged to him. He put the SUV in *Park*, cut the ignition, then stared at the split level in front of them.

The house looked like any other average split-level house, with nothing to set it apart from the houses they'd passed to get here. A sidewalk lined with the remains of summer flowers led to the door. The landscaping at the front of the house was well-maintained and clipped back.

It was nothing more than a regular house, which almost disappointed Kelsey. For some reason, she'd been expecting something more...fortified? Unusual? She had no idea. The only thing out of the ordinary was the uphill drive to reach it—Daryl's house sat off by itself at the top of a steep hill, far away from any neighbors. And the view—now that, at least, was impressive. She could see the main street below, the tops of houses and buildings and, in the distance, rolling hills painted in the muted oranges and reds of leftover fall color.

But Kelsey wasn't here for the view. She wasn't sure why she was here, period, except that Daryl felt the need to bring her someplace safe. She didn't care about being safe—all she cared about was getting to her daughter. That wouldn't happen until Daryl took her there because he was the only one who knew where

Paige was.

And right now, he wasn't moving.

Kelsey glanced over at him, studied the rigid set of his shoulders and jaw, watched the way his hands tightened around the steering wheel. He looked as on-edge as she felt. Tired and weary, an impression made even stronger by his disheveled appearance. Thick stubble covered his strong jaw and his hair—shorter than it had been in the Caribbean—looked like he'd been raking his fingers through it for the past five hours. For all she knew, he had been doing just that because the last few hours were nothing more than a blur to her.

Then he turned his head and those amber eyes met hers, strong and fierce and unreadable. Had she honestly just thought he looked tired and weary? She had never been more wrong. The man staring at her was a predator, dangerous and intense, nothing at all like the man she had met a few months ago. She *knew* that, had known it the second she landed flat on her back behind the tiny cabin with his familiar weight stretched out on top of her. Yes, she knew it—and she could never let herself forget it.

She forced her gaze from his and looked at the house in front of them. "Who lives here?"

"I do." He opened the door, climbed out then paused, looking at her once more. "You'll be safe here."

Safe from everyone else, yes. But would she be safe from him?

Kelsey pushed that thought from her mind—he'd given her no reason at all to think she wouldn't be safe from him. Even when she had fought him earlier this morning, he'd been holding back, careful not to hurt her no matter how much she struggled and hit and kick.

She climbed out of the SUV, tossed her bag over her shoulder then followed him up the sidewalk. He didn't say anything as he unlocked the door, as he stepped inside and quickly punched in a long string of numbers on the alarm panel. He held the door open, motioned her inside with a casual wave of his hand.

"I haven't been home for close to two weeks. The place probably needs to be aired out."

"Why so long?"

"Business." The answer was curt, leaving no room for more questions. Fair enough, since she hadn't planned on asking in the first place.

She stepped around him, hesitated then made her way up the short flight of steps. The upstairs was a large open floor plan: living room and combination country kitchen and dining room to her right, a short hallway to her left. What she saw was tastefully decorated in masculine earth tones—rusts and dark greens and light tans. Framed artwork hung in clusters on the walls, landscapes and a few abstracts mixed together.

It looked...normal. She didn't know why that surprised her, unless she'd been subconsciously expecting animal heads and military paraphernalia.

"Bedrooms are back this way."

She hesitated for a brief second, only slightly panicked until she realized what he had said: *bedrooms*. Plural. Sure enough, he stopped at the first closed door on the right, twisted the knob and pushed it open.

"This one has its own bathroom. The other bathroom is here—" He motioned to the closed door to the left then pointed to another door on the right. "And the second spare room is right there. Bed's smaller, though, and it doesn't have its own bath."

Kelsey nodded, motioned to the fourth door at the end of the hall. "What's down there?"

Daryl's intense gaze met hers long enough that heat filled her face. "My room."

He adjusted the large pack on his shoulder then continued down the hall, paused just outside his room and turned back. "There should be plenty of fresh towels in the bathroom closet. If you have anything that needs to be washed, toss it in the hamper and leave it outside the door. I'll do a few loads in a little bit."

She stared at his bedroom door for several long minutes after he disappeared through it, wondering if she had understood him correctly. Had he just offered to do laundry for her?

Yes, he had. Kelsey wasn't sure whether to laugh or cry—or throw herself into his arms and thank him.

All three were absolutely ridiculous.

She stepped into the bedroom, closed the door behind her, then looked around with something close to stunned amazement. The reaction was completely unwarranted, a sure sign that she was still too tired and drained to think rationally.

The bedroom was nothing more than a regular bedroom, maybe just a tad smaller but that was probably because it had its own bathroom. A double bed was centered against the far wall. A thick comforter with a subdued gray-and-white geometrical design covered the bed. Plump pillows—four of them—rested against the pale wood headboard. Identical nightstands in the same pale wood flanked the bed and a matching dresser was placed against the wall to her right.

The walls had been painted pale gray, several

shades lighter than the thick carpet under her feet. Artwork covered the walls in here as well, ink drawings and sketches all tastefully framed. Despite the color, the room was anything but depressing.

Or maybe she only thought so because it had been too long since she'd been in a real bedroom. Not since that night—

She stopped herself before she could go down that crazy path of thought and moved toward the bed. Her pack needed to be emptied and reorganized, her clothes sorted through.

She started to upend the pack on the bed, changed her mind at the last minute and sat on the floor instead. She carefully dumped everything in front of her, checked the several pockets and emptied their contents as well.

Then she methodically went through everything, sorting and organizing, checking each item against the master list in her head. It didn't take long because she didn't have much.

Two pairs of jeans, neatly rolled.

One pair of sweatpants, also rolled.

One sweatshirt. One flannel shirt. One denim shirt. Three plain t-shirts.

Scarf. Baseball hat.

Six pairs of socks and four pairs of underwear, neatly stored in a sealed plastic bag.

Other than what she had on, the few pieces of clothing scattered in front of her completed her entire wardrobe. She stared at them for a minute then grabbed the sweatpants, a t-shirt, and a pair of socks and placed them to her right. Everything else she gathered into a pile and sat to her left. They weren't *dirty* but a cycle through a real washing machine wouldn't hurt.

She grabbed the remaining items and began sorting them.

Two boxes of ammunition for the pistol she no longer had. One knife secured in a leather scabbard. A pack of strike-anywhere matches. A set of folding eating utensils. A flashlight and spare batteries. A small first aid kit containing nothing more than the very basics.

A few MRE's that she'd taken from the cabin, just in case.

Personal toiletries, all neatly enclosed in a heavy-duty plastic organizer: deodorant, shampoo, conditioner, soap. Toothbrush, toothpaste, mouthwash. A small travel-sized brush. Nail clippers and nail file—not that she needed them.

She tossed the toiletries on top of the sweatpants then reached for the final waterproof pouch. This one was bigger, sealed against any possible damage from the elements. She opened it, carefully removed the thick stack of contents, and placed them on the floor in front of her.

Her and Paige's birth certificates and social security cards. The tiny plastic bracelet the hospital had placed around Paige's wrist after she'd been born. A small envelope holding the curl from her very first haircut.

A stack of pictures. One of Kelsey and Blaine when they had been dating. One of the three of them in the hospital, right after Paige had been born. Another of her and Paige when she had turned one, both of them pointing at the camera with silly smiles.

A picture of the three them—Blaine and Paige and her—taken not long before Blaine died. They'd been at a carnival with some friends, had posed for the picture in front of the merry-go-round. Paige was standing between them, grinning at the camera, her mouth and cheeks pink from the sticky cotton candy Blaine had given her.

Another picture, this one of her and her Dad taken at her high school graduation.

Kelsey wiped at her eyes with one hand then carefully gathered the pictures in a neat pile. The packet she had taken from her father's house twelve days ago was next. She slid her finger under the clasp and opened it up, pulled out the contents and studied them again.

Two passports, one for her and one for Paige, only with different names—different even from the passport she had used this summer. Social security cards for both of them, the names matching those on the passports. A single sheet of paper, neatly folded, the note inside scrawled in her father's bold handwriting—written in a code she couldn't read.

Another sealed envelope, the words *For Paige* printed across the front in her father's writing. She smiled, wondering what kind of note he had left for his granddaughter. She thought of opening it, of reading it. No, the letter was for Paige. She'd hold it for her daughter until she was old enough to read it.

She studied the final item, her stomach once again tilting at the sight. Cash—a grossly obscene amount of cash, all large bills. A way for Kelsey and Paige to disappear for good, to go anywhere Kelsey wanted to take them and start all over.

All she needed was Paige.

She tucked everything back into the envelope then stared at it, once again wondering where her father had gotten everything. Where he had come up with the money. He'd told her six months ago, the night she had given him Paige to hide, that he was working on something. On some kind of failsafe that she could fall back on. Had made sure she knew exactly where to look to find it.

Was that why he sent her the cryptic message to meet? To give her the packet and tell her where Paige was so they could finally be free of Grady Byrne? So they could disappear for good?

Maybe. But would she have gone? Would she have been able to leave her father, completely cutting all ties with him, knowing she might never see or talk to him again? Kelsey didn't know, couldn't answer that question. She thought she would have, if it meant keeping Paige safe.

It didn't matter now. Her father was gone and there was nothing stopping her.

She just needed to get Paige. Once she had her daughter, they could truly disappear.

Kelsey placed everything back into the weatherproof pouch, sealed it and secured it in the inside back pocket of her pack where it would be safe. Everything else except the clothes followed.

She pushed to her feet, grabbed the pack and placed it in the corner near the bed—then hesitated. The bag was never out of her sight. Ever. Should she take into the bathroom with her?

She reached for it, hesitated again, finally grabbed it. Maybe it was foolish but she couldn't leave it unattended. Did she think Daryl would go through it if he found it? No—but she still wasn't comfortable with leaving it.

Kelsey carried it into the bathroom then went to

grab her toiletries and both piles of clothes. The sweatpants and t-shirt and socks she placed on the small vanity counter; everything else went into the hamper—including the clothes she had on. She set the hamper outside the bathroom door, closed it, then stepped into the shower.

Water washed over her, caressing skin and easing muscles. She adjusted the temperature, making it as hot as she could stand it, then closed her eyes and stood under the stream and let the water pound her body.

Let the water wash away her tension. Her fears. Her worries.

She waited as long as she dared before the water could turn cold and shampooed her hair, digging her fingers into her scalp, working the shampoo into a thick lather. Conditioner followed and she used her fingers to work through the tangles, wincing when she came to a particularly stubborn one.

She had forgotten how relaxing a shower could be. Had forgotten how it felt to take her time instead of rushing. Instead of worrying about conserving water.

She'd forgotten a lot of things beyond basic survival these last few months.

A loud knock echoed in the room, making her jump. She braced a hand against the tile wall for balance, brushed the water from her eyes with her free hand. Instinct had her reaching for the faucet, ready to run and fight and flee—

"I've got your dirty clothes. Do you need anything else?"

Daryl's voice, coming through the door. Drifting through the stream and pebbling her skin. She shook her head, realized he couldn't see her so she poked her head around the edge of the shower curtain. "No.

Thank you. I-I'm almost done."

"No need to rush. I'll be in the kitchen. Come grab something to eat when you're done."

"Um. Okay. Sure." She focused on the closed bathroom door. Watched the handle to see if it turned. Wondered if he would come inside—

Footsteps retreated away from the door, faded into silence a few seconds later. Kelsey yanked the shower curtain closed then stepped under the stream of water again. Her heart was racing too quickly and she felt feverish despite the way her skin pebbled.

Not from the cooling spray of water but from *him*. From the memory of that night three months ago. She had taken a long shower then, too—with Daryl. Had watched with burning eyes as he explored every inch of her body. As he kissed and touched and caressed while streams of water washed over them from every direction.

Had he been thinking of their time in that exquisite shower while he stood outside the bathroom door? Or was she the only one who held those memories close?

She was a fool. An absolute fool. That night had meant nothing. Not to her, certainly not to him. It wasn't supposed to mean anything. It had been nothing more than a brief interlude. A few stolen hours where she'd been able to feel human again.

Where she'd been able to *feel*, period.

The water was turning cool now so she rinsed off, still thoroughly berating herself for being so foolish. Feeling guilty for craving—just for a second—some normalcy. A gentle touch. A soft caress. A warm embrace. She had no business remembering those things, even less business wanting them, if even for a second. Her priority was her daughter.

Finding Paige.

Keeping her safe.

Disappearing forever.

Nothing else mattered but that.

She quickly dried off and pulled on her clothes. Ran the brush through her damp hair then bent over and finger-combed it. Brushed her teeth then studied the stranger in the mirror staring back at her.

She had changed so much in the last three years that she had trouble recognizing herself. The change had been expected, at least to a degree—you didn't go on the run the way she had and *not* change.

The few extra pounds she had kept after Paige was born were gone now—and quite a few more on top of them, to the point she almost looked *too* thin. Her hair was shorter, wavier—easier to maintain, especially since it was usually hidden by a baseball cap. No mascara coated her eyelashes, no blush colored her pale cheeks. If she used any cosmetics at all, it was a simple swipe of plain lip balm. She didn't have the room—or the money—for useless cosmetics, not anymore.

But it wasn't the physical changes that always caught her off-guard, it was how she had changed as a person. She looked...hard. Wary. Suspicious. Even more now than she had six months ago. At least then she'd had Paige. Now, she had...

Nothing.

But that would change soon enough. As soon as Daryl took her to Paige, they'd leave. Start over. Go somewhere far away. Someplace where Grady Byrne would never find them.

Kelsey nodded at the stranger staring back at her

then turned on her heel and left the room.

Daryl was in the kitchen, as he had said. He glanced over his shoulder, his gaze meeting hers for a brief second when she walked in.

"Lunch will be ready in a few minutes. Have a seat."

Kelsey considered telling him she wasn't hungry then thought better of it. There was no point in spiting herself just because she was stubborn. She *was* hungry and whatever he was cooking smelled—maybe not *delicious* but definitely appetizing.

She moved over to the table, pulled out a chair and sat down at one of the place settings. Placemat. Silverware. Two glasses, one filled with water and the other with a darker liquid. She reached for the second glass, raised it to her mouth and took a cautious sip. Iced tea. Strong and unsweetened, with just the faintest hint of lemon. She took another sip, longer this time, then cradled the glass in both hands, not sure what else to do. It was unsettling, sitting here doing nothing. Worrying about nothing.

Having someone else wait on her.

She cleared her throat, winced at how loud just that small noise seemed. "Do you need help with anything?"

"Nope, almost done." He looked over at her again, the barest hint of a smile curling the corners of his mouth. "I hope you like grilled cheese and tomato soup. I was running low on everything else."

"That's fine. Thank you."

He turned back to the stove and she busied herself with looking around. Studying the room was a hundred times safer than watching him.

But no matter how hard she tried, her gaze kept

returning to him. To the broad back covered by a black t-shirt. To the muscled-arms that moved so gracefully as he worked in front of the stove.

Like her, he had taken a shower. His hair was damp and his jaw was smooth, the days-old scruff gone. Sweatpants rode low on lean hips, clung to a firm ass and hugged muscular thighs.

Kelsey yanked her gaze away once more, forced herself to focus on the placemat in front of her. There was no reason to be staring at Daryl. No reason for the sudden yearning pulling at her. She had only one priority: her daughter. Nothing else mattered.

She couldn't *let* anything else matter.

A shadow fell across her and she jerked back in surprise, felt her face heat in embarrassment when Daryl looked down at her with a frown.

"Didn't mean to startle you." He slid a plate and a soup mug in front of her, turned away before she could say anything. A minute later, he was sitting across from her, his own lunch in front of him. "I'd offer you some chips but they're stale as shit."

"This is fine." And she meant it. It was more than fine. She took a bite of the sandwich, held back a sigh at the rich taste of gooey cheese and tangy mustard. She finished half the sandwich and reached for the soup, looked up and noticed Daryl watching her.

She dropped her hands into her lap, bowed her head and wondered if she'd eaten too fast. If she'd made a fool of herself by devouring just that little bit of food.

"Is the sandwich okay?"

"Yeah. It's fine. Thank you."

"Then eat up before it gets cold. Same with the soup."

Kelsey shook her head. "I'm not—"

"What was the last thing you had to eat?"

She frowned, trying to remember. "Oatmeal."

"When was that?"

She looked away from his steady gaze, stared at the plate in front of her. "Last night."

"And before that?"

"I—I don't remember." Peanut butter crackers, probably. Or maybe a can of soup heated up on the cookstove back at the cabin. She honestly couldn't remember, not when the days ran together, blended into one long nightmare.

"Eat, Kelsey." It was an order. Phrased gently, yes, but still an order. She almost balked at it, stopped herself when she realized how stupid that would be.

She picked up the spoon and started on her soup.

"I can make another sandwich if you're still hungry. And there's soup left, too, if you'd rather have that. I'll make a grocery run tonight. If there's anything you want—or don't want—let me know."

Kelsey looked up, the food forgotten. "A grocery run? I thought—I mean, you said we were going to get Paige—"

"And we are."

"Then you don't need groceries. Not if we're leaving right away—"

"We're not leaving right away, Kelsey." There was a finality in his voice that chilled her—but not as much as the stony expression in his eyes. She dropped the spoon, ignored the wave of soup that splashed over the side as she gripped the edge of the table.

"You said you would get my daughter. You said you would help—"

"And I will. But things need to be planned first."

"No." She shook her head, pushed away from the table. "No. I'm not waiting. Just tell me where she is and I'll get her."

"And manage to get her killed in the process?" His low voice vibrated with subdued anger. "Is that what you want?"

Kelsey shook her head in denial. No, that wouldn't happen. He was just trying to scare her. To make her wait.

She thought of the passports in her bag. The cash. Two stepping stones to freedom—all she needed was Paige. Once she had her daughter, they could disappear within hours. They could finally be safe—for good.

"That won't happen. We'll both be gone before Grady can find us."

"Is that what you think?" Daryl propped his elbows on the table, stared at her with those amber eyes she had thought were so mesmerizing a few months ago. They weren't mesmerizing now—they were lethal. Dangerous. The eyes of a powerful predator. "Grady's men found your little hiding place. How long do you think it'll take before he finds you again? Especially if you go tearing off across the country."

"I've stayed ahead of him for three years."

"Have you? How? By running? By hiding? Is that what you're going to do again? Take your daughter and run, knowing you'll always be looking over your shoulder? Never knowing when he might show up and take her away. Never knowing when you might lose her for good."

There was a hard edge to his voice that made the hair on the back of her neck stand up. She pushed the feeling away, dismissed it as nothing more than a scare tactic. He was wrong. With the package her father had left her, she could make them both disappear forever. They could leave the country, start fresh somewhere else and never have to worry about Grady Byrne again.

Or could she? Was she merely fooling herself? Was the idea of freedom so tempting that she was refusing to face reality? Would she find a place for her and Paige to settle down and call home, only to constantly look over her shoulder, the way Daryl warned?

Kelsey's shoulders sagged as her dreams of freedom were crushed under the weight of reality. Disappointment washed over her and with it, the sudden certainty that this nightmare would never end. Daryl was right—she would always be looking over her shoulder. Always waiting for the monsters to show up.

And they would. They always did.

"I can keep you safe, Kelsey." Daryl's voice softened, gentled into the voice she remembered from that night so long ago. "Both of you. But you can't fight me. And you have to trust me."

Trust.

He said it like that was something so easily done. It wasn't. She didn't know him, couldn't trust him—even if her father did. Especially not with the most important thing in her life.

But she didn't have a choice. Not in this.

She nodded but said nothing. There was nothing to say, no words she could utter that wouldn't be an outright lie.

"Finish eating."

"I'm not hungry." That, at least, was the truth. The thought of putting any food in her mouth made her stomach clench and roll in distaste. Would he push her? No—he just simply watched her for a few minutes then shoved his own plate away.

"I have a meeting in a few hours to discuss strategy. Come up with a plan. Before then, I plan on getting some sleep. You should probably do the same."

"I'm not tired."

"Is that why you look like you're ready to collapse right now?"

Did she? Maybe. But she didn't care. She started to say as much but Daryl stood, started clearing the table as he talked.

"At least lie down. You might surprise yourself. If you don't sleep, that's fine. You have the run of the house. And just so you know—everything's alarmed, Kelsey. One door opens, one window cracks, and I'll know."

Was that meant as reassurance—or as a warning? She studied his strong face, saw no indication of either and decided to take it as a warning. If she tried to leave, he would know about it.

And he'd stop her.

Fair enough. She wasn't planning on going anywhere. She couldn't, not when the only person alive who knew her daughter's location happened to be standing there, studying her with those calculating eyes.

Kelsey nodded, stood up and left the room without saying another word. She didn't need to, not when it was clear he saw her understanding of the subtle warning.

CHAPTER SEVENTEEN

The shift from sleep to awake was instantaneous. No startling, no jerking, no grunt of surprise. Daryl's body had been floating in the blackness, insulated from consciousness—

But aware. Always aware.

That awareness shifted to alertness as he lay in bed, listening to his surroundings, searching out whatever had caused him to come awake. He didn't need to search, he already *knew*.

But he remained still, listening anyway.

A sob, quickly muffled, followed by a soft sniffle.

The noise came from the guest room—the room he had given Kelsey.

He swallowed back a groan and turned his head to the side to glance at the clock. He'd been asleep for two hours—longer than he thought he'd sleep, but nowhere near enough to catch up on the rest his body needed from the last seventy-plus hours of hell.

Fuck it. Sleep was overrated anyway.

He swung his legs over the side of the bed, grabbed the sweatpants from the floor where he had dropped them and pulled them on. Then he stood there, torn between indecision and worry.

Another sob, this one even softer than before. Fuck. Kelsey was crying. Should he go to her? Ask her what was wrong? Offer comfort?

Yeah, that would be like comforting a viper. He hadn't missed the flash of anger in her gaze earlier, when he had told her they weren't leaving right away.

Flash? Fuck. It had been a hell of a lot more than a *flash*. She had wanted to do bodily harm—and his was the body in question. Part of him understood—she was a momma bear and he was keeping her from her baby cub. Of course, she'd be pissed. If he were honest with himself, he'd be pissed, too. But if she stopped to actually think about what he'd said, she'd understand. She was Davis's daughter, she must have inherited at least some of his reasoning skills.

Yeah, he could hope. Just like he could hope that those skills asserted themselves tomorrow when he told her she wasn't going with him when he went to get her daughter. Fuck. Now there was something he wasn't looking forward to.

He grabbed his t-shirt, pulled it over his head as he made his way to the bedroom door. There was no noise when he opened it but Kelsey must have heard anyway because the quiet sniffling coming from her room silenced immediately.

He started toward the kitchen, intent on ignoring the woman in the guest room and walking right past that closed door. Pretend he hadn't heard anything and go put on some coffee, let the caffeine burn away the remaining rough edges he couldn't quite shake off.

Except for some reason, his damn feet weren't working and instead of making it to the kitchen, he was standing right in front of Kelsey's door.

Listening.

Waiting.

He swallowed back a sigh. Called himself every name he could think of. Told himself *not* to be stupid, to move, to keep walking.

And then he knocked on the door, just a quiet rap

that wouldn't wake her if she was actually sleeping. Yeah, because he'd only imagined those noises.

Silence answered his knock. He started to move, heard a rustle, then—finally—a muffled voice.

"Yeah. Come in."

And fuck, that wasn't what he expected to hear. Not even close. At best, he thought maybe she'd say she was fine. At worst, he expected her to tell him to get lost.

But *come in*? Not even close.

He ignored the warning voice in his head and reached for the knob. Turned it and pushed the door open, just enough to poke his head in. Kelsey was leaning against the headboard, her knees drawn to her chest—much like she had been this morning, after he cornered her in the cabin. Even now, he had trouble reconciling the woman he was watching with the woman he remembered from three months ago. Not just because of the physical differences—it was more than that.

The woman he'd met in the Caribbean had been quiet, reserved. Maybe even a little shy—at first. But there had been a small playful spark there, too. A light in her eye that seemed to hint at an appreciation for life.

At least, that's what he'd told himself at the time.

The woman he watched now was nearly the complete opposite. Despite the way she had fought him this morning, despite the strength he sensed deep inside her, this woman seemed almost...hopeless. Dejected.

Battered and worn, like she no longer had the strength to fight everything being thrown her way.

Sympathy welled inside him and he ruthlessly

quashed it. He needed to keep the two different women separated in his mind. Hell, he just needed to completely forget the woman he'd met three months ago, put her out of his head for good.

Yeah, sure. He'd get right on that.

He cleared his throat and focused his gaze on the wall just above her shoulder. "You okay?"

She nodded, which was good enough for him. So why wasn't he moving? Why wasn't he backing out of the room and closing the door behind him?

Because she *wasn't* okay and he knew it. And then he made the mistake of meeting her gaze and dammit, he felt like he'd been sucker-punched in the gut. Hard. The expression in those green-ringed hazel eyes did him in.

He stepped into the room, cautiously made his way over to the bed. Still waiting for her to tell him to get lost. Waiting, hell—he was *hoping* she'd tell him to get lost.

But she didn't. And dammit, she was still watching him, looking at him like he was her last chance at saving the world.

He reached the side of the bed, sat on the edge—close but not too close. "Anything you want to talk about?"

She shook her head, reached up with one hand and wiped her face. Shook her head again. "I just—I miss Paige."

"You'll be with her soon enough."

She looked up, the hope in her eyes mingling with something else. Fear. Worry. Disbelief. "Will I? And then what? Do I keep running? Keep looking over my shoulder like you said?"

"Maybe not." Not if he had anything to do about

it. Not if he could remove Grady Byrne from the picture permanently. And yeah, he really was losing his fucking mind, just like Chaos accused him of on the plane.

She started to say something, clamped her mouth shut and shook her head. Took a deep breath and let it out. "Sometimes I wonder if maybe Paige isn't better off where she is now, without me. And then...then I wonder if Grady already has her—"

"He doesn't."

"That's what I keep telling myself. He wouldn't be after me if he did, right? He wouldn't have gone after Dad—" Kelsey squeezed her eyes closed and took another deep breath. Opened them and met his gaze. "I'm sorry, I'm not usually such a mess. I just—I haven't—the last two weeks..."

Since she found her father. But she couldn't seem to say the words. Could Daryl blame her? No, he couldn't. "You don't have anything to apologize for."

"How—how did you know Dad? He never told me."

"He was my old CO. When I was stationed in Texas."

"Texas? That was one of Dad's last duty stations. Almost—" She hesitated, her lips moving as she silently counted. "Seven years ago, I think."

"Nine years ago. For me, I mean."

"Nine?" Her head shot up, understanding flashing in her eyes. "When you lost—"

"Yeah." Daryl cut her off before she could finish. "Your dad got me through a pretty rough time."

"I didn't realize—I'm sorry."

He shrugged off her sympathy, forced a cold smile to his face. "It was a long time ago."

Kelsey watched him for a long minute. What did she see when she looked at him? When she studied him with those clear eyes? Fuck, he didn't want to know. Didn't care. And he sure as hell didn't want to bring his past up again. He started to move. Stopped, frozen in place, when she spoke again.

"What was her name?"

He didn't have to ask who she meant—he *knew*. And he didn't want to go there. Didn't want to bring up memories better left forgotten and buried. "Kelsey, I don't—"

She reached out, placed her hand on his bare arm. In sympathy. In understanding. Holding him place when all he wanted to do was run. "Please."

One simple word. One simple word, spoken in her low voice, was all it took for his will and resolve to crumble. It made no sense, this sudden need to share with her details he had never shared with anyone else.

He forced his gaze away from hers, stared down at the hand resting on his arm. Pale, her long fingers trembling just the faintest bit. Warm. Comforting.

She was comforting *him*, when it should be the other way around. His past was just that: in the past. Nothing he could do would ever change what happened. But there was still a chance for her—for Kelsey and her daughter.

Maybe Chaos was right, maybe he really had lost his mind to even think of doing what he wanted to do. But he knew, right here at this moment, that he would stop at nothing to get Kelsey's daughter back. To make sure all threat to them was eliminated.

Not for the woman waiting patiently to hear his story—

But for the little girl with light brown eyes who

never had a chance.

He closed his eyes, pushed the last memory of his daughter from his mind, searched for another memory. And just like that, the gates opened, flooding his mind with memories he had convinced himself were better off forgotten.

The sight of Layla's tiny fists waving in the air, her eyes squeezed tight the day they brought her home from the hospital.

The time she reached for him with chubby little hands and smiled her first smile.

When he'd been so worried because she was feverish and cranky, only to learn that she was cutting her first tooth and the only way to keep her calm had been for him to hold her and rock her.

Her first word. Not *Daddy*, not *Mommy*, but *BaBa*—the name of her stuffed bunny.

Her first steps. The way she had gone from cautious toddling to full-out running in what had seemed like a matter of hours.

Memory after memory assailed him. Instead of filling him with regret and sorrow and anger as he'd been afraid of all these years, they filled him with a tender happiness. The sorrow and loss were there as well, but their sharp edges were tempered, no longer as painful as they'd been for all these years.

He opened his eyes, surprised to see that Kelsey's hand was in his now, that their fingers were threaded together. Had she taken his hand—or had he reached for hers?

Did it matter?

"Her name was Layla. She was three-years-old when she—" *No, don't think of that. Remember something else.* "She was the most precocious child you've ever seen. So inquisitive, always getting into things, trying to figure out how things worked. It used to drive Melissa crazy."

"Melissa was your wife?"

"Yeah. She, uh, she didn't always have a lot of patience." Daryl frowned, shook his head. No, he couldn't paint Melissa as a villain. Not now. Yes, she bore a lot of the blame—but he carried his own, as well. "In her defense, I wasn't around a lot. She hadn't really known what to expect as an enlisted soldier's wife, I don't think. There were a lot of times she felt like a single parent. She, uh, she couldn't handle the fact that I was getting ready to deploy again. That's why she was leaving, taking Layla—"

No! He forced that particular memory away, refused to remember the pain and agony, the way he had come unglued and lost all control.

He squeezed Kelsey's hand, slowly released it. "Like I said, your dad was my CO at the time. I'm not sure I would have made it through if he hadn't been there, riding my ass. He's the one who pulled strings, put my packet together for the Rangers."

Where Daryl had learned to pull from the rage eating him alive, had learned how to turn it into something else. Something constructive.

Something deadly.

Kelsey was no longer watching him, focused instead on the frayed hem of her sweatpants. She fingered it, pulled a thread loose and slowly balled it between her finger and thumb.

"Dad told me a little about you." She looked up at him, offered him a fleeting smile that didn't touch her eyes. "Nothing personal, not like that. Just that he knew you and trusted you. That you could help if I needed it. I—I think he was preparing for the worst, that a part of him knew I'd need more help than he could give me."

"Is that why you were you there this summer?"

She lowered her gaze again. Because she heard the underlying accusation in his voice, no matter how hard he tried to hide it? Or for another reason?

"Yeah. I had no idea who you were. And as much as I trust my dad, I still had to see for myself. Had to decide if I could trust you the way he did."

At least she didn't try to deny it. And her reasoning even made sense—to a point.

Daryl shifted, asked the question he wasn't sure he wanted to know the answer to. "Did you? Decide, I mean."

"Yeah." Kelsey nodded, shot him a shy glance and quickly looked away. "Yeah, I did."

"And?"

"I think Dad was right. At least, that's what I thought then."

"Then? But not now?"

"No, now too. At least, I think so." She sighed, tossed the tiny thread ball onto the nightstand and wrapped her arms around her bent legs. "It would have been easier to trust my instincts if we hadn't, you know, slept together."

A small burst of anger shot through him. Daryl pushed it away, did his best to hide his reaction. But there was no hiding the defensiveness in his voice when he spoke. "If you're blaming me—"

"No, I'm not." Kelsey shook her head hard enough that her hair flew into her face. She swiped at it, tucked a few waves behind her ear, shook her head again. "I'm not. That was pretty much all me."

The anger and defensiveness left him as quickly as it came. "Pretty sure it was both of us."

"No. When you came over to me—"

"You kept staring. I thought you were interested—"

"I didn't mean to. Stare, I mean. And then you came over and I didn't know what to do. Part of me wanted to run away."

"You almost did."

"Yeah. But then you started to walk away, after you asked my name, and I—" She stopped, lowered her gaze with a shrug. "I didn't want you to. But I hadn't planned on anything else happening. That wasn't why I went there. And then it did and..."

Daryl waited, the silence stretching around them. He leaned forward, met her lowered gaze. "And what?"

"It made me question all my impressions. I couldn't figure out if I trusted you based on what I had seen and learned so far—or if I only thought that because we slept together."

What she said made sense, in an odd kind of way. Yeah, he could understand why she would question herself, why she would second-guess her instincts. Hell, wasn't he doing the same damn thing in a way?

He reached for her left hand, stretched it out between them and turned it palm-up so her tattoo was visible. He traced the bold lines surrounding the eye with the tip of one finger then looked up, caught Kelsey's surprised gaze.

"Your tattoos. The Eye of Horus here. The triquetra on your shoulder. They're symbols of protection."

She pulled her lower lip between her teeth, nibbled on it for a brief second then finally nodded.

"I asked you then what you were protecting yourself from. You said nothing. Everything. Do you remember that?"

She nodded and Daryl kept talking.

"I also asked if you needed protection from me. Do you remember what you said?"

Another nod. A quick sigh, a brief lowering of lids over wide eyes. "I said no, not you. Not tonight."

"*Not tonight*. Not then. But what about now, Kelsey? Do you need protection from me now? Can you trust me? *Do* you trust me?"

Her gaze—filled with hesitation, wariness, uncertainty—met his. For a long moment, she said nothing. Then, finally, she nodded, just the slightest motion. "I—yeah, I do."

For now.

Because I have no choice.

No, she didn't say those words out loud but he still heard them. Saw them in her eyes. Felt them in the still air floating between them.

Fair enough. He couldn't expect anything more, not yet.

He released her hand and pushed off the bed. "Get some more rest if you can. We've got a lot of planning to do in a few hours."

She didn't say anything as he walked out of the room but he felt her eyes on him, knew she was following him with her gaze.

Knew she kept staring at the door, even after he closed it behind him with a quiet *click*.

CHAPTER EIGHTEEN

Kelsey stared at the door for a long time after Daryl left.

Fighting the urge to go after him.

Telling herself she was a fool.

Convincing herself she didn't need him. That she didn't want him.

She stared at the tattoo on her inner wrist, at the eye staring back at her. She could still feel his touch on her tender flesh as he traced the lines, hear his deep voice as he asked her if she needed protection from him.

Like a fool, she had said no.

But she did. Oh God, she did.

Because he made her want. Made her need.

Made her forget the nightmare of the last three years; the fear and loneliness and uncertainty that had been with her since the day of Blaine's funeral.

The day Grady Byrne had offered to buy her daughter. *His* granddaughter.

It wasn't just that he made her forget—he made her *feel*. That was what she hadn't shared with him when they talked about the few hours they had shared three months ago.

He made her *feel*. And that was dangerous.

Yes, she could have walked away when he came over to her that day. Could have ignored him like she had initially planned, when she first stood and quickly gathered her things.

But she hadn't—because he made her feel.

Made her pulse race when he looked at her.

Made her skin pebble when he smiled at her.

Made her lungs squeeze and her breath quicken when he said her name in that rich voice.

And when he had touched her, when his hand briefly rested against the small of her back—her heart had jumped and skipped as heat filled her. As need blindsided her.

The same way it had only moments ago when he gently traced the lines on her inner wrist. The only difference between then and now was that then, she had only wondered how he tasted, how his body would feel stretched out along hers.

Now...now, she knew.

And the hunger filling her was ten times stronger than it had been three months ago.

She swung her legs over the side of the bed and moved toward the door. Quickly, before she stopped and thought about what she was doing—what she was about to do. If she stopped, she'd have time to think about how selfish she was being, about how foolish she was.

She didn't want to think. Not now. She just wanted to...to feel. To forget.

Daryl was leaning against the counter, a mug of coffee in one hand, a cell phone in the other. He looked up when she walked in, frowned and tossed the phone onto the counter. "What's wrong?"

"Nothing. I—" She stopped talking, kept moving toward him before she lost her nerve. His frown deepened and he turned to the side, placed the full mug next to the phone before turning back to her. Then she was in front of him and his hands closed around her waist.

To pull her closer? To push her away? She didn't know. Didn't want to know.

"Kelsey—"

She pressed against him, leaned up and brushed her mouth against his. Once, twice. Waiting for him to respond. Hoping he'd take over. Deepen the kiss. Sweep her off her feet and make her forget.

He turned his head to the side, held her away from him—but he didn't move his hands from her hips, didn't push her away. "Kelsey, this is a bad idea."

"Please. I just—I need—"

You. This. Us. Just for now. For a little while. To forget.

But she didn't say the words, couldn't get them past the lump in her throat. Maybe she didn't need to. Maybe Daryl could see what she needed. Maybe he understood without hearing the words.

His gaze dropped to her mouth, shot back to hers. The amber of his eyes deepened as he watched her. He shook his head—but he still didn't push her away. "Sex is only going to cloud the issue, Kelsey."

Would it? Yes, probably. Definitely. But she didn't care, not right now. Not when she needed to forget. Not when she just needed to *feel*.

Him. Her. *Them.*

Her lips parted and she swiped her tongue along her bottom lip, her gaze never leaving his. "Please."

He didn't say anything, just kept watching her with that steady gaze that took her breath away. Then, just when she was ready to back away, to apologize for making a fool of herself, he dipped his head and closed his mouth over hers.

Soft. Gentle. Hesitant, as if seeking permission. She sighed and leaned into him, sighed again when his arms tightened around her and pulled her closer. Chest against chest, hips against hips. Her hands closed over his arms, hard muscle and hot flesh beneath her fingers. Need swept over her, raw and primal. Urgent.

More. She needed more. All of him. Here. Now.

But he simply kissed her, taking his time, teasing her with his lips and tongue. In control.

She eased away, stared at him through eyes glazed with need. She didn't want to be teased, didn't want him to be slow or gentle. She wanted him to claim her, the way he had in that small bungalow in paradise.

"Please, Daryl."

Could he see what she wanted? What she needed? She didn't think he could, was afraid he didn't understand, that she would have to tell him—

And she couldn't do that. Couldn't put voice to those inner thoughts and yearnings.

Disappointment surged through her when he moved his hands from her hips. She started to pull away, to turn around and run and hide, the way she'd been doing for three years. But he wouldn't let her. He cradled her face between his hands, caught her mouth with his—

And she was lost. *This*. This is what she needed. What she craved. He deepened the kiss, claiming her. His tongue delved between her parted lips, met hers in a battle of wills she quickly seceded.

Yes. *This*.

Him. Her. *Them*.

He threaded his fingers through her, tilted her head back, trailed his hot mouth along the sensitive skin of her throat until she was breathless with need. Mindless with want. More, over and over, until she clung to him. Until there was nothing else except his touch, his taste. The sound of his harsh breathing, mingling with hers.

This.

Him. Her. *Them.*

He broke the kiss, bent down and scooped her into his arms. His gaze—hungry and needy—never left hers as he carried her back to his bedroom.

He lowered her to the bed, claimed her mouth once more in a kiss that ended too soon. He leaned back, watched her with the eyes of a hungry animal. "I'm not a saint, Kelsey."

No, he wasn't. He was a warrior, hardened by things she could only imagine. Did he think she didn't know that? Was he asking her to acknowledge it?

She didn't know. Didn't care. She didn't need a saint—

She needed *him.*

She lifted her hand, cradled his cheek with her palm. "I know."

He watched her for the space of a few heartbeats, a few seconds where she feared he would pull away and send her back to her room. Then his mouth crashed against hers. Claiming hers. Claiming *her.* Demanding a surrender she willingly gave.

He reached between them, grabbed the hem of her shirt and pulled it up. Broke the kiss long enough to pull it over her head. This his mouth was back, trailing hungry kisses along her throat. His teeth nipped tender flesh. Lower, along her collarbone. Lower still, sending flames shooting across her skin. One large hand closed over her breast, kneaded and teased as his mouth closed over her nipple. Licking. Sucking. Nipping. Her back arched and she reached for him, tangled her fingers in his hair as he sucked and nipped.

Over and over until her breathy moans of need filled the warm air. Need grew, spiraled. She rocked her hips against his, sighed at the feel of his erection, hard and thick and long.

"Please." She heard the throaty plea, felt heat rush to her face when she realized it had come from her. Her hands pulled at his shirt, dragged it up his back, needing to feel bare flesh against bare flesh,

Needing *him*.

He pushed to his knees, yanked the shirt over his head and tossed it behind him. Kelsey's gaze landed on the leather cord around his neck and she froze.

Trembling fingers reached for the rough black stone, gently caressed it as her eyes met his. "You kept it."

"I haven't taken it off since the morning you left."

There was something in his voice, something in his eyes when he looked at her—then his mouth was on hers once more and she could no longer think, she could only feel.

His hands, caressing her bare skin. Teasing the points of her nipples.

His knuckles, grazing her thighs as he peeled the sweatpants from her legs.

The soft strands of his hair under her fingers, teasing the sensitive flesh of her inner thigh.

His mouth, so hot and wet between her legs. His tongue, swirling against her sensitive flesh.

The hard muscles of his arms holding her, whispering words of reassurance in her ear as she fell apart.

The shifting of the mattress as he reached for the nightstand. The tear of a wrapper as he opened a condom.

The weight of his body as he stretched out on top of her. The feel of his erection, so hard and thick as he drove into her. Hard. Deep. Fast. Over and over until there was nothing but *this*.

Him. Her. *Them*.

She screamed his name, clung to him as her body shattered. As she came apart again and again. His arms tightened around her, held her close as he drove into her a final time. As he called her name on a low moan, his lean hips pumping his release.

She closed her eyes, felt herself drift off, secure in the cradle of his arms.

Only then did she make sense of the look in his eyes, the tone in his voice when she had first seen the obsidian hanging from the leather cord around his neck. When she had uttered the surprise that he had kept it.

When his gaze had met hers, never wavering as he answered.

I haven't taken it off since the morning you left.

It had been possessiveness.

Kelsey didn't care. Not now, when she rested safely in his arms. Not now, when she knew Daryl would let nothing happen to her. Not now, when she knew he would soon be taking her to get her daughter.

She drifted into the blackness and, after three long years, finally found peace as she rested.

CHAPTER NINETEEN

The neighborhood was...disappointing. Strictly middle-class, with nothing to set it apart from any other middle-class neighborhood anywhere else in middle America.

Even so, it was several steps up from the rat-infested slums where Grady Byrne had grown up, the youngest of four children of a poor single mother who cared more for the alcohol and drugs running through her veins than she did her own kids. She'd been nothing more than a whore, spreading her legs for any man with a dick to shove in her overused pussy—provided they had money to pay for the lack of pleasure she provided.

And if it wasn't *her* pussy they wanted, she would barter with them, strike a deal and offer up either of her daughters, shoving a needle in their thin arms until they could no longer fight. Until they spread their own bruised legs as readily as their mother. Until they craved the drugs as much as the traitorous whore did.

And if a man had no taste for pussy? If he craved a taste of young cock or had an urge to ram his dick in an untried ass? Well, his mother had two sons for that and would readily oblige the men—for a price.

Grady shuddered in distaste and pushed the memory away. The young boy known as James Kelly was dead now, pulled from the slums by one of the very men who had used his mother. Seamus Byrne had witnessed his mother's crimes, had made her pay before brutally ending her life and dragging the boy away with him.

He'd been reborn in the weeks that followed, given a new home—and a new name. Grady Byrne had started small, acting as nothing more than a messenger and errand boy for Seamus. He'd been given more responsibility as he grew older, proving himself time and time again until Seamus had made him second-in-command.

Until Grady had taken over the business when Seamus passed away.

That had been over twenty years ago and now...now Grady was in danger of losing it all. He refused to let that happen. The fools who had been careless enough to whisper behind his back, to sow the seeds of discontent in men once loyal to him, would soon learn how much they had underestimated him. Yes, they would learn. As soon as he had his granddaughter. When he had her, his legacy, he could put the rest of his plan into motion.

It was time.

He glanced around the neighborhood, searched the quiet streets. Everyone was safely behind closed doors, oblivious to the dangers around them. Grady swallowed his contempt for their carelessness and nodded to Daniel. The other man got out of the car, came around and opened the door for Grady.

The walk to the house was a short one. If anyone happened to look out their window, they would see three businessmen, impeccably dressed in tailored suits. But nobody was looking.

Nobody was paying attention.

Grady knocked on the door, waited patiently as he listened to the woman moving around inside the house. A shadow passed in front of the window and Grady smiled, knowing the woman would be looking through the tiny peephole in the door.

Knowing she would be reassured by the sight of the well-dressed older gentleman standing patiently, harmlessly, on the other side.

A lock turned and the door slowly opened. A woman's face appeared around the corner of the door. Short dark hair framed a full face. A row of piercings lined her right ear, another one glittered from the edge of her nose. Grady hid his disgust, widened his smile and saw the woman visibly relax.

"Can I help you?"

"I hope so. I was looking for Theresa Martin." The name rolled from his tongue, carefully wrapped in an exaggerated lilt. A brief smile lifted the corner of the woman's mouth, quickly disappeared in her confusion.

"I'm Theresa."

"You were a friend of Allen Davis?"

"Yes, but—"

"I think you may have some information I would find very useful."

The woman's brows pulled low over eyes suddenly filled with wariness. She shook her head, started to close the door. "I'm sorry but I can't help you—"

Grady slammed his hand against the door, the smile never wavering from his face. "I believe you can."

Fear crossed the woman's face and she tried to shove the door closed. It was a useless gesture. Grady shoved his shoulder against the wood, pushed the door open and stepped inside as the woman ran for the other room. Daniel moved around him, caught the woman by the arm and held her in place as Grady quietly closed the door—and locked it.

Dark eyes widened in fear as Grady approached her. He smiled, a genuine smile this time as the woman cowered in Daniel's strong hold. He reached for her hand, cradled it gently between his own.

"As I was saying, Ms. Martin—you have some information that would be very useful to me." He took one of her fingers between his own and twisted, felt bone crack and tendons snap. Smiled when the woman screamed. "And we won't be leaving until I get it."

CHAPTER TWENTY

"Jesus. Are you fucking kidding me?"

Daryl glanced over his shoulder, frowned when he noticed Chaos staring at something down the hall. The man turned toward him, dark brows slashed low over chilling blue eyes.

"You have got to be fucking kidding me." Chaos repeated the words, drawing the attention of the other three men standing around: Mac, Boomer, and Wolf. Chaos ignored the curious glances and moved closer to Daryl, his voice lowered in a harsh growl.

"You really think fucking her is a good idea?"

Daryl didn't think, he reacted. His fist shot out, clipping Chaos on the jaw before the man could move. All hell broke loose in the space of two seconds—Mac jumped between them, grabbing Daryl and shoving him backward. Boomer did the same to Chaos, aided by an arm around the man's throat.

Wolf quietly stood there, a fucking shit-eating grin on his face as he watched.

Daryl shrugged off Mac's hold, leaned around the bigger man and pointed at Chaos. "You need to shut the fuck up."

"Me? Seriously? I'm not the one fucking—"

Daryl lunged for him again, only to be grabbed once more by Mac.

"Both of you knock it the fuck off." Mac shot a warning look at Chaos, turned that same look on Daryl. "What the hell is he talking about?"

Daryl shook his head, started to say he had no clue and that it was nobody's damn business anyway but Chaos jumped in and started spouting off at the mouth. "I'm talking about the woman who just snuck out of his room and hurried into the guest room."

Daryl shot the man a scathing glance that would have any other normal man slinking away. The problem was, Chaos wasn't like normal men, not by a long shot. "You need to mind your own damn business and shut the fuck up."

Boomer pushed Chaos back. "Wait. Hang on. Is he talking about the girl from this morning?"

"Who the fuck else would I be talking about?"

Boomer ignored Chaos, turned back to Daryl with a surprised grin. "Seriously? After she tried to shoot me? You've got balls, Zeus, I'll give you that. I mean, I know you two got together after Mac's wedding but still."

"Knock it off. Everyone." Mac's gravelly voice sliced through the air, silencing everyone—not that anyone else had been talking. He leveled a questioning glance at Daryl then shook his head. Yeah, Daryl heard the unspoken recrimination in that glance.

Too damn bad he didn't give a shit. Yes, clients were off-limits; sleeping with them was the best way to have things go sideways in a heartbeat.

Tough shit. Kelsey wasn't a client. She was—

Daryl frowned. He didn't know what the hell she was, but she definitely was *not* a client. Regardless, Chaos was right—sleeping with her had probably been a mistake. Not because he was helping her, but because they'd done it for the wrong reasons.

To be more precise, *she* had done it for the wrong reasons. Daryl had slept with her because he wanted her. Because he hadn't stopped wanting her since that night in the Caribbean. And how fucked up was that? It had been a one-night stand—wasn't supposed to be anything but that. Yeah, right. That's why he'd been obsessing over her for the last three months. So when she asked—

Bullshit. He couldn't blame anything on her. He knew exactly what she had been trying to do: use him to forget. Use him to feel human. Use him so she could feel normal. Yeah, he knew exactly what she'd been doing. If he had been any kind of gentleman, he would have turned her down. Pushed her away.

But he hadn't—because he wanted her. It was as simple as that.

As complicated as that. Because, fuck it, Chaos was right. It had been a bad idea. Daryl had known it right from the start. Had known it would lead to a whole separate set of issues, especially when Kelsey found out she wasn't going with them when they left in the morning to get her daughter.

He pushed away from Mac, grabbed the small file from the counter and moved to the table. Four sets of eyes followed him and he knew without looking that all four men were trying to figure out what the fuck he was doing. They'd find out soon enough.

He tossed the file on the table, pulled out a chair and sat down. "We have plans to make. Let's get to it."

One by one, the four men joined him—Chaos last. He met the other man's chilled stare, returned it with one of his own. Neither of them said a word—there was nothing to say, not when they both knew the other had been wrong.

Daryl opened the file, pulled out the small map and information on the children's home. "The home is here, not quite an hour outside the city. The closest airport is right outside Portales so we'll fly in, rent a car, and drive the rest of the way. We should be in and out in four hours, tops."

Mac leaned forward, studied the paperwork, looked up. "Who's *we?*"

"I'm taking Wolf." Daryl held up his hand to stop the questions before they could start. "He's the least physically intimidating—"

"Hey—"

Daryl cut off the man's objections with a quick look. Why the hell was he even arguing? With his shaggy blonde hair and ridiculous dimples, Wolf looked like a fucking surfer-boy-turned-cover-model and he knew it. "This isn't up for discussion."

Chaos leaned back in the chair, folded his arms in front of him. "That sounds too damn easy."

"Because it is. All we're doing is getting the girl, bringing her back here. Nothing complicated about it." Daryl stared at the papers spread out in front of him, finally shook his head. "It's the next part that gets complicated as fuck."

"What's that?"

Daryl looked over at Boomer, met the man's steady gaze. "Flushing out Grady Byrne and putting an end to this once and for all."

Boomer shook his head. "Yeah, Chaos was right earlier: you've lost your fucking mind. What's stopping his second-in-command from stepping up and taking his place? How does eliminating Byrne take care of anything?"

Daryl nodded at Chaos. "You want to fill them in?"

"I did some more digging when we got back this

morning. Turns out that Grady Byrne isn't as well-liked by his minions as he probably thinks. His entire organization has been dwindling the last few years—they're nowhere near as powerful as they used to be. I reached out to a few contacts and learned that his command staff—or whatever the fuck they like to call themselves—wouldn't mind seeing Byrne meet with an accident."

"Then why the fuck haven't they made that accident happen themselves?"

"Apparently that would make them look bad and create dissension in the ranks."

"Are you fucking shitting me?"

Chaos held his hand up, palms out, warding off Mac's question with a careless shrug. "I'm just telling you what my contacts told me."

Nobody bothered to ask Chaos who his contacts were. They didn't need to know—and the man wouldn't have told them anyway. Chaos had moved in the darkest of circles before joining Cover Six Security, had seen and done shit the rest of them couldn't even guess at—which was saying a hell of a lot, considering their combined backgrounds.

"Byrne does have a few loyal followers but not more than a handful. I don't think we'd run into any issues if they all happened to disappear." Chaos looked around the table. "That is, if we want to go that route."

"Yeah, I'm fine with that." Boomer nodded then looked at Daryl. "The question is, how do you flush the bastard out?"

Daryl met the other man's eyes and said nothing. He didn't need to, not when he knew each man could see precisely what he had planned in the steel of his gaze, in the set of his jaw.

"Jesus." Chaos swore softly, shook his head. "That's fucking cold, Zeus. And you wonder why I called you out on fu—"

"Enough. If you have a better idea, I'm all ears." Daryl glanced around the table, hoping—praying—that one of them would jump in with something better. But all four men were silent.

Fuck. He didn't want to use Kelsey as bait. Wouldn't, if he could think of any other way. But he didn't see any other way to do it. He just needed to use her to draw Byrne out, just long enough to set up a meeting. Kelsey would never be in any danger. He'd keep her safe—they all would.

But fuck, as far as plans went, he didn't like it. There were so many things that could go wrong.

Fine. They'd just have to make sure they were ready for anything.

Daryl ignored every single misgiving that sent chills skipping along his spine and turned back to Chaos. "Have you been able to figure out how they found the cabin?"

"No. There's nothing. I did a search under Davis' name, under any possible aliases. I even used your girl's name. Her mother's name. Hell, even her daughter's, as well as the baby-daddy's name. Nothing. I have no idea how he did it, but there is no record anywhere of Davis—or any possible relative of his—ever owning property in West Virginia. Or anywhere else for that matter."

"The cabin isn't my dad's."

Daryl's stomach clenched with some unnamed emotion when Kelsey turned the corner of the hallway and stepped into the kitchen. Their gazes met, held for a long minute—long enough that he was able to figure

The Guardian: DARYL

out what was causing those knots in his gut.

Guilt. Pure, simple, guilt.

How long had she been standing around the corner, unseen? How much had she heard?

Maybe not all of it—but enough. He saw that much in her gaze as she watched him. That wasn't all he saw in those green-ringed eyes staring back at him.

Anger. Surprise. Hurt.

Betrayal.

He started to stand, stopped himself at the last second. There was nothing he could say to explain himself. Certainly not in front of the four men who were currently shifting in their chairs, looking like they suddenly wished they could be anywhere else but here. And even if they weren't here—if it was just the two of them—Daryl wasn't sure he'd explain. Wasn't sure he *could*, not enough to remove those incriminating emotions from her eyes.

"What do you mean, it's not your dad's cabin?" The calm question came from Chaos—the only one of them who seemed to be able to focus at the moment. Kelsey's gaze held Daryl's for a second longer then slid to the other man's.

"Just that—it's not my dad's. The cabin belonged to Theresa's husband, before he died."

"Who the fuck is Theresa?"

If Chaos's language surprised her, she showed no signs of it. She crossed her arms in front of her and leaned against the wall with a shrug. "Theresa Martin. She's a friend of my dad's."

No, they were more than just friends.

And *fuck*. Why hadn't Daryl thought of it before?

He turned to Chaos, who was already opening his laptop and hitting keys. "Find out how easy it is to trace the cabin to her. Boomer, get Ninja on the phone. Tell him to standby. I may need him to go wheels-up."

"On it. Destination?"

"Just outside St. Louis."

Boomer nodded, already heading to the living room as he punched in numbers on his phone. Kelsey pushed away from the wall, the anger and betrayal on her face morphing to panic and fear.

"Do you think Theresa's in danger? Do you think—"

"I think she's fine. This is just a precaution." Daryl forced a conviction to his voice that he didn't feel and hoped like hell he wasn't lying.

"Got it." Chaos's voice was grim, the words sharp. "Traces right back to her, no buffer at all."

"Fuck. Dammit all to hell. *Shit*." Daryl pushed away from the table, issuing orders as he made a mental list of what he needed. "Chaos, see if you can figure out if anyone's accessed that information. I need to know who and when. Boomer, tell Ninja to get moving. I'll text him the info. Wolf, change of plans. We're leaving in ten."

"Daryl—"

He ignored the plea in Kelsey's voice, ignored the fear in her eyes as she watched him. He turned to Mac, didn't bother to hide the concern from his eyes when he spoke in a low tone. "I need you to take Kelsey, make sure she's safe."

"Daryl—"

He approached Kelsey, reached for her then dropped his hands when she jerked away from him. Fine. He'd deal with that later—he had other priorities to take care of first.

Like making sure everyone was safe, especially the

woman currently staring at him with a mixture of anger and panic in her eyes.

"Kelsey, I need you to go with Mac—"

"No." She shook her head. "No. Not until you tell me what's going on. Is Theresa okay? Has something happened to her?"

"She's fine." And Christ, he hoped he wasn't lying when he said that. "But I think Byrne's men were able to trace the cabin through her."

"I don't understand. What does that mean?"

"It means that if Byrne knows about her relationship with your father, he may have done a search on her name and found the cabin that way."

"What do you mean, *if* and *may*? Is she in danger?"

"I don't think so, no. But I'm sending one of my guys to be with her, just in case."

Kelsey wrapped her arms tight around her middle and nodded. Some of the fear and panic left her eyes, edged out by anger.

By suspicion.

"And where are you going?"

"I have something I need to do. You'll stay with Mac—"

"No. You're lying."

"Kelsey—"

"I'm going with you when you get Paige."

Dammit! How did she know? Had she heard? Or had she merely guessed? Did it matter? No, it didn't.

Daryl tightened his jaw. Stepped closer and lowered his voice. "You're staying here—"

"No, I'm not. You can use me as bait all you want, I don't care about that. I'll do whatever you need me to do to draw Grady out. But you are *not* getting Paige without me."

Fuck! She had heard. And there wasn't a damn thing Daryl could do about it, nothing he could say to explain. Not here, in front of everyone. Not now.

Maybe never.

But that didn't change things. He shook his head, met her stubborn gaze with his own chilled one. "You're not going, Kelsey—"

"She's *my* daughter—"

"And I'll keep her safe—"

"Like you kept your own daughter safe?"

Daryl reeled under the impact of the words, the pain as sharp and as real as if she had taken a knife and plunged it into his chest. Silence filled the air around them, thick with tension.

Thick with unasked questions.

He ignored the questioning glances from the four men watching them. Ignored the regret filling Kelsey's eyes with unshed tears. She reached for him, dropped her hand before he could brush it away.

"I didn't mean—"

He turned away from her, moved down the hall with clipped, measured steps. "We leave in ten minutes."

It took all his control not to slam the bedroom door behind him. He didn't even bother to close it, just simply moved to the closet and pulled out his go-bag, unzipped it to make sure he had everything he needed.

But he wasn't seeing the contents of the bag—he was seeing a pair of tear-filled brown eyes.

"Wanna stay, Daddy. Wanna stay with you."

"I know, Bean. But you need to go with Mommy for right now. Just for a little bit. Then Daddy will come get you."

"Promise?"

"You're my Bean. Of course I promise. And Daddy never

breaks his promise."

Heavy steps pulled him from the painful memories. He didn't have to look to know who was standing in the doorway. It was Mac—and he must have wanted Daryl to know he was coming. If he hadn't, Daryl would have never heard him. For someone so damn big, the man could be as quiet and still as death when he wanted to be.

"Chaos and Boomer already took off. Wolf is waiting outside."

"Good." Daryl yanked the zipper of the bag closed. Stood there staring down at it. Didn't move. How the fuck could he move when he could barely fucking breathe?

"I'm not going to ask what that was about."

He sucked in a deep breath, felt some of the tightness in his chest ease. "Good, because it's none of your damn business."

"Yeah, which is why what I'm going to say next will really piss you off." Mac stepped inside the room, gently closed the door. "You're too fucking close to this. Let me take Kelsey. We'll both go with Wolf, you stay here—"

"Not happening."

"Which part?"

"All of it.

"Care to tell me why?"

"Kelsey stays here with you. I go with Wolf—"

"Are you even listening to what you're saying? It's her daughter. Did you even stop to think what would happen when you got to this children's home? Do you honestly think they're just going to hand over a kid to some fucking strangers?"

"They won't have any choice."

"Yeah? And what are you going to do? Shoot the place up? Kidnap the damn girl?" Mac laughed, the sound rough and low. "Dammit, Daryl, what the hell is going on? Since when don't you fucking *think* before acting?"

Daryl closed his eyes, forced his jaw to relax. Forced his hands to unclench. "Is that what you think?"

"No—it's what I *know*. Who the hell is this woman to you?"

"I told you—she's my old CO's daughter."

"That you just happen to be sleeping with."

"*Slept*. Past tense."

"I hate to break this to you, buddy, but a few hours ago isn't *past tense*. And don't even try to tell me you just hadn't rolled out of bed with her when I got here. This is me you're talking to. I know better. Now who the hell is she?"

Daryl finally turned around to face Mac—but he couldn't quite meet the other man's eyes. "If you think there's something more going on, you'd be wrong. We met after your wedding. Had one night together. I haven't seen her or talked to her since—not until I found her this morning."

"Yeah, sure. That's why she seems to know a hell of a lot more about you than the rest of us." Mac ran a hand through his short hair, shifted his weight from one foot to the other. "You've been obsessing over this woman for the last three months. Don't fucking deny it."

"If that's what you want to think—"

"Stop with the bullshit. We've been through too much for that."

"Then what the hell do you want me to do?"

"I want you to fucking stop and think. I want you to admit you're too fucking close to all of this and let me go in your place."

Daryl stepped toward him, stopped when he saw Mac tense and shift his weight forward, ready to go on the offensive. He blew out a deep breath, ran both hands over his face. "Would you have stayed back and let me handle things when TR was in trouble?"

"That was different—"

"The hell it was."

"Yeah, it was. That fucking asshole already had TR. No way in hell would I have let anyone else go in—"

"Yeah, exactly. Which is why you're staying back here. With Kelsey."

"She needs to go—"

"She's staying here." Daryl grabbed his pack, tossed it over his shoulder. "And I'm done with this discussion."

Mac started to say something else but Daryl simply pushed past him and tore open the door. He stumbled to a stop, choked back an oath when he saw Kelsey standing at the end of the hallway, her own pack tossed over her shoulder. The blood froze in his veins when he saw the papers in her hand.

The map—with the name and location of the children's home clearly marked on it.

He met Kelsey's chilled gaze, swallowed back another oath when he saw the determination in her eyes.

"I either go with you—or I get her by myself."

CHAPTER TWENTY-ONE

Kelsey shifted in the seat, trying to get comfortable—an impossible feat when she had so much nervous energy shooting through her.

In a few short hours, she'd see her daughter. She'd be able to hold Paige in her arms. Hug her. Run her fingers through that mop of unruly auburn curls.

Six months had gone by. Six long months. A lifetime to a five-year-old. Would she have grown? Yes, of course she would have. But how much? An inch? More? Had her hair grown in that time, or had someone trimmed it? Had Paige convinced whoever was taking care of her to chop it off? She had tried that once with Kelsey, insisting over and over that she wanted it cut short because the curls would get tangled in her face.

Kelsey hoped not. She hoped whoever had been looking after her little girl refused to give into Paige's demands. But she could be so adamant sometimes, so stubborn—

Had she started school? It was almost November now, she must have. Worry swept through Kelsey when she thought of Paige's education. Would her daughter be on the same level as the other children, or would she be behind? Kelsey had tried so hard when they were on the run, teaching Paige her letters and numbers and colors and shapes. They had both started teaching her those things—her and Blaine—long before Kelsey had been forced to take her daughter and run. Kelsey had tried her best to keep up with everything. Paige was such an inquisitive child, always asking questions, thirsty for knowledge. Had it been enough?

Or had she failed her daughter in that as well?

She'd have the answer to that—and to every other question burning inside her—in just a few short hours.

In just a few short hours, she'd have Paige back and this would all be over—

No, it wouldn't be over. It wouldn't be over until Grady Byrne was gone. Out of their lives permanently. She still had to worry about him.

But not for much longer. Please God, not much longer.

She shifted again, slid her gaze to the left and studied the man asleep next to her. The men had called him *Wolf* but he'd told her his name was Sebastian. Neither name fit him. With his shaggy blonde hair and deep green eyes and dimples that had surely made many women swoon and simper, he looked like he belonged on a California beach somewhere. Or maybe in the pages of a magazine, modeling men's underwear.

He certainly didn't look like he belonged with the small group of men that she'd seen this morning and again an hour ago. That was why she had chosen to sit next to him—because he looked harmless. Because he had smiled at her and winked and patted the empty seat with the tip of one long finger.

He was perfectly nice to her, engaging her in light conversation, even flirting with her a little and calling her Cinderella. The teasing name brought back a memory and she realized she had met him before—not just him, but two of the others as well—at the resort in the Caribbean the same day she had met Daryl.

Sebastian had simply laughed, the sound deep and warm, and said he was glad he'd made such a lasting impression on her.

But the more she talked to him, the more she realized she had been completely wrong about him. His golden good looks were nothing more than a mask, hiding the predator within. There was something about him, something about the way his eyes remained too steady and too emotionless, even when he smiled, that made her realize he was *exactly* like those other men.

Maybe even more dangerous than the others, even the one with the surprisingly blue eyes. At least the other men looked exactly like what they were: warriors. Men accustomed to war and violence. Men who would stop at nothing to get what they wanted.

Kelsey shifted again, turned her head the slightest bit to the right. She could just make out Daryl's profile in the seat ahead of her. He was facing toward the dark window. Asleep? Maybe. Or maybe, like her, he was alone with his thoughts.

Alone with his own demons.

She shouldn't care. Shouldn't feel any sympathy for him at all. He had planned on leaving her behind. On handing her off to someone she didn't know or trust while he went to get her daughter. Paige was *her* daughter, and he wasn't even going to take her with him.

She had been angrier about that—was still angry—than she had been when she overheard his plan to use her as bait to draw out Grady Byrne. No, he hadn't said as much, not in those exact words, but she still understood what he *hadn't* said. So had the other men. What did it say about her that she didn't care? That she actually agreed with Daryl? *Yes*, she had wanted to scream. *Use me. Anything. As long as it keeps Paige safe.*

Anything, as long as it kept her daughter safe.

No, she wasn't angry about that part, even though a small rational piece of her mind said she should be. Her anger—her *fury*—was because Daryl had planned on keeping her from her daughter. So she had lashed out, had thrown his own personal tragedy in his face, trying to hurt him the way she was hurt.

And it had worked. God, it had worked too well. She had seen the pain in his eyes. Sharp. Brittle. Had *felt* it, straight to the center of her own heart. She had wanted to take the words back as soon as they left her mouth—*before* they left her mouth. Wished she had never said them to begin with. How could she have been so deliberately cruel, knowing what the loss of his daughter had cost him? Her own anger wasn't an excuse for what she'd done, not when she knew exactly how he felt.

But it was done. Over with. She had thrown the words in his face, had hurt him. There was nothing she could do about it now. And she shouldn't care. He was nothing to her, just a means to an end. The way she was nothing to him, nothing more than a distraction.

Kelsey closed her eyes, leaned her head against the seat.

She was such a liar. Had been lying to herself for the last three months. If he really meant nothing to her, she would have stopped thinking about him the morning she left his bungalow. But she hadn't stopped. Instead, she'd done something totally idiotic and completely out of character for her.

She'd fallen in love.

Not with the man himself, not really. She didn't

know him, couldn't possibly fall in love with him. But it had been thoughts of him that had kept her going these last three months.

And maybe that was the problem. Maybe she had built up a huge fantasy surrounding him, this man her father trusted. A man who would protect and guard her. A man strong enough to slay the fiercest dragon of all time. A hero. No, not just any hero—

Her hero.

Yes, that was exactly what she had done. Created a fantasy, weaving it with unbreakable threads of hopes and dreams and promises, building on the fairytale until she had fallen in love with the mythical hero who would swoop in and save the day. The hero who would rescue her and her daughter.

Except he wasn't a mythical hero—he was a flesh-and-blood man with his own weaknesses. His own demons. A man very capable of feeling real pain.

Pain she had caused.

Oh, Daddy, what have I done?

She waited, needing to hear her father's voice. Needing his advice, now more than ever. But her father was silent.

Kelsey opened her eyes, glanced over once more at Daryl. He hadn't moved, was still staring out at the darkness visible through the small window. She pushed to her feet, made herself move before she lost all courage.

She sat down next to him, careful to keep space between them—not an easy thing to do on such a small airplane. Not an easy thing to do when the man beside her took up so much room. He still didn't move, not even to glance her way. Did he even know she was there?

Of course, he knew. How could he not?

She shifted in the seat. Cleared her throat. Shifted again. "I—I shouldn't have said—"

"Go back with Wolf. Get some rest." His voice was low. Flat. Completely emotionless. A chill ran over her, pebbling her skin. Kelsey tugged the sleeves of her coat over her hands, curled her fingers into her palms.

"I'm trying to apologize—"

"Don't." He finally turned his head, amber eyes meeting hers. Her heart slammed into her chest as a surprised gasp stuck in her throat. What she saw in those eyes scared her—

Because they were completely empty. Completely emotionless. *This*—this was the predator she had sensed below the surface, even when she had first met him three months ago. Common sense told her to move, to do exactly as he had instructed and return to her seat.

To forget all about fantasies and heroes who could slay dragons. To focus on reality.

On survival.

But she couldn't move, not when those cold eyes held her in place.

He finally broke that eerie eye contact. Kelsey pulled in a deep gulp of air, realized she had been holding her breath the entire time he held her gaze. That she was lightheaded and dizzy because of that, not because of the dead expression in his eyes.

Dead expression? No, she was being melodramatic. Overreacting. Daryl was right, she should go back to her seat. Close her eyes and at least pretend to rest. She'd been running for too long, had been teetering on the edge of breaking down for far too long. Hadn't been sleeping right, hadn't been eating right—

And now she was being dramatic. Weaving fantasies, falling in love with mythical heroes—and seeing death in eyes the color of liquid amber.

But she couldn't make herself leave. Not yet. She had to apologize, had to at least *try*, one more time. If he didn't accept it—or at least acknowledge it—then that was on him. She could return to her seat knowing she hadn't just simply quit.

Kelsey reached out, gently rested her trembling fingers on his arm, felt the muscles bunch under her touch. "Daryl, I—"

He stiffened, moved his arm so her hand fell to the side. He didn't say anything, just stood and climbed over her. He paused in the narrow space that passed for an aisle, reached up and removed something from around his neck. He held it in his hand for a long minute then carefully dropped it in her lap.

"We'll be landing soon. Get some rest."

Kelsey watched as he took the seat next to Wolf, kept watching long after he leaned his head back and closed his eyes. Then she dropped her gaze to her lap, surprised at the tears burning the back of her eyes when she saw the chunk of raw obsidian hanging from a leather cord.

Her necklace.

No, *his*. The one she had carefully placed on the pillow next to him before leaving his bungalow that morning all those months ago.

I haven't taken it off since the morning you left.

Until now.

She scooped the necklace into her hand, cradled the obsidian in her palm. Instead of being cold like she expected, the stone was still warm. From Daryl. From the heat of his body. His essence.

The Guardian: DARYL

She curled her hand around the stone and closed her eyes, tried to tell herself it didn't matter.

And tried to convince herself that she hadn't just lost something she didn't even realize she had.

CHAPTER
TWENTY-TWO

Daryl rapped his knuckles against the adjoining door then pushed it open, not bothering to wait for an answer. Wolf looked up from the paper he was reading, one eyebrow raised in silent question.

Daryl ignored him and looked around the small motel room. The bed closest to the door was rumpled and messy, the comforter hanging halfway off the mattress and dangling on the floor. The sheet was off at one corner, revealing the aged mattress cover. Both pillows were stacked on top of each other, shoved against the cheap lacquer headboard.

The second bed looked like it had barely been slept in. The right edge of the comforter was only slightly crooked, as if someone had pulled it back into place. A single pillow bore a small indentation mark. If not for those two signs—and the well-known fact that Wolf was a fucking slob—Daryl would have been convinced that the two people in the room had shared just one bed.

He swallowed back an irrational surge of jealousy and pinned one of the people in question with a steely look. Wolf looked back at him, a dimple popping with the sly grin he gave Daryl.

"Don't look at me. You're the stupid ass who insisted I share a room with her."

"Where is she?"

"In the bathroom getting ready. For what it's worth, I don't think she slept at all." Wolf dropped the paper in a careless heap on the cheap table then stood and stretched. "Neither did I. That fucking mattress was uncomfortable as shit."

Then that made three of them who hadn't gotten much sleep. Daryl had spent most of the night staring at the stained ceiling of the small motel room, wondering what the fuck had possessed him to be so fucking stupid. Wondering why he had insisted that Wolf share the room with Kelsey. Wondering why Kelsey hadn't even blinked an eye at the suggestion, let alone argue about it.

Would she have agreed as quickly if he'd told her *he* was sharing the room with her instead? Probably not.

Why the fuck did he even care?

He pushed the thought away and strode across the room, placed the cardboard tray holding three cups of coffee and a bag of breakfast sandwiches on top of the newspaper Wolf had carelessly tossed down. How the hell the man had survived military life was a mystery because he was a fucking slob.

"Is the coffee any good?" Wolf didn't bother to wait for an answer, just grabbed one of the cups from the tray and peeled back the lid. He took a sip, grimaced, then reached for a handful of sugar packs.

"Do that in the other room."

Wolf paused, looked up. "Do what?"

"Fix your damn coffee. In the other room."

"You trying to get rid of me?"

"Yeah. Get lost."

"Not a problem." Wolf grabbed his coffee cup and enough sugar packs to give a dentist a mouth full of cavities and headed toward the adjoining door. He stopped, came back to grab a sandwich from the bag, then headed for the door again. He paused, turned back to Daryl. "Am I coming to your rescue when she beats the hell out of you for being such a dick?"

"Fuck off. And close the damn door behind you." Daryl thought about throwing something at the other man when he laughed but Wolf closed the door before he could find anything sharp enough. What the hell. It wasn't like Daryl didn't deserve it—he *had* been a dick. Acting like a fucking baby who'd had his feelings hurt.

Rude. Cold. Indifferent.

Pissed.

Fuck. He was still pissed—at himself. Mac had been right—he was too fucking close to this. Why, he didn't know. But he needed to distance himself from everything, starting now.

Now? Hell, he'd been trying to do that since last night, when they'd left his place to head back to the small airport to meet the charter plane. Only it wasn't working and he didn't know why. He'd never had this problem before. Had always been able to control his reactions, no matter what. Cool. Calm. Rational—that was how he operated.

So why was this so fucking different? Why had he acted like a fucking two-year-old throwing a damn temper tantrum because he'd had his feelings hurt?

He was afraid he knew why—and no way in fucking hell was he going there. He pushed those thoughts out of his mind, pushed everything away except the next few hours.

Leave here, drive to the children's home.

Get Kelsey's daughter.

Go back to the airport where yet another charter would be waiting for them.

Get Kelsey and her daughter back home—

No, not back *home*. Get them someplace safe. That wasn't the same thing as *home*. And it sure as hell didn't mean his home.

Okay, yeah. Get them someplace safe, then finesse the plan to flush Byrne out and end this thing once and for all. Kelsey and her daughter would be safe. His obligation to Davis would be fulfilled.

And Daryl would go on a nice long vacation somewhere. To the mountains, maybe. Someplace where nobody could find him. Someplace where he could just fucking disappear for a month to get his fucking head on straight because he was obviously losing his fucking mind.

Yeah. Sure. No problem.

He pulled out a chair and lowered his weight onto it, holding his breath until he was sure it wouldn't collapse under him. Then he sat back and waited for Kelsey to finish whatever the hell she was doing in the bathroom.

He didn't have long to wait—maybe five minutes at the most. The bathroom door opened and Kelsey came out, a frown on her face as she smoothed the front of the denim shirt she had on.

"Do you think this is okay? I don't want to look like I'm homeless—" Her voice trailed off as she came to an abrupt stop, her eyes briefly widening in surprise before narrowing. "Where's Sebastian?"

Daryl ground his back teeth together. *Sebastian*. Fuck. Just the way she said his name made him want to storm into the next room and rip Wolf's head from his fucking shoulders.

Yeah, so much for being in control.

He forced his jaw to relax and motioned to the chair across from him. "Wolf went next door. Have a seat. We need to talk."

She looked like she wanted to argue with him. Hell, could he blame her? But she bit back whatever she had been ready to say and slowly made her way over to the chair—and pulled it back a good two feet before sitting in it.

He swallowed back an oath and pushed the paper bag toward her. "Breakfast. Eat up."

"I'm not hungry—"

"You haven't had anything since yesterday afternoon, and all you had then was half a sandwich and two spoons of soup. The last thing I need is you passing out on me. Now eat."

Kelsey didn't bother to hide her scowl—but she reached for the bag and dug out a sandwich, which was all he cared about. He waited until she unwrapped it, raised it to her mouth and took a small bite.

He took advantage of her distraction to study her. She looked different this morning. Not as tired. Her cheeks were filled with color, no doubt from the anticipation of finally seeing her daughter again. Her hair still had that tousled, wavy look but it seemed shinier, smoother. Less windblown and a little more controlled. Maybe the jeans she had on were a little too loose, the denim shirt just a little too faded—but despite her fears, she didn't look homeless.

His gaze dropped to the open collar of her shirt, the smooth column of her neck. Her father's dog tags were tucked inside her shirt, with only the chain visible. Another necklace circled her throat, a black leather cord with a chunk of raw obsidian hanging from it.

The necklace she had left for him. The one he had so carelessly dumped in her lap last night on the plane.

He pulled his gaze away and focused on the edge

of the cardboard tray resting on the table. "We'll leave in fifteen minutes, go straight to the home. Make sure you take everything with you because we're not coming back here. We'll get your daughter, head back to the airport."

She nodded, grabbed one of the coffee cups and took a long swallow. "Okay."

Should he count that as progress? Probably not—there was no reason for her to argue with him, not when they were doing what she had wanted him to do all along.

"When we get back ho—to Maryland, we'll take you and Paige someplace safe until Byrne is taken care of."

She lowered the sandwich, stared at him with carefully hooded eyes. "Not back to your place?"

"No, I don't think that's a good idea."

She nodded and lowered her gaze—but not before he saw the disappointment flash in her eyes. And fuck, he didn't need to see that. Didn't even understand why the fuck she'd be disappointed.

He ignored the twisting in his gut and kept talking. "Once Byrne is taken care of, we can help you get to wherever you want to go. Find a place for you, help get you on your feet and settled in—"

"I don't need help. Dad left me—he, uh, he left some things to help me with that."

There was something in the way she said it, something in the way her eyes wouldn't quite meet his that made him wonder exactly what Davis had left. A will, definitely. Life insurance? Probably. But she wouldn't have been able to access either of those things if she was still on the run, not without alerting Byrne to her whereabouts.

Which meant there was something else, too, something that went beyond the usual considerations a father would leave a daughter.

Daryl didn't bother to ask what. It wasn't his business—and he doubted she would tell him anyway.

"Finish your breakfast. We'll leave when you're ready." He pushed to his feet, headed toward the connecting door. Stopped and turned back. "Kelsey? You, um, you look nice."

Nice? What. The. Fuck.

He ignored her stunned look and pushed through the door, nearly slammed into Wolf before the other man could move back. Daryl closed the door and shot him a warning look—which Wolf simply ignored.

"Oh man, Prince Charming you're not. That was fucking pathetic."

"Shut up and get your shit together. I'll be out in the car waiting." Daryl dragged his bag from the bed, tossed it over his shoulder and stormed out of the room, slamming the door behind him—

And drowning out Wolf's roar of laughter.

CHAPTER
TWENTY-THREE

Mac stared at his watch. Tapped the face then shook his wrist. No way was the damn thing right.

Except it was. A quick glance at the clock hanging on the wall in his office told him that much. Besides, the fucking thing had never failed him—and he'd put it through some serious shit, including one hell of a fireworks display in the sandbox.

He ran a hand over his jaw, barely noticing the network of scars now. And wasn't that some weird shit? Not that he'd ever really been bothered by them—at least, not much—but he'd always known they were there. Had always been aware of them. Now, not so much.

He had TR to thank for that. TR, with her love and laughter and total acceptance for who he was, inside and out. Yeah, he'd been fucking lucky that she hadn't stopped when he pushed her away.

His gaze slid to the picture sitting on the edge of his desk—the only damn thing that could pass as decoration in the plain office. It had been taken three months earlier, right after their wedding.

Gazing at it brought a smile to his face—one big enough that he'd catch a shit-ton of grief from any of the guys if they happened to see it.

Fuck it. He didn't care. He loved his wife, why the fuck wouldn't he smile at her picture? And if the guys caught him, he'd tell them they could only hope to be so fucking lucky. Hell, he *had* told them that, numerous times.

Not a single one of them believed him.

Too damn bad. That was their problem, not his.

Right now, he had a different problem to worry about altogether.

He tapped the face of his watch again and frowned. Where the fuck was Ninja? He should have heard back from the man by now. Hell, he should have heard something hours ago. The fact that he hadn't yet was starting to worry him.

Mac slid out from behind the desk—he hated that damn thing, would much prefer to be out in the field kicking ass without taking names—and made his way through the hallway maze to the front reception area. He pushed through the secure door and paused long enough to catch his breath, to let the racing of his heart settle down just a bit.

Yeah, the sight of his wife did that to him, every damn time.

"Hey babe—"

"No, he hasn't called yet." She looked up from the monitor she had been studying and offered him the sweetest damn fucking smile he'd ever seen. For one brief second, he entertained the thought of tossing her over his shoulder and hauling her back to his office for some personal time.

Yeah, he enjoyed going all caveman on her. So sue his ugly ass for being politically incorrect. As long as TR didn't mind, he'd keep doing it—and she had yet to complain.

But now wasn't the time or the place—it never was, not here—so he pushed the thought from his mind and sat on the edge of her desk.

Her desk. Except it wasn't. This whole

receptionist-slash-assistant thing she was doing was only supposed to be temporary. She was a fucking reporter, not a secretary. But she didn't seem to be too eager to start a new job search and that worried him, more than he cared to admit. TR was still a little too skittish, thanks to that fucking asshole who had wreaked havoc on their lives ten months ago. The scar across her cheek had faded, barely noticeable unless you happened to really look for it. But he more than anyone knew that it wasn't the scars you could see that caused the most damage.

So he wouldn't push her. Not yet. Just like he wouldn't say anything about the damn weapon she always carried now—a Taurus G2C 9mm. It made her feel safe and she knew how to use it—had become damn good at it, as a matter of fact—so he just accepted it. Maybe, hopefully one day soon, she wouldn't feel the need to carry it. Just like, one day, she'd realize she was meant for something a hell of a lot more meaningful than organizing the daily shit that the rest of them couldn't seem to keep up with.

Until then, he'd continue to support her with whatever she needed. Besides, he kind of liked having her so close by.

Except for now, when she was staring at him like she was waiting for him to say something. She gave his leg a gentle nudge then leaned back in the chair.

"You're worried."

It was a statement, not a question, but he nodded anyway. "Yeah. Ninja should have checked in by now. The fact that he hasn't—and that he's gone totally silent—can't be good. He was just supposed to go out and check on the woman, that was it."

"You think there's a problem."

"I think this whole thing is a huge fucking problem." He swore again—under his breath this time—and pulled the wallet from his back pocket. He peeled off a five from the stack of bills and handed it to TR, who promptly put it in the envelope she kept tucked in one of the top drawers. She was convinced he'd stop swearing if he had to pay her every time she caught him—except in bed, that didn't count, thank Christ. So far, it wasn't working because that damn envelope was at least an inch thick by now.

"So why is the whole thing a problem?"

"Because Daryl isn't thinking straight. He's too damn close to everything. If shit goes sideways, he's not going to see it in time."

"Maybe he's in love."

"Bullshit. Daryl doesn't do love. He doesn't do emotion, period. He's too damn controlled for that."

"Actually, Wolf is the one who doesn't do emotion." TR leaned forward, rested one elbow on the desk and propped her chin in her hand. "You really haven't noticed how different Daryl's been since our wedding?"

"He hasn't been different, just distracted. And tired. The damn fool has been wearing himself out, going on jobs he doesn't need to go out on."

"Yeah, keeping himself busy. You don't think that means anything?"

"It sure as hell doesn't mean he's in love. Christ, he only met the woman one time."

"Sometimes that's all it takes."

Mac opened his mouth to argue, quickly snapped it shut. TR was right—sometimes one time was all it took. The two of them were perfect examples of that. At least, *he* was. TR swore she had fallen in love with him the first time she had seen him but he still didn't believe it. *Couldn't* believe it.

He was just grateful that she loved him now, and counted himself the luckiest man alive because of it.

She laughed, the sound soft and delicate. "No comeback for that one, huh?"

He answered with a low growl, leaned forward and brushed his mouth against hers for a fleeting kiss. "I'm going to the back to workout. Get rid of some of this damn tension. Let me know if Ninja calls, or if you have any luck getting through to him."

She nodded, gave him a saucy wink that promised a workout of a different kind when they got home, then turned back to the computer.

Mac forced himself to walk away, pushed through the secure door leading to the back. The faint whisper of his boots against concrete floated around him, the sound an ominous accompaniment to the hairs that were starting to stand on the back of his neck.

And fuck, that was never a good sign.

CHAPTER TWENTY-FOUR

The main lobby was open and airy, filled with sunlight streaming in through the wall of windows behind them. The tile floor gleamed and the faintest scent of lemon and pine lingered on the air. Clusters of potted plants native to the area added warmth and the framed prints on the wall—obviously drawn and painted by children—added color, giving the space a warm, welcoming feel.

The woman seated behind the desk, however, did not.

Long black hair threaded with silver fell below her shoulders. Dark brown eyes watched them from below delicate brows. The appearance of faint lines at the creases of those eyes hinted at laughter and warmth—both of which were completely absent as the woman stared down all three of them.

Daryl wasn't used to being stared down, especially not by a woman who was at least fifteen years older and an entire foot shorter than he was. He took firm reign on his temper, drew in a deep breath, let it out calmly and started again.

"If you could just check your records—"

"There's no need for me to check my records. Without proper identification and the necessary paperwork, I absolutely will not give you any information—especially not about one of our children." There was a finality in her softly accented voice that told him there was no way in hell this woman would budge. He could hold at her at gunpoint and offer her a million dollars in cash and she still wouldn't budge.

Which was great. Absolutely fucking wonderful and more power to her. She was serious about protecting her charges. Serious about doing her job. Terrific.

That didn't help them one damn bit.

And why the *fuck* hadn't he even considered this? He should have—who the hell would just hand over a child to a stranger, especially in this day and age with all the twisted fucking sickos out there? Nobody. Hell, even Mac had brought it up, had warned him of the possibility. But Daryl had never once considered that the child's own *mother* wouldn't be able to get her.

The mother in question—the woman he had nearly left behind and thank God he hadn't, or they'd really be screwed—was close to having a meltdown of major proportions. Daryl couldn't blame her—to be this close to the daughter she hadn't seen in six months, only to be turned away? Yeah, she had good reason for that panicked desperation that pretty much oozed from her. But having Kelsey meltdown—or worse, come completely undone and start throwing things— wouldn't help them one bit.

He stepped behind her, placed one hand on her shoulder and held his breath, wondering if she'd brush it off. Because yeah, that wouldn't look good, either. But she didn't do anything except turn to him, her eyes filled with silent pleading.

Fuck. What the hell was he supposed to do now? Tear the place apart until he found the girl then kidnap her?

Wolf slid a glance his way, one dimple creasing his

cheek as if he knew exactly what Daryl was thinking. "There's always option number two."

Yeah, the son-of-a-bitch *did* know what he was thinking.

Kelsey stepped away from him, moved closer to the woman and curled her hands around the edges of the desk as she leaned over it. "Please. She's my daughter. I haven't seen her in six months. Her name is Paige Davis. My dad brought her. To hide her. To keep her safe. I just want—"

"Ma'am, I'm sorry. Without the proper paperwork and authorization, there's nothing I can do."

Kelsey's hand curled into a fist and she banged it against the desk. "I just want—"

"Ma'am, if you don't leave now, I'm going to have to call security."

Shit. Kelsey was two seconds away from going into full momma-bear meltdown, the way she had back at the cabin. That was the last fucking thing they needed. Daryl stepped forward, offered the woman what he hoped was an apologetic smile, then wrapped his hand around Kelsey's arm and tugged.

"Kelsey, this way."

"But I want—"

"I know. Just—I need you to calm down and follow me for a minute."

She started to say *no*, started to struggle—then caught herself at the last second and nodded. Thank God for small favors.

He led her over to a small alcove that provided at least an illusion of privacy then dropped her arm. "You said your father left some things for you. To help get you started again. What did he leave?"

She pulled her lower lip between her teeth,

The Guardian: DARYL

chewed on it for a second, then shook her head. "It wasn't anything that would help with this."

"Are you sure?"

"Yes, of course. I think I'd know—"

"Do you have it?"

"What?"

"Whatever he left for you. Do you have it with you?"

A long pause. A slow nod. "Yes but—"

"Where is it?"

"I don't think—"

"Where is it, Kelsey? I need to see what he left."

"But—"

Daryl cut her off with a cold look. He leaned closer, lowered his voice so only she could hear. "Listen, lady, I did not plan on coming here to stage a coup on a goddamn children's home, which is something I'd like to avoid at all possible costs. So if you're father left you something, I need to know what. *Now.*"

She must have seen the threat in his eyes, or maybe heard it in his voice, because she finally—thank God—nodded. "It—it's in my pack. In the car."

Daryl straightened, tossed a bright smile at the receptionist who was watching them way too closely. "Excuse us. We'll be right back."

He marched Kelsey out the door, Wolf bringing up their rear, and led her straight to the Crossover SUV. The alarm beeped as he thumbed the key fob. He hit another button to release the latch on the rear hatch. Kelsey's pack was tossed in the back with his and Wolf's. He grabbed it, shoved it at her. "Let me see it."

She hesitated then unzipped the pack, rummaged

through it one-handed then pulled out a waterproof document bag, maybe two inches thick. The look she gave him telegraphed her reluctance as she handed him the pouch. Handed? Hell no, that would have been too damn easy. She practically slammed the thing into his chest.

She was pissed. Too damn bad, she'd just have to get over it.

He unsealed the pouch, removed the contents one at a time and placed them on top of his pack. An envelope containing several pictures: Kelsey and her father. Kelsey and a cute little girl who must be her daughter. Another picture, this one of Kelsey and the girl with a young man, taken in front of a Merry-Go-Round. Man? Hell, he looked more like a kid, certainly not old enough to be a father. Good looking in a nerdy way—and with the same laughing eyes and crooked smile as the little girl. Yeah, he was definitely the girl's father.

The man Kelsey loved.

Daryl ignored the flare of jealousy twisting his gut and carefully placed the pictures back in the envelope. He grabbed the second envelope and opened it, thumbed through the papers. Paige's birth certificate and social security card. Kelsey's as well. He folded the flap on the envelope and handed it to Wolf then reached for the third. This one was thicker, heavier. Kelsey shifted beside him, staring at the edge of the trunk as he opened it—

Holy fucking shit. This is what Davis had left her? No wonder she didn't want him to know about it. He thumbed through the wad of cash—well over ten grand, probably at least twice that amount, all in big bills. Shit. Yeah, that would definitely go a long way to helping someone start over.

So would the passports. He pulled one out, opened it, stared at the name printed next to the picture. *Kelsey's* picture—only, according to this, her name was Katy Anderson, from Richmond, Virginia.

Son of a bitch.

He slid a glance at Kelsey, thought about asking her if she was planning on going somewhere, thought better of it. She wouldn't give him a straight answer no matter how many times he asked.

Did she even realize the significance of the last name? Or hadn't she given it any thought at all? Watching the small blush spreading across her cheeks, his bet was on the former.

He thumbed past the second passport—he didn't even want to know what fucking name Davis had picked for that one—and pulled out the letter stuck to the back of the envelope.

"I—I can't read that one."

Of course, she couldn't read it. The damn thing was in Davis's fucking code—and addressed to him.

"It's not for you." He skimmed several long paragraphs. Read them again, slower this time, and swore to himself. Clenched his back teeth hard enough to shatter them. Damn the man. God damn him.

He folded the letter, shoved it into the front pocket of his jeans, then placed the money and passports back into the document pouch. He didn't miss Kelsey's small sigh or the way her shoulders sagged in relief. Had she thought he would take it? Probably.

Nothing was saying he wouldn't—later.

That left one more envelope. *For Paige* was written across the front in Davis's bold handwriting. He reached for it, started to open it—only to have Kelsey's hand close over his wrist, stopping him.

"You can't open that! It's for Paige. He left it for Paige."

"Yeah—*for* Paige. Not *to* Paige."

She frowned, reached for the envelope again when he held it away from her. "It's the same thing."

Was it? Maybe. Maybe not. In this case, Daryl was betting on the *maybe not*, especially after reading that damn letter. He slid his finger under the flap, unsealed it, pulled out the thin sheaf of papers and quickly scanned them.

Yeah, there was definitely a difference between *for* and *to*.

He folded the papers and put them back, reached up and closed the hatch door. "This is what we need. Let's go."

"But—" Kelsey stared at the envelope in his hands, looked up at him with tear-filled eyes. "I didn't know. I had them and I didn't know. I didn't want to open them, thought he left them for Paige—"

"He did." And shit, why the hell did she look so upset? Daryl wanted to pull her into his arms, tell her it was okay. Let her know that she wasn't *supposed* to know, that her father had counted on it.

Yeah—the wily son-of-a-bitch had counted on one hell of a lot. But she didn't need to know the rest of it. Especially not now. Maybe never. Except she was going to discover at least one part of it in about fifteen minutes—and he wasn't looking forward to the shit storm that was going to hit when she did.

He caught her gaze, started to reach for her arm then stopped. "Do you trust your father?"

"What? Of course, I do. Why wouldn't I?"

"Then just remember that everything he's done has been for a reason. Promise me you'll remember that."

"Promise? I don't understand. What are you talking about?"

"Nothing." Yeah, sure. *Nothing*, his fucking ass. Damn the sneaky bastard. "Come on, let's go get your daughter."

He turned and headed back across the parking lot, held the door open for Kelsey and started to follow behind her only to be stopped by Wolf. "Did I really see what I thought I saw?"

"Yeah."

"Holy fucking shit. Um, yeah. I'll just go wait in the car—"

"The hell you will." Daryl grabbed his arm and dragged him inside, snatched the first envelope from his hand. "I need you with me every second from here on out."

"Why? Afraid she's going to kill you?"

"You could say that, yeah." He dropped Wolf's arm and marched back to the desk. He pulled the sheaf of papers out and passed them to the woman, followed them with Paige's birth certificate and his own license.

The woman accepted the papers, scanned them, then looked from him to Kelsey and back again. She pushed away from the desk and motioned for them to follow her. "I'll call our manager then get Paige. You can wait in here. Ms. Edmunds will have some paperwork for you to sign, Mr. Anderson."

Daryl nodded, ignored Kelsey's questioning glance as he pulled out a chair and motioned for her to sit. At least Wolf was smart enough to start a rambling conversation, drawing Kelsey in, keeping her occupied so she wouldn't ask the fucking question he'd seen in her eyes.

Yeah, but for how long? Ten minutes? Fifteen? Maybe more but he wouldn't count on it. He just hoped to hell she didn't make a scene. If she did, the woman in charge—whoever she was—might start asking questions. Questions he couldn't answer.

That was the last thing they needed.

The minutes dragged by, Kelsey's impatience increasing with each one. Every time someone moved down the hall, she would jump and slide to the edge of the chair, like she was ready to bolt out of it. Could he really blame her? Hell, no. Not when he knew how much this meant to her.

He leaned over, grabbed her hand and gave it a gentle squeeze. Surprise flashed across her face and he expected her to yank her hand away, to tell him not to touch her. Instead, her trembling fingers threaded through his and she squeezed back, holding on like he was some kind of lifeline.

He leaned closer, ignored the way her head dipped toward him and dropped his voice to a whisper. "Just remember to trust your father. Remember he had his reasons."

Confusion creased her face and she opened her mouth. Whatever she'd been ready to say was drowned out by the quick knock against the door. They turned—all three of them—and stared at the woman standing in the doorway.

At the young girl with wide green eyes clinging to her hand.

"Paige! Paige, oh my God!" Kelsey launched from the chair, stumbled and dropped to her knees in front of the little girl. A second went by, then another. Did

Kelsey see the girl's confusion? Her uncertainty? For her sake, Daryl hoped not.

Then the little girl's face cleared, the uncertainty disappearing behind a wide smile as she ripped her hand from the woman's and launched herself at Kelsey. "Mommy!"

A memory slammed into him from nowhere, knocking him to the side. Stealing his fucking breath.

A sunny Spring day, just warm enough to finally shed the light jackets they'd been forced to wear the last few weeks. A small hand held his, tiny fingers wrapped around his larger ones because Layla's hand wasn't really big enough to hold his yet. She skipped along, her hair blowing in the breeze as she pulled him with her toward the swings. She loved the swings. Loved going higher and higher, holding on tight while she leaned back, making him laugh and giving him heart failure at the same time.

She dropped his hand and skipped over to the bench near the swings, carefully placed BaBa Bunny in his usual seat of honor and dropped a kiss against the fake pink fur. Then she was back, already climbing onto the swing without any help.

"Real high today, Daddy."

"Yeah? How high?"

"Higher than the angels, Daddy."

It was what she said every time. He made sure the belt was clipped and started to pull the swing back, only she stopped him with an impatient command.

"Come here, Daddy."

He bent down, wondering what secret she'd tell him today. "What is it, Bean?"

But there was no secret, not today. She quietly clapped her small hands against his cheeks and pressed a noisy kiss against his lips.

"I love you, Daddy."

"I love you, too, Bean. Forever and ever."

And then he sent her flying, higher and higher, her joyful giggles dancing in the air around them.

Higher than the angels, never knowing that his baby girl would become one two weeks later.

And shit. *Fuck*. Daryl looked away, pressed the edge of one hand against his eyes and struggled to draw air through his closed throat. Struggled against the fucking weight sitting in the middle of his chest while laughter and cries of joy echoed around him in a homecoming he'd never have.

"Mr. Anderson."

He heard his name, drew in a sharp breath. He needed to get his fucking act together, needed to get his fucking head on straight. A second went by, then another and another, time moving too damn slow as he shoved the memory—all the memories—into that little fucking box he kept hidden deep inside. He slammed the lid closed, drew in one last deep breath, then lowered his hand.

The woman sitting across from him offered him a gentle smile, like she knew exactly why he was so overcome with emotion. Only she didn't know shit, had no fucking clue. Nobody did.

"I just need you to sign some paperwork then you can take your daughter home."

His daughter.

He slid a glance to his left, saw Kelsey's body stiffen as she looked up. She was still clinging to the little girl in her arms, holding her like she'd never let her go.

His daughter.

Fuck. The little girl with a mop of wild curls the same color as her mother's wasn't his daughter. The little girl sending him shy looks with her father's wide green eyes wasn't his daughter.

His daughter was dead. Taken from him in one selfish moment that had destroyed his life.

Only the little girl still watching him *was* his daughter—because that son-of-a-bitch Allen Davis had signed over guardianship of her to *him*.

Fuck.

Kelsey stood, scooped the girl off her feet and rested her on her hip. And she was going to fucking blow it, ruin everything by opening her mouth and asking what the fuck was going on. Daryl knew it.

And Wolf did, too. Thank God the man was there, was thinking a hell of a lot faster on his feet than Daryl could. He made his way over to Kelsey and the little girl, both dimples showing as he smiled and gently took Kelsey's arm and guided her out of the room, talking nonsense about some cartoon Scottish princess that he said looked just like Paige.

Daryl ignored them, focused on the paperwork the woman pushed across the desk. He signed his name, over and over, the woman's words nothing more than a senseless droning in the background until, finally, he was done.

She said something else, reached down and grabbed a small backpack and a stuffed bear from the floor and handed it to him. "These belong to Paige. She must have forgotten them."

"Uh, yeah. Yeah. Thanks." He took the pack and the stuffed animal, tried to hide his surprise. Fuck, that was it? All her worldly possessions were contained to one small backpack and a fucking stuffed bear?

He held them both in one hand, made his way down the hall and pushed through the doors. Kelsey was standing there waiting, anger clear in her eyes.

"What was that about? What did she mean?"

"Nothing." He moved past her, kept walking.

"Don't tell me it was *nothing*. She said *your*—"

He spun on her, his own anger jumping to the surface. "Not. Now."

"I deserve to know—"

"It was nothing. Just a fu—" He stopped, swallowed back the oath and sucked in a deep breath. "It's just a formality. A matter of paperwork. I'll make it right when we get home."

"Make what right? What did you do?"

"Lady, don't even think about putting this on me. This was all your father's doing."

"What was? What are you talking about?"

Dammit! Couldn't she leave well enough alone? Couldn't she fucking wait?

He started to ask her that, stopped when the phone in his pocket started ringing. He swore to himself, shoved the fucking pink backpack and stuffed animal at Wolf, then grabbed the phone, answered it with a sharp, "Yeah."

"You've got problems."

Yeah. No fucking shit he had problems. He had a woman ready to rip his head from his shoulders and piss down his neck and a daughter he didn't want. He started to say as much when the urgency in Mac's voice finally registered, stopping him in his tracks.

"Talk to me."

And damn if Kelsey wasn't still coming after him, demanding answers he wasn't ready to give. Wolf grabbed her, shook his head, started walking her toward the car.

"I've been trying to reach you for two fucking hours."

The Guardian: DARYL

"Cell reception hasn't been the greatest—"

"Ninja checked in. That woman you sent him to check on? She's been worked over pretty damn bad."

"What? What the fuck happened?"

"Looks like Grady Byrne paid her a visit."

A blast of icy air washed over him. He looked over at Wolf, motioned for him to get in the car, *now*. "What? When?"

"Sometime yesterday. Maybe an hour or two before he got there."

"Fuck. Is she going to make it?"

"She's out of surgery. Beyond that, who fucking knows."

"Okay, keep me posted—"

"Yeah, that's not the problem."

"Mac, you better start fucking talking and not stop until I know everything."

"Ninja was able to talk to her. Byrne knows everything. Your name. That you're the one who grabbed Kelsey from the cabin. The name of CSS. All of it. Chaos found the name Byrne used to get into the country and he's been tracking it. He got here yesterday afternoon."

"Fuck. Fucking goddamn son-of-a-fucking—"

"Daryl—Chaos thinks Byrne found you. He's not sure how, but Byrne's on the way there now. To New Mexico."

He didn't wait to hear anything else, just rushed to the car and pushed Kelsey in, jumped in behind her and pointed at Wolf.

"Drive. Now. And don't fucking stop."

CHAPTER TWENTY-FIVE

Daryl met Wolf's gaze in the rear-view mirror and quickly shook his head. Yeah, the man knew something was up—but Daryl couldn't tell him, not yet.

Not when Kelsey was staring at him like he'd lost his mind. She finished buckling Paige into the car seat, ruffled the girl's hair, then frowned at Daryl while she fastened her own seatbelt.

"I think you owe me an explanation."

"I'll explain later—"

"Not later—*now*. What did she mean when she said *your* daughter?"

Holy shit. *That* was what she wanted to talk about? Didn't she realize—?

No, she didn't. There was no reason for her to realize anything. Hell, she probably thought he'd pushed her into the car just so they could leave. That he'd ordered Wolf to start driving because he was in a fucking hurry.

Shit.

He met the other man's gaze once more, saw Wolf shake his head and utter a low oath.

"Kelsey, there are bigger things I need to focus on right now."

"Bigger things—" Her mouth snapped closed, those green-ringed hazel eyes going wide for a fraction of a second. The color drained from her face and she shot a panicked look out the back window. "Do you mean—but how? Why?"

The Guardian: DARYL

"I'm not sure." He leaned between the front seats, stretching until his fingers caught the latch of the glove box and flipped it open. It was empty except for the rental paperwork. "Dammit. I need a map."

Wolf nudged him out of the way, tapped the center console. "Try in here."

Daryl rolled to the side, yanked the lid open. Nothing. "Dammit. Doesn't anyone believe in maps anymore?"

"Not when they can simply use their phones, no."

"Phones aren't an option right now."

"You think he can access them?"

"I can't risk it. Not right now."

"Then if you have a better idea, I need you to share it because I'm coming up on the turn for the airport."

Shit. Daryl clenched his jaw, trying to figure out their best option. Should they head to the airport and hope that Byrne wasn't there waiting for them? Or head in the opposite direction, ditch the car for another one then drive like hell for the state line and cross into Texas?

He closed his eyes, pulled up a mental image of the map he had briefly studied before leaving home. Christ, he wished he had that fucking map with him now instead of relying solely on memory, because what he was remembering wasn't very reassuring.

Because there wasn't a hell of a lot of anything between here and there—unless you counted a lot of empty highway.

"Zeus, I need an answer."

Fuck.

He met Wolf's gaze, nodded. "Airport."

"You sure?"

"No, but it's our best bet."

Wolf hit the brakes, cut the wheel to the left and fishtailed as he made the turn. Kelsey lurched forward, caught herself as Daryl swore.

"Dammit, Wolf, you've got passengers back here."

"Yeah. Sorry. My bad."

For her part, Kelsey looked relatively calm. Pale and shaken, yes, but still surprisingly calm. The little girl was a different matter—her wide green eyes filled with tears and her lower lip trembled. She pulled the stuffed bear closer to her, holding it tight enough to decapitate the fuzzy head, and reached for Kelsey with her other hand.

"Mommy."

"It's okay, sweetie. I'm right here. We're just going for a quick ride, that's all."

Daryl uttered a quick prayer that she wasn't lying. That they'd reach the airport with no issues. That they'd be in the air and out of harm's way within an hour.

He'd feel a hell of a lot better if this area wasn't quite so remote. Nothing but fields and brush, with an occasional house so far off the road you could barely see it. And they didn't have any options for backroads because there simply wasn't any, not unless they decided to make their own.

Yeah, that wasn't an option, either.

Daryl turned in the seat, stretched behind him for his pack and reached into the outer pocket for his weapon and an extra clip before grabbing Wolf's from the other pack. He tried to be discreet about it, used his body to shield both weapons from view when he passed Wolf's up front—

But Kelsey saw anyway. Her eyes widened, panic flaring in their depths before she quickly hid it.

The Guardian: DARYL

"It's just a precaution." He meant the words to be reassuring, figured it would have sounded a hell of a lot better if he believed it himself. But she didn't say anything, just turned her head and started talking to her daughter in a low voice, keeping up a stream of one-sided conversation.

How much farther? It had taken them forty minutes to get to the home from the small motel this morning. The airport was only ten minutes from the hotel—but they had to pass the hotel to get there. Fifty minutes then? No, less than that with the way Wolf was driving, pushing the small SUV to its top speed of nowhere-near-fast-enough.

Daryl twisted in the seat, glanced out the back window, saw nothing but empty road behind them. He looked at his watch, jerked his head up at Wolf's low oath.

"Car's coming our way."

"Just keep going, doesn't mean anything."

Daryl focused straight ahead, breath held as Wolf shortened the distance between them. Fifty yards. Thirty. Ten—

"It's slowing down—"

"Just keep going." He cradled the weapon in his hand, slid the rack to chamber a round.

"Daryl." Kelsey's voice. Soft, holding the faintest tremor. He looked over, his gaze holding hers for the space of a few heartbeats. Then he looked at the little girl, felt his heart slam into his chest when she stared up at him with those tear-filled eyes.

She wasn't his daughter. His daughter was dead and buried, her life cut entirely too short by a tragedy he'd had no control over. This time was different—this time, he was the one in control.

And he'd die before allowing something to happen to this girl. Before allowing something to happen to her mother.

He met Kelsey's eyes once more, wondered if she could see the determination in his gaze. If she could see the unspoken promise in his eyes.

Wolf swore, the sound sharp and angry. "They just spun around to follow us."

"How many?"

"I saw three visible."

Daryl nodded, a deep sense of calm falling over him. Three against two were damn good odds—except for the two passengers with them.

"Kelsey. I need you to keep your head down. I need you to keep calm, no matter what happens. Is that understood?"

She nodded then leaned to the side, draping herself over her daughter, her fingers squeezing the edge of the car seat so hard that her knuckles turned white. Daryl shifted in place, focused on the car behind them.

"Wolf—"

"This is as fast as it goes, Zeus."

Shit. Not good. Not when that car was gaining on them.

Sunlight flashed off something a split-second before he saw another flash, before he felt the impact of something hitting the back of the SUV. There was a ping of something hitting metal, the sound of plastic splintering. What was left of the SUV's taillight bounced on the road behind them, disappeared under the tires of the encroaching car.

The SUV swerved, quickly straightened as Wolf gained control of the wheel. Daryl bit back an oath, held his breath as he willed the small SUV to go faster. Faster—

Another shot. The SUV lurched as shredded rubber fell away behind them. The car swerved—no, not the car. It was the SUV, bouncing from one side of the road to the other as Wolf fought to control it.

They went off the side of the road, bounced across a small ditch and pitched sideways. Kelsey screamed, the sound drowning at the frightened cries of her daughter. Daryl grabbed for the seat, the console, anything to anchor himself as the small vehicle tilted sideways. As it rolled—

Pain shot through his left shoulder. His cheek. His left temple. Screams echoed in his ears as the world around him tumbled and bounced with dizzying speed before abruptly righting itself.

Before coming to a deadly stop.

He blinked, shook his head then looked around. They were sitting off the road in a rough patch of scrub and dirt, pointing in the opposite direction they'd been heading. The car that had been following them had come to a stop five yards away. Doors opened and three men got out, two of them holding weapons—pointing them at the SUV.

He glanced toward the front, blinked until Wolf came into focus. Blood streamed from a gash in the man's head but other than that, he seemed fine. He was leaning over the wheel, swearing as he pressed the ignition button over and over.

"Wolf—"

"I'm trying."

Trying—but it wasn't working. Even if the other man could get the SUV to start, they had nowhere to go.

"Kelsey, are you okay?" He turned his head, saw her nod. The little girl was crying, quiet sobs that shook her small shoulders. Kelsey leaned over her, tried to quiet her as she sent a pleading look in Daryl's direction.

"Kelsey, get Paige out of the car seat. Go out the door and stay down."

"But—"

"Do it. Now." He turned to Wolf but the other man was already scrambling across the front passenger seat and opening the door. Daryl waited until he was out then quickly looked around, searching for his weapon. There, just under the front seat. He leaned down for it—

And the glass of the door window shattered above his head.

"Fuck!" He closed his hand over the grip of the pistol and dove out the open door head-first. Kelsey was crouched near the front tire, her body curled protectively around her daughter. Wolf was in front of her, weapon at the ready.

Daryl scrambled toward the rear tire, took cover and peered around the crushed bumper. The men hadn't moved. Damn fools. If Daryl had been in their shoes, he would have already flanked the SUV, come at them from both sides while they were still inside, trapping them.

They had made a huge tactical error by not moving in when they had a chance—and now they were going to pay.

"Gentleman, my fight was never with you—not until you disposed of my men. I'm willing to forgive that error as long as you give me the woman and the girl." The voice was clear, well-modulated, with the faintest trace of a lilt.

Daryl glanced over his shoulder, met Wolf's what-the-fuck gaze with one of his own. He nodded, held his left fist out to the side with a grimace and slowly raised his fingers.

One.

Two.

Three—

Daryl and Wolf spun toward the men at the same time, firing off several quick rounds each. A grunt. A scream. A string of curses abruptly cut off before someone was smart enough to return fire.

Then silence. Long. Tense. A minute went by, then another, until the silence was finally broken by a muffled whimper of pain. Even that was cut short, abruptly silenced by a single shot.

Daryl risked a glance around the rear of the car. Just a quick one but it was enough to confirm his suspicions. Holy shit. Fuck. Grady Byrne had just shot his own fucking man in the head.

That made it two against two—and Byrne's second man looked like he'd been injured, shot in the arm. Ready to run if given the opportunity. What had Chaos said? That only a few men were loyal to Byrne?

Yeah, maybe not.

"That's another man you've cost me. My patience wears thin, gentlemen. Give me my granddaughter."

"She's not your granddaughter! She'll never be yours!"

What the fuck? Daryl turned toward Kelsey, tried to catch her eye and tell her to shut but she wasn't looking at him. She was still curled around Paige, a fierce expression etched onto her pale face. And fuck, they needed to end this. Now. Before she did something completely stupid.

He nodded at Wolf, got into position—

"Ah, Kelsey. You're such a stubborn lass, aren't you? But we both know you're lying, don't we? The girl is my bastard son's offspring—which means she's mine."

"No, she's not! She—"

Enough of this fucking shit. He signaled Wolf, launched himself around the rear of the SUV and opened fire. One shot. Two. Three.

Byrne's man fell in a crumpled heap, his weapon no longer a danger to anyone. That left Byrne himself.

Daryl watched, detached, as Byrne raised his weapon and fired. Felt fire explode in his left shoulder, ignored it as he pulled the trigger again. Felt another blast of fire, this one in his arm. He kept firing, watching through blurred vision as the other man toppled over backward, blood spraying from his chest.

Daryl dropped to his knees, swayed and fell sideways. Tried to catch himself but his arm wasn't working, the fucking thing just twisted and collapsed as he landed on it. And fuck. Yeah, that fucking hurt.

But not as much as the pain in his side. What the fuck? Had he fallen on something? A piece of glass, maybe? He tried to lift himself up, tried to roll so he could see what the fuck he'd fallen on but he couldn't move because his fucking arm wasn't working.

Fuck.

He blinked. Shook his head. Blinked again but he couldn't make out anything more than shadows. His ears were working just fine though because he heard Kelsey screaming, heard a little girl crying.

Heard Wolf's calm voice telling him to stop fucking moving.

Daryl opened his mouth, ready to tear Wolf a new one, to tell him to watch his fucking language, but no words came out. He tried again, finally gave up and closed his eyes.

Felt himself floating.

Higher. Higher still.

Higher than the angels, where a little girl with wide brown eyes smiled down on him.

CHAPTER TWENTY-SIX

Four weeks later.

"How's the shoulder?"
"Fine."
A pause. "How's your arm?"
"Fine."
"And your side?"
"Fine. Everything is fucking fine." Daryl spit the last words, reached across the desk for another file and winced. Mac grunted but didn't say anything, just sat there and watched him.

And kept on fucking watching him.

Daryl narrowed his eyes, shot him a dirty look designed to make the other man turn tail and run. Mac didn't budge. Of course he didn't. He wasn't fucking smart enough to know when to run.

No, scratch that. He was smart enough—he just didn't give a fuck. And it wasn't like Daryl was in any condition to kick his ass and throw him out of his office. The damn man knew it, too.

He blew out a sigh, slammed the file shut and leaned back in the chair. Managed to do it without wincing, too. Thank God for fucking progress.

"What's everyone's status?"
"All present and accounted for, except for Boomer and Ninja. They went to retrieve a package."

Daryl frowned, searched his mental database for any job that had come in requiring a package retrieval

The Guardian: DARYL

and came up empty. "I don't remember seeing anything about a retrieval—"

"This is a two-legged one." Mac shifted in the chair, his lips curling in a scowl. "Boomer has personal ties to this one. Tore out of here about three hours ago. They already went wheels-up."

"Personal?" *Dammit!* Was Daryl going to have to institute a new rule about personal missions? They needed to be off-limits, effective immediately. Nothing good came from personal missions—he was a perfect example of that.

And hell, so was Mac—only Mac's mission had ended a thousand times better, considering he was now married to TR.

He stared at the man still sitting across from him. Still watching him. He narrowed his eyes and glared. "Why are you even here? Don't you have something better to do with your time?"

Mac ran a hand over his jaw then shook his head. "Not particularly."

"Then maybe you should go find something. I don't need you sitting there, staring at me."

"That's because you know I'm right."

Shit. Was he really going to start this again? Daryl grabbed another file. Flipped it open and pretended to read, did his best to ignore Mac. But the other man didn't know when to quit because he leaned across the desk, snagged the file, and tossed it to the side.

"It was a stupid fucking move."

"Yeah, well. I wasn't planning on getting shot."

"That's not what I'm fucking talking about and you know it."

Yeah, he knew it—but he wasn't discussing it. Not now. Just like he hadn't discussed it the other fifty fucking times Mac had brought it up over the last two weeks. No, probably more than that. The problem was the first week was still pretty fuzzy.

At least, most of it was. It would be ten times better if he couldn't remember all of it.

"You should have gone after her."

Daryl blew out a sigh, ran a hand through his hair. It was getting too long, he needed a fucking haircut—

"What? Nothing to say?"

Daryl slammed his hand against the desk. "No, dammit, I've got nothing to say. There's nothing *to* say. She left. She's gone. End of story."

"Only because you let her."

"*Let her*. Yeah, uh-huh. What was I supposed to do? Tie her down and hold her prisoner?"

"Telling her how you feel would have been a good start."

"How I feel?" Daryl laughed, the sound sharp and bitter. "There is no *feel*. Okay? There was nothing there. I don't know why you're so fucking convinced there was."

"*Is*, not *was*. Bullshit yourself all you want but I know better. In all the years I've known you, I have never seen you like this."

"Like what?"

"Distracted. Out of control. On edge."

"I haven't been—"

"Yeah, you have. Deny it all you want but the only one you're lying to is yourself."

"There's. Nothing. There." Daryl forced the words through clenched teeth, trying to get them through Mac's thick skull. But the other man just sat there, watching him with dark eyes filled with disbelief. "Fuck. We don't even know each other. We've

The Guardian: DARYL

probably spent less than ninety-six hours in each other's company—"

"Who are you trying to convince now? Me? Or yourself?"

"Dammit, Mac. Just let it go. She's gone, to God only knows where." Could Daryl blame her for running again? She'd taken off damn near as soon as they returned to Maryland, thirty-six hours after the confrontation with Byrne.

Twelve hours after he'd signed guardianship of her daughter over to her. It was nothing more than a formality as far as he was concerned—the paperwork Davis had drawn up would never stand up in court. At least, Daryl didn't think so. But just in case, he'd signed the paperwork. *That* memory was pretty damn clear. So was the relief in Kelsey's eyes when he'd slid it across to her.

Everything after that was still a blur. He *thought* she had stayed with him, his hand cradled in hers while she held Page on her lap. *Thought* he remembered the feel of her lips brushing against his. *Thought* he remembered her saying...something.

Yeah. That was nothing more than his mind playing tricks on him because Kelsey was gone. She'd taken off again, leaving nothing behind.

Nothing except a chunk of raw obsidian hanging from the leather cord around his neck.

No, he couldn't blame her for taking off. Kelsey was safe now, but it would take her time to realize that. Take time to get used to the fact that she didn't have to run anymore. Didn't have to look over her shoulder. The bad guy was dead, her nightmare was over. She could settle down, build a life for her and her daughter. Start fresh, just like she had hoped.

Mac stood up, slid the chair against the desk hard enough that it bounced back with a squeak of springs. "I never thought I'd see the day when you just fucking gave up without even trying."

"Fuck you. I'm not *giving up* anything."

"Yeah. Sure. Whatever. Suit yourself."

Daryl started to say something, slammed his mouth closed when Mac stormed out of the office. Fuck it. There was nothing to say. Mac was fucking delusional, so in love with his own fucking wife that he thought everyone else should be, too.

Yeah. Fuck it.

Life didn't always work out that way. Daryl had learned that lesson years ago.

CHAPTER
TWENTY-SEVEN

Kelsey ran a strip of tape along the top of the box, sealing it. That was the last box.

The last bits of a life well-lived.

She straightened, looked around the empty house. At the bare walls and clean floor. Nothing of her father remained.

Nothing except memories.

Most of the furnishings had been donated, along with his clothes. She found a veteran's organization who had gladly accepted them, had even come out to pick everything up. She thought her father would have liked that.

His personal belongings—those that held sentimental value—had been carefully boxed up. It wasn't much—her father had been a minimalist. He'd spent too much time in the military to be anything but. And he'd never been one for collecting things, had always told her that his memories were more than enough.

Memories.

Yes, she had plenty of those. A lifetime of memories to pull out and look back on. To laugh and smile about and even some to cry over. But what about her daughter?

She was only five. Did she remember Blaine? Her grandfather? Or were they nothing more than hazy images that floated to her in a dream? Images that would fade in time?

Kelsey vowed to make sure they were much more than that. To keep their memories alive in her daughter's mind.

She looked over at Paige, sitting quietly under the window, coloring. A brief spurt of panic washed over her and she nearly yanked her daughter away from the window—then stopped herself. The danger was gone. The nightmare was over.

They were free. Finally.

Would this whole thing be nothing more than a bad memory for Paige? Or would she somehow come to forget about it? How many images from the last three years would follow her through life? Would they form who she'd become in three years? Five? Ten? Would they make her stronger?

Or would they do the opposite and make her afraid to take chances?

Paige pushed to her feet, ran over with a brightly colored sheet of paper in her hand. "Look, Mommy. For you."

Kelsey crouched next to her daughter and accepted the paper, studied the flowers and rainbow and the stick figure of a woman holding a little girl's hand. She smiled and pulled Paige into a hug, dropped a kiss on the top of her head. "Thank you, sweetie. It's very pretty."

Paige nodded, took it back and carefully placed it in the folder with her other drawings.

Were the colorful drawings a good sign? Kelsey could only hope so.

She pushed to her feet, lifted the small box from the floor, and looked around one final time. There was nothing left for her to do here. The things she was keeping were already packed up and stored in the back of her car. The real estate agent had left a little while ago, Kelsey's phone number stored in her contacts. The house was officially on the market as of this morning and the agent was optimistic it wouldn't take long to sell.

Maybe. Time would tell.

She rested the box against her hip and dug the keys from her front pocket. There was one thing left for her to do and then they could leave. "You ready, sweetie?"

Paige nodded, stuffed her folder of drawings into her backpack, and carefully zipped it. She pulled on her coat, grabbed the bag and her stuffed bear and hurried over to Kelsey, staying close by her side as they walked out of the house.

Instead of going to her car, Kelsey made her way down the sidewalk, her steps slow enough for Paige to keep up. The early afternoon was sunny, the air crisp and clean. A few houses in the neighborhood had already decorated for the holidays, garland and lights covering windows and doors, reindeer and sleighs carefully placed on the small front lawns.

But not the house they were going to.

Kelsey moved up the front walk, stopped in front of the door and hesitated. She started to knock but the door was already opening, revealing a bruised and swollen face still healing from violent injuries more than four weeks later.

Kelsey blinked back tears, forced a smile as she greeted Theresa. "I wanted to say goodbye before we left."

The woman nodded, stepped back to let them in. She smiled, but only the left side of her mouth moved—the right side was partially paralyzed, possibly permanently. It was a miracle the woman was out of the hospital—

No. It was a miracle she was still alive after the brutal beating she had suffered at Grady Byrne's hands.

"I was hoping you would." Theresa closed the door behind them and moved over to the sofa, her gait slow and uneven as she balanced herself on the cane. She sat down, shifted with a slight grimace, then patted the cushion next to her.

"We can't stay long." Kelsey took a seat, glanced at the private duty nurse hovering a few feet away, then turned back to Theresa and offered her the box. "I wanted to drop this off."

"I don't understand—"

"They're some of Dad's things—"

"Kelsey, no. I couldn't."

"Please. He would have wanted you to have them." The mementos in the box were meant for the woman across from her, keepsakes from the time her father had spent with her. A few pictures. A black t-shirt from Sturgis, South Dakota, that still held the faint scent of her father's spicy aftershave. A black nylon lanyard with collector's pins from several National Parks—places her dad had visited with Theresa on motorcycle. Memories of a life they had shared—

A life Kelsey hadn't even known about.

She placed the box on Theresa's lap, swallowed against the lump in her throat when the woman reached out and gently caressed the lid. Kelsey could see the love in her misty eyes, could feel it shimmering in the air between them. On impulse, she grabbed the woman's good hand and squeezed it.

"I'm glad he had you in his life. For however long

it was, I'm glad he had someone to love and someone to love him back. I'm glad he had you."

"Oh, Kelsey." The woman leaned forward, pulled her into a hug with a strength that surprised her. "I am so, so sorry. For everything."

Kelsey wrapped her arms around her, squeezed her eyes closed and held on tight. "No, don't be. Please. It's not your fault. None of it's your fault."

They stayed that way for a long time, holding onto each other while Paige clung to Kelsey's leg. They finally separated, each wiping at their eyes, bound together by their shared love of a strong man.

"Have you decided where you're going yet?"

Kelsey pushed to her feet, shook her head. "No, not yet."

"You'll let me know when you decide? You'll keep in touch?"

"Yes, of course." And she would—as soon as she figured it out.

Kelsey took Paige's small hand in hers and let herself out, waving a final goodbye to the woman who meant so much to her father. She walked back to the car, stopping for one last look at her father's house.

Wondering, for just one minute, how things might have been different.

Stop the damn nonsense, Katydid. You can't live in the past, and you can't build a life on regrets. You just need to move forward and make the best of every damn day that you have.

She didn't bother turning around—her father wasn't standing next to her. But he *was* close by. He would always be close. Would always be with her.

A small smile curled her mouth as she unlocked the back door and buckled Paige into her car seat. Kelsey climbed behind the wheel and started the engine, sat there for a long moment as her father's words echoed in her ear.

It was time.

Time to put the past behind her.

Time to move forward.

She put the car in gear and headed east.

CHAPTER TWENTY-EIGHT

His ass was dragging.

No, it was more than that. More than being physically tired from pushing himself. More than doing too much on his way to full recovery. More than—

Hell, Daryl didn't know what the fuck it was. All he knew was that it felt like something was missing. That he'd misplaced something important, even though he didn't know what the fuck it was, and he couldn't find it.

He snorted, reached for the coffee pot and topped off his mug even though he hadn't taken more than two swallows of the stuff.

What the hell was his problem? Was it some kind of gray funk? The start of another downward spiral? No, not that. At least not yet.

Was the potential there? Maybe. He could feel *something*, hovering around the edges, calling to him. Beckoning him. But this was different from what he'd experienced nine years ago, when his heart had been ripped from his chest and shredded into a million tiny pieces, so many fucking pieces he didn't think he'd ever get it back again.

But he had.

Hadn't he?

Maybe not. Maybe that feeling of normalcy, the one he'd struggled so hard to recapture, had been nothing more than an illusion. Maybe the steel control he prided himself on was nothing more than a fucking fantasy he'd convinced himself was reality.

Yeah, sure. Or maybe he was just losing his fucking mind. Wasn't that what he had thought right after being shot? When he was floating into nothingness, higher and higher? Feeling nothing, caring about nothing—

Until he saw Layla. She'd been sitting on a swing, pushing it back and forth with the toe of one bright blue sneaker. Only she couldn't be because her feet had never been able to reach the ground, she'd been too young, too small.

But she could reach it now. She placed her foot on the ground to stop the swing and looked up at him, a bright smile lighting her face.

"*Daddy! You're not supposed to be here, you know.*"

He moved closer to her, ruffled her hair with his hand and sat on the swing next to her. "*No? And why not?*"

"*Because you're not.*"

"*But it's my dream, Bean. I can be anywhere I want in my dream.*"

Layla laughed, the sound light and musical and filling his heart with so much love, he thought he'd burst from it. Not just love, but sadness, too. Sadness that he'd never see his little girl again. Never get to hold her or watch her grow up.

Layla's tiny hand cupped his cheek and he looked up, surprised to see that she was standing in front of him now. "*Don't be sad, Daddy. You can always see me. Whenever you want. You just need to close your eyes and open your heart. Not just to me, but to them, too.*"

"*Them? Them, who, Bean?*"

"*You know who. You just need to let yourself admit it.*"

He shook his head, forced a smile to his face. Started to question her again, started to ask her why she sounded so different. It was Layla's voice, but older. Wiser. But this was a dream. Who was he to question a dream?

"If that's what you want to believe, Daddy." Layla laughed again, clapped her hands against his cheeks and pressed a noisy kiss against his mouth. "I love you, Daddy."

"I love you, too, Bean. Always."

Layla smiled. Reached for his hand, tugged him to his feet and led him to the swing she had been sitting on a few minutes earlier. "Push me, Daddy. Nice and high, just like always."

"Yeah? How high?"

"Higher and higher. Higher than the angels, Daddy."

Then she was gone, her voice fading away as someone yelled at him. Wolf, telling him to stop fucking moving before he hurt himself—

Shit.

Daryl sat the mug on the counter, reached for the towel to mop up the hot coffee he had splashed over his hand and shirt. What the fuck was wrong with him? It had been a dream, nothing more than a fucking dream.

He needed to get back in the field. Go do something other than sitting around doing *nothing*. That was his problem—too much inactivity. Daryl had never been the kind of man comfortable with sitting behind a desk and that's all he'd been doing since he got out of the hospital. Hell, he hadn't even been to the fucking range.

He tossed the kitchen towel onto the counter and started for his bedroom. He'd change, call Mac or Chaos or Wolf and see if they wanted to go with him. They could run some mock scenarios or hell, just empty clip after clip into those damn paper targets.

He was halfway down the hall when the doorbell rang. He swore under his breath, changed direction and bounded down the short flight of stairs. Maybe it was

Mac, coming to give him shit again. Fine, let him. The mood Daryl was in, he'd have no problem getting into a damn wrestling match right here in the fucking entranceway.

He yanked the door open, ready to give the man a shit-ton of grief. The words died in his throat and he stood there, his mouth hanging open, wondering if maybe he was fucking hallucinating.

Kelsey stood on the small porch, her hand wrapped around her daughter's. Sunlight glinted off her hair, shooting back reds and golds and browns. Green-ringed hazel eyes stared back at him, filled with uncertainty. She blinked and the uncertainty disappeared, replaced by something else he couldn't quite make out.

"Kelsey."

"Hi." She raised one hand, dragged it through the loose waves framing her face. "Um, can we come in? Or is this a bad time?"

"What? Oh, no. No, it's—yeah, come on in." He stepped back, held the door open as they moved past him. Kelsey hesitated for a brief second, her gaze catching his before she led Paige upstairs. Daryl closed the door, followed them with slower steps. Tamped down the confusion swirling through him as Kelsey got her daughter settled in the living room, spreading out some coloring books and plain paper and crayons on the coffee table. Then she turned to him, the uncertainty back in her gaze.

"Do you mind if we go into the kitchen to talk?"

He shook his head, grimaced, changed it to a nod. "Yeah. Sure. Is everything okay? Did something happen?"

"Everything's good." She followed him into the

kitchen, leaned against the counter and folded her arms in front of her. "I'm selling Dad's house. The real estate agent came out two days to finalize everything."

"Selling it? You didn't want—"

"No." She shook her head, offered him a shaky smile. "No, I couldn't stay there. Not after—well, I just couldn't."

Daryl heard what she *wasn't* saying, understood her reasonings—she couldn't stay there, not after finding her father. Not knowing that he'd been murdered there.

"I saw Theresa."

"How's she doing?"

Kelsey shrugged. "Healing. Moving forward, one day at a time. By the way, thank you."

"For what?"

"For the private duty nurse. She didn't say as much, but I know you arranged for her to have one."

Daryl crossed his arms in front of him, dropped his gaze to the floor. Yeah, he'd arranged for the nurse, for as long as Theresa needed her. It was his damn fault she'd been hurt in the first place. If he had acted sooner, if he'd sent Ninja out there earlier or—

"It's not your fault. What happened to Theresa. What happened, period. None of it's your fault."

Daryl looked up, met Kelsey's gaze, saw the truth of the words in the depths of her eyes. Maybe she didn't think so, but he knew better. He wasn't going to argue the point with her, not now.

"So where are you heading off to now? Have you decided?"

"I'm not really sure." She shrugged, looked around the kitchen then stepped closer to him. Close enough he could feel the heat of her body, smell the faint scent of her shampoo.

He stepped back, needing to put distance between them, and collided with the refrigerator. A small smile teased Kelsey's mouth, there and gone so quickly he thought he might have imagined it. But she kept talking, acting like she hadn't noticed the way he'd moved away.

"I was thinking about heading out to the coast. Either California or maybe Oregon. We spent some time there—Paige and I—when we were running. Paige likes the beach and the water."

California? Christ, that was on the opposite side of the country. "Yeah, the beach would be nice."

"Then I was thinking about maybe the mountains. I've always liked the mountains. The crisp air, the sense of peace and solitude." She smiled, lifted one shoulder in a careless shrug. "One place that definitely isn't on the list is a big city. I've never liked big cities, even before all this. I—I don't think I'll ever be comfortable around that many people."

Daryl nodded. Yeah, he could understand that. What he *couldn't* understand was why she was here, standing a foot away, telling him all this. "I'm sure you'll figure it out."

"Probably. But whatever I decide has to be soon because I need to enroll Paige in school." She inched closer, rested her hip against the edge of the counter and tilted her head to the side. "I did some research and learned something pretty interesting."

"You did?"

She nodded, that small smile once again teasing the corners of her mouth. "Yeah, I did. Did you know that Maryland has a coastline with beaches? Bumps right up to the Atlantic."

Daryl swallowed back a surprised laugh. "Yeah, pretty sure I knew that."

"It has mountains, too. Did you know that? And—" She leaned closer, close enough that her shoulder brushed against his arm. "Did you also know that central Maryland puts you just around two hours away from both the ocean *and* the mountains?"

"I—"

"Isn't that where we are now? Central Maryland?"

"Yeah." He nodded, called himself a fool for letting his heart race in his chest. For jumping to conclusions. "Yeah, we are. But, um, that two-hour calculation might be a little off, especially for the ocean. Especially—"

"Maybe, but it's close enough."

Close enough. What the fuck was she saying? What was she trying to tell him? Was he just imagining things when he looked at her? Was that a flicker of need in her eyes—or just wishful thinking on his part? Should he push her way—or risk making a fool of himself?

Daryl shook his head, started to push away from the refrigerator, to put distance between them. Something stopped him—the echo of a small voice, from somewhere deep down inside him. He dug his fingers into his arm, stared at a spot over her shoulder because he was afraid to meet her eyes.

"Kelsey, what are you trying to say?"

A hand reached for his, soft and warm, the touch light and hesitant. He looked down, saw her fingers trembling against his. He hesitated, slowly turned his hand palm-up and folded it around hers.

"I'm not sure. I just...when I first saw you, this past summer, I—I had this image built up in my mind, from everything Dad told me about you. You were Zeus, this mighty hero who could slay dragons and—"

"I'm not a hero, Kelsey—"

"But you are. You always have been—to me. I kept building you up in my mind, convinced myself that you were this larger-than-life mythical god who would swoop in and rescue me—"

"A mythical god?" Daryl laughed, the sound filled with bitter sarcasm. God save him from that stupid fucking name. *Zeus*. What a fucking joke. "Do you know how I got that name?"

"I—"

"It was your father. Him and his stupid damn sense of humor." He squeezed her hand, released it and stepped away. "Kelsey, that name was nothing more than a joke. It was during my first deployment. We'd been over there for two months when a bunch of us had gone out and had a few too many cheap beers, had thought going back to the barracks and wrapping sheets around us like togas was the funniest damn thing ever. Your father caught us—caught *me*. I was waving around a damn mop like some drunken gladiator fending off a pack of hungry lions."

The memory came back, crystal clear. Davis, standing at the entrance of the barracks like a silent sentinel, his clear eyes scanning the dozen men who thought they were so fucking smart. They had no idea how long he'd been standing there but the heavy silence quickly spread around the room once the first man noticed him.

Except for Daryl. He'd been facing the other way and suddenly spun around, wielding the mop like a sword—and came damn close to catching Captain Davis in the chest with it. The mop fell from his hands, hit the floor with an ominous sound. And Davis just stood there, watching him with eyes that missed nothing.

"Let me guess. You're the head asshole in charge of all these other assholes. Is that right?"

Daryl had started to answer—whether with 'yes, sir' or 'no, sir', he hadn't yet decided, wouldn't know until the words fell out of his mouth. But Davis had stopped him with a simple shake of his head. "Forget it, son. You want to be the head asshole, I won't stop you. I'll just call you Zeus from here on out."

Daryl finished the story and turned back to Kelsey, expected to see disappointment flash in her eyes. She was laughing instead, her mouth curled into a smile and her eyes dancing with amusement.

She stepped closer, reached for his hand and threaded her fingers with his. "I know. He told me the story years ago. Told me again last year when he said I could go to you if I ever needed help."

"He told you?" Daryl tried to step away, couldn't make his feet move. "Then you know the entire name was nothing more than a joke. I'm not some mythical god, Kelsey. I'm not even a hero."

"But you are. And that's what I was trying to say. I had built this image of you in my mind so that when I finally met you the first time, you were already larger than life to me. Meeting you, in person, only reinforced that. For those three months—from the time I first met you until you showed up at that cabin—I fantasized about you. About how you'd find me, how you'd help me slay those dragons and end my nightmare. And during that time, I fell in love with you."

His heart slammed into his throat. He shook his head, squeezed her hand then tried to let it go. "Kelsey, you don't love me—"

"I love the man I thought you were, the larger-than-life hero I had built up in my head. But somewhere along the line, I started to realize I could very easily fall in love with the man you really are."

"Kelsey—"

"We never got the chance to really get to know each other, Daryl. Not under normal circumstances. That's all I'm asking for—a chance to see what we might have together." She finally released his hand and stepped back, uncertainty flashing in her eyes as she watched him. "If—if you want to, I mean."

If he wanted to.

The gray fog that had been hovering around him for the past four weeks—no, for the past nine years—finally lifted. Fell away from him in tatters, disappearing into the light surrounding him.

If he wanted to.

Yeah. Yeah, he did. But he couldn't get the words out, wasn't even sure what words to use—so he did the only thing he could think of. He reached for Kelsey's hand and tugged her toward him. Wrapped one arm around her waist and cradled her cheek with his hand. Then he lowered his face and caught her mouth with his for a kiss. Deep. Warm. Filled with promise. Lingering, turning to something else—

Until the sound of a young girl giggling broke them apart.

Daryl looked down into a pair of wide green eyes, felt a hesitant smile curl his mouth as the little girl studied him. Kelsey eased out of his hold, knelt next to her daughter and ruffled the girl's hair.

"Paige, do you remember Mr. Daryl?"

The little girl's fingers tightened around the edges

of the drawing in her hand. She shot him another shy smile and nodded then buried her face against Kelsey's neck.

"You can say hi if you want. It's okay, sweetie. You can trust him." Kelsey's voice was soothing, reassuring. She looked up, offered him a smile that made his heart lurch in his chest. "Mommy does."

Daryl recognized the words for the gift they truly were. He pressed one fist against his chest, rubbed to relieve the unexpected tightness beneath his breastbone. Then he crouched down next to Kelsey, his gaze on the little girl as he smiled.

"Hi, Paige."

She turned her head, offered him a shy smile. "Hi."

She watched him for a few more seconds, her smile growing bigger. Then she lunged toward him, nearly knocking him over as she held the drawing out to him. He took it, his mouth twitching with amusement as he studied the colorful images.

A full rainbow of purples and reds and greens and oranges. Below that was a little girl with curly hair, holding a dog on a leash. A woman with wavy reddish-brown hair stood next to the girl, holding her hand.

And next to her, holding the woman's hand, was the figure of a man with amber eyes.

Above all three was a big heart. Crooked and oddly sized, but unmistakably a heart.

Daryl titled his head back and laughed.

And somewhere else, high above the angels, another little girl laughed along with him.

EPILOGUE

Five years later.

A shrill screech emanated from somewhere near the front of the house, slicing through the conversation and making every adult wince. Heads turned toward each other, wary eyes silently questioning as the adults tried to identify which child the scream had come from.

Mac sighed and pushed to his feet. "My turn to go see who's murdering who this time."

He made it three feet before the sound of running steps slapping against refinished plank floors filled the room, growing louder as the large group of children surged toward the vast kitchen of Mac's restored farmhouse. Could six even be considered a large group? Daryl chuckled and shook his head.

Under normal circumstances, no—but the group of children rushing into the kitchen would never be considered normal. The responsibility for *that* fell directly on their parents' shoulders.

At ten, Paige was the oldest—and usually the ringleader. Her wild mop of curls had fallen from the ribbon Kelsey had carefully placed there this morning. Wide green eyes scanned the room, her impatience clear until her gaze finally landed on Mac.

With a dramatic sigh, Paige swung her arm up, stood on her toes, and pointed one skinny finger in Mac's direction. "It's *your* son's fault!"

The adults in the room choked back their

laughter—both at Paige's dramatic announcement and at the look of sheer terror that briefly crossed Mac's scarred face. He ran one large hand over his jaw, covering a loud sigh.

"What did Lucas do this time?"

Claire—Jon and Sammie's nine-year-old daughter and Paige's accomplice in almost everything—jumped in, her voice a little more serious. "Lucas pushed Alyssa down and told her she couldn't play with his trucks because she's a girl."

Mac closed his eyes, took a deep breath, no doubt ready to bellow his son's name. The boy stomped into the room, his face a combination of mutiny and contrition.

"Lucas, did you push your sister?"

"She was playing with my truck and wouldn't give it back."

"That's not what I asked." Mac crouched next to the little boy. "Now answer the question. Did you push your sister?"

Lucas's lower lip trembled and tears welled in his eyes. "Yes but—"

"No *buts*. You know better. Now go sit in your chair until I tell you it's time to get up."

"But Dad, you have to tell them!"

"Tell them what?"

Lucas pointed an accusing finger at the five girls behind him. "Tell them that girls can't play with trucks because they're not boys!"

The five girls moved in closer, surrounding the single male like sharks circling helpless prey.

Paige and Claire.

Claire's five-year-old sister, Tessa.

Alyssa, Mac and TR's youngest and, at only two,

the youngest of the bunch.

And three-year-old Caroline, who stared back at the young boy with all of her mother's sass—and her father's amber eyes. She stepped closer, standing toe-to-toe with him even though he was almost a head taller.

"Can, too. Wucas."

Mac covered his mouth with his hand, shot a pleading look at TR. "Babe—"

"Oh no. This one's all on you."

Mac's mouth moved, no doubt in a silent oath. He scooped Lucas into his arms seconds before the females closed in for a kill. "Son, I think it's time we had another little chat. And after that, you're going to sit in your chair as punishment for pushing your sister."

"But—"

"And after *that*, if you have any sense in that thick skull of yours, you'll learn to play nice and realize when you're outnumbered." Mac paused in the doorway and shot a scowl at the laughing adults over his shoulder. "At least until some of your uncles decide to even the odds for you."

Mac carried Lucas from the room, the girls following him. There was more laughter, accompanied by the clink of silverware against plates as the adults returned to their dessert.

Kelsey leaned over, nudged Daryl in the side with an elbow. "Let's take a walk."

"Now?"

The smile she gave him set him on fire from the inside out—the way it had every day for the last five years. Daryl dropped the fork to his plate, swung his leg over the side of the long bench, and offered Kelsey his hand.

He ignored the teasing comments as he led his wife through the back door and out to the large deck Mac had added to the house a few years ago. "How far are we walking?"

"Right here is fine." Kelsey leaned against the railing and pulled him closer, wrapped her arms around his waist and lifted her head for a kiss. Daryl captured her mouth, deepened the kiss and sighed when she pressed herself even closer. Temptation made his knees weak and it was a struggle not to lift her in his arms and carry her away from the house.

Carry her to someplace private.

No, he couldn't. Not here. But later.

Definitely later.

He pulled away with a soft groan, reached up and brushed the hair from her cheek. "As much as I love kissing you, something tells me that's not why we came out here."

Kelsey smiled, shook her head. "No, it's not. It's, um, about what Mac said."

"What Mac said?" Daryl frowned, tried to recall the other man's words. He was still trying to figure it out when Kelsey's hand closed over his—and pressed it against the flat of her stomach.

Daryl blinked. Swallowed. Blinked again as a shit-eating grin spread across his face. "Are you trying to tell me what I think you're telling me?"

Kelsey laughed. "If you think I'm trying to tell you I'm pregnant, then yes."

Daryl's whoop of excitement was loud enough to be heard inside. He reached for Kelsey, spun her around then placed her on her feet before giving her another kiss. "Do you know—"

"No, not yet. It's too early. And—I wasn't sure if

you wanted to find out. Beforehand, I mean."

Did he want to know? Did it matter if it was a boy or a girl? No, it didn't.

He pressed his hand against her stomach once more, imagined he could already feel the life moving beneath his palm. His gaze caught Kelsey's, held it. "Allen. If it's a boy, his name will be Allen."

Tears filled Kelsey's eyes and she quickly blinked them away. "I think Dad would like that."

"*Think*? Shit. Kelsey, he had this planned all along."

"Had what planned? What are you talking about?"

Daryl pulled her back into his arms and held her. This is where she belonged. Where *he* belonged.

And it was time he told her.

"Do you remember that letter he left with you? The one with the fake passports that you couldn't read?"

"I—" She frowned, tilted her head to the side then slowly nodded. "I think so. It was the one you found the day we picked up Paige from the children's home, right?"

"Yeah. The one addressed to me."

"I remember." She playfully nudged him in the chest. "You never did tell me what it said."

No, he hadn't—because he'd been furious. Because he'd been convinced his old CO was playing games.

And because he'd been afraid to hope. "I didn't tell you because you would have turned and run and never come back if I had."

"Why would I do that?"

"Because your father knew us both better than we thought."

"Daryl, enough already." She cupped his face in her hands and kissed him. "What did the letter say?"

He closed his eyes, saw the letter clear in his mind. Davis's bold handwriting, the words jotted down in his own personal code.

> If you ever get around to reading this, one of two things will have happened. I'll hope for the best because the alternative doesn't bear thinking.
>
> You don't owe me anything, son. You never did. Everything you've done, you did on your own. But I'm putting them into your care anyway. My daughter. My granddaughter. My family. They mean the world to me and I know they will never replace what you lost. Nobody can and you shouldn't expect them to. But they're yours now. To love and cherish. Even if you only become their guardian, they're yours to protect as if they were your own. I hope it's more than that. I hope that damn stubborn streak you have doesn't keep you from being happy. I hope the same damn thing for Kelsey, who can be too damn independent for her own good sometimes.
>
> I take the blame for that—she is my daughter, after all. And I'm damn proud of her. Damn proud of you, too.
>
> There you have it. A dying man's wish. Take care of my family like they're your own. Maybe one day, they really will be. I'd like that. Just don't wait until it's too late to find happiness. And remember that sometimes, what you need the most has been right in front of you the whole damn time.

Daryl opened his eyes, met Kelsey's curious gaze. "The gist of it was—he wanted me to have you. Both of you. I think he was hoping that by putting me in charge of your safety, we'd become a real family. That we'd find happiness together."

Kelsey was quiet a long time—almost too long. Daryl started to wonder if he should have told her after all. Or maybe he'd botched the explanation—

His wife leaned up on her toes, gently brushed her mouth against his. "I think Dad was a very smart man who knew exactly what he was doing."

"Yeah. Yeah, I think so, too." He squeezed Kelsey's hand, tugged her toward the house. "Let's go inside, tell everyone the news."

He had opened the door, was ready to follow Kelsey inside when something made him stop and pause. Daryl looked up, saw a shooting star streak across the night sky high above him.

And he swore, for just one second, that he heard laughter.

A young girl's childish giggles, accompanied by an older man's gruff chuckle.

You did good, Daddy.
Yes, he did, Layla. He certainly did.

~ The End ~

About the Author

Lisa B. Kamps is a *USA Today* Bestselling Author who writes steamy romance with real-life characters and relatable stories that evoke deep emotion. She likes her men hard, her bed soft, her coffee strong, her whiskey neat, and her wine chilled...and when it comes to sports, hockey is the only thing that matters!

Lisa currently lives in Maryland with her husband and two sons (who are mostly sorta-kinda out of the house), one very spoiled Border Collie, two cats with major attitude, several head of cattle, and entirely too many chickens to count. When she's not busy writing or chasing animals, she's cheering loudly for her favorite hockey team, the Washington Capitals--or going through withdrawal and waiting for October to roll back around!

Interested in reaching out to Lisa? She'd love to hear from you:

Website: www.LisaBKamps.com

Newsletter: http://www.lisabkamps.com/signup/

Email: LisaBKamps@gmail.com

Facebook: https://www.facebook.com/authorLisaBKamps

Kamps Korner Facebook Group:
https://www.facebook.com/groups/1160217000707067/

BookBub:
https://www.bookbub.com/authors/lisa-b-kamps

Goodreads: https://www.goodreads.com/LBKamps

Instagram: https://www.instagram.com/lbkamps/
Twitter: https://twitter.com/LBKamps

Amazon Author Page:
http://www.amazon.com/author/lisabkamps

THE PROTECTOR: MAC
COVER SIX SECURITY BOOK 1

These men never back away from danger—and always fall hard for love in *Cover Six Security*, an explosive new series from *USA Today* Bestselling Author Lisa B. Kamps

Gordon "Mac" MacGregor swore an oath to protect and defend—an oath he continues to uphold as a former Army Ranger specializing in dark ops private security with Cover Six Security. Danger is a constant companion—and one of the few things that make him feel alive. He doesn't expect that danger to come in the form of the Tabitha "TR" Meyers, the only woman who sees him for who he truly is—and the only woman he's ever sworn off.

TR rarely abides by the rules, not when there's something she needs—and right now, she needs Mac. She enlists his help for one night, thinking she can simply walk away when it's over. But that one night is just the beginning, thrusting both of them into a dangerous web of scandal and cover-up with roots that run deeper than either of them expects.

When TR becomes an unwitting pawn in a game of deception and revenge, Mac will do anything to protect her—even if it means risking his own heart.

Don't miss the exciting launch title of the Cover Six Security series, *The Protector: MAC*, available now.

THE DEFENDER: RYDER
COVER SIX SECURITY BOOK 3

These men never back away from danger—and always fall hard for love in *Cover Six Security*, an explosive new series from *USA Today* Bestselling Author Lisa B. Kamps

Ryder "Boomer" Hess: former Army Ranger. Demolitions expert. Problem solver...and the unluckiest bastard around when it comes to love. Meeting women is never a problem but actually surviving a relationship? Not happening. And all because of his kid sister's best friend.

Hannah Montgomery: professional volunteer. Humanitarian activist. Eternal optimist...and a woman who lost her heart years ago to her best friend's brother. She's learned to turn that heartache into something useful and now loses herself in helping others...until *he* shows up and turns her world upside down.

When Ryder gets a call that his sister—and Hannah—could be in trouble, he drops everything and rushes to their rescue—and quickly learns that he might be the one who needs rescuing the most. But danger of another sort looms on the horizon and it's up to Ryder to save them. And if he fails, he'll lose a lot more than just his heart this time.

Don't miss the third sizzling title in the Cover Six Security series, *The Defender: RYDER*, now available.